CW01391576

THE
EPSILON
TWISTOR

THE
EPSILON TWISTOR

MARTIN SMALLEY

BROWN DOG BOOKS

First published 2025

Copyright © Martin Smalley 2025

The right of Martin Smalley to be identified as the author of this work
has been asserted in accordance with the Copyright, Designs & Patents
Act 1988.

All rights reserved. No part of this book may be reproduced, stored in
a retrieval system, or transmitted in any form or by any means, digital,
electronic, electrostatic, magnetic tape, mechanical, photocopying,
recording or otherwise, without the written permission of the
copyright holder.

Published under licence by Brown Dog Books and
The Self-Publishing Partnership Ltd, 10b Greenway Farm,
Bath Rd, Wick, nr. Bath BS30 5RL, UK

www.selfpublishingpartnership.co.uk

ISBN printed book: 978-1-83952-927-6
ISBN e-book: 978-1-83952-928-3

Cover design by Kevin Rylands
Internal design by Mac Style

Printed and bound in the UK

This book is printed on FSC® certified paper

MIX
Paper | Supporting
responsible forestry
FSC® C013604

Contents

Chapter 1

The Six O'Clock News

It was ludicrously hot in the minibus.

"Can't you turn the bloody heating down?" O'Malley asked the driver.

"Sorry, Grace, it's on or off, nothing in between."

"Well, how about off, then?"

"I'd rather have it off."

"Wouldn't we all?"

"O, funny, ha, ha."

It was obvious which passengers were the miners, who were the middle-class do-gooders from the South Oxford Labour Party and which ones were the students. South Oxford had been twinned with the Maerdy pit and the Welsh miners were quiet, looked resigned. They knew the struggle was already going against them and yesterday's successful food collection in the narrow streets of terraced houses off the Abingdon Road had done little to raise their spirits.

"Well, let's at least open a window."

"But it's bloody freezing out there."

It was indeed a misty, moisty morning, typical of the weather in the squelchy bog of Oxford. Martina shivered as the front passenger seat's window was cranked down. She had been chewing on her lower lip ever since they had set off a quarter of an hour ago and was now peering gloomily into the mist shrouding the banks of the dual carriageway.

"Great start, eh, Martina" said Grace. "We're going to need teamwork on the picket lines and we can't even agree about the temperature in the van. Pity it seems to be in a quantum on/off condition. Maybe if we don't observe the temperature, we can get the heating into a superposition of states…"

"Well, I'm cold" grumbled Martina.

She looked it, too. It had been warm when she left Barcelona.

"Must be your Spanish blood, eh?"

"I'm not Spanish. I'm Catalan."

Grace blushed, a rosy colour on her blackish face, which had tinges of her pugnacious Irish squaddie father and softer tones of her Jamaican mother, a care worker in London, where Grace had been born. She hated it when people assumed she was English.

"Sorry…"

"Where's Richard?"

"I don't know. I think I saw him getting into the big Williams coach down at the lower end of the high street."

"We'll probably meet up with him there."

"Are we nearly there yet?"

"About five minutes, I reckon."

The minibus had pulled off the dual carriageway and was now bumping along the B road into Didcot. Martina and one of the students were looking off-whitish, with an unhealthy tinge of green.

"Only a couple of minutes, Martina" said O'Malley. "We'll be there soon."

"What the hell" said the driver, slamming on the brakes.

"Police roadblock" said Tegid to one of his mates, the first word spoken by any of the miners during the half hour drive.

"O, well, at least no one's going to chunder before we get there" said O'Malley flippantly, but the crack in her voice betrayed a certain fear.

2

It was all very well to have seen the cavalry and truncheon charges at places like Orgreave and Brodsworth on the telly, but to see the array of visors and riot shields blocking the road, still a couple of miles from the power station, was a daunting sight. The smoking stacks lit eerily in silhouette behind him, a senior policeman wearing a bright yellow flak jacket detached himself from the squad and approached the minibus with his right arm raised, palm facing outwards.

"Let's run the bastard down" said Grace.

"Calm down, Grace" said Julian, the leader of the South Oxford Labour Party, "and let me do the talking."

The driver killed the ignition and after the noisy engine had spluttered out, there was a moment's silence, followed by the crunching of the approaching policeman's heavy boots. Julian slid the door back and jumped out a little clumsily and self-consciously.

"Morning, officer" he said.

"Morning, sir" said the policeman. "May I be of assistance to you?"

He wasn't wearing any identification tags.

Julian replied

"Certainly, officer. We are looking for Didcot Power Station. Could you give us any directions?"

In the flat landscape of Oxfordshire, Didcot Power Station could be seen from just about anywhere in the county on a clear day. Even in the morning fog, the stacks were broodily dominant. The policeman obviously didn't appreciate Julian's sense of humour. The superficial smile disappeared from his lips and his mouth took a downward turn.

"There's no way into Didcot Power Station today. I'm advising you to turn around and head back where you came from."

"This is a public highway" said Julian, warily. "You have no right to prevent us using it."

"Yeah" said O'Malley, "no right whatsoever."

The minibus had now disgorged all its fifteen occupants, including the six beefy looking Maerdy pit men, one of whom muttered something incomprehensible, probably in Welsh, to the policeman. It didn't sound very complimentary. The policeman's lips turned into a sneer.

"When I need a lesson on rights, I'll ask for one, girly."

O'Malley was nearly thirty and didn't like being addressed as girly. She started to square up, the way her father had taught her. The policeman turned and made a signal to the squad of men at the brow of the low hill, then turned back to Julian and Grace and said

"Get lost. You heard. You've got thirty seconds. Then I'm moving you on."

The policemen on the low bridge on the edge of the village were already shaping up into formation, drawing their long staves. Julian turned to Tegid and said

"I think we'd better head back. Maybe there's another way round to the power station."

"There is" said O'Malley. "When I was a student, I worked at a canning factory round here. It'll be about five miles, but I reckon we could sneak around this lot and still get up onto the main concourse where the coal lorries arrive."

"Great" said Tegid. "Let's try that."

"My God" said Julian. "Here's trouble."

Grace and Tegid looked up to see three lines of policemen, about twenty in each, advancing towards the van.

"Look, officer" said Julian, towards the back of the senior policeman. "We're just on our way. We need a couple of minutes. One of our party isn't well."

Martina was standing by the side of the van, vomiting onto the grass verge. The senior policeman marched busily back and was soon behind the sixty advancing men, who were now less than fifty yards from the minibus.

"My God" said Emily, "my cousin's in the second row. He's a para. I thought he was on duty in Northern Ireland. Quick, the camera."

The camera was passed to Emily, who hurriedly screwed the telephoto lens into place and took up a squatting position about ten yards in front of the van. The policemen, now about thirty yards away, suddenly broke into a trot and made a kind of 'gurk, gurk' noise.

"Run for it, Emily" said Julian.

It was too late. As Emily turned, the first stave smashed into the side of her head and the camera was stamped on. The open-mouthed Julian was struck in the belly with a stave used in a spear-like fashion and collapsed to the ground groaning. A heavy boot crunched into his midriff. As another of the students crashed to the ground under a heavy blow, the Maerdy men pitched in. O'Malley joined them. In trying to clear a path through to Emily, she ducked inside a haymaker from one of the long truncheons and flipped up the visor on the policeman's face shield with her left hand. The man's face had a split second to register surprise before O'Malley's right fist smashed into his cheekbone. Then another truncheon from the left side caught O'Malley's left shoulder and as she turned she was clubbed in the side of the face.

Jack Milton was the new professor at the Nuclear Physics Laboratory in Oxford. He had done some mediocre work on nuclear magnetic resonance in the mid-sixties and had made his name by jumping on the carbon-thirteen bandwagon at the right time. From a professorship at a small London college in the seventies, he'd leapt up to be a division leader at the Rutherford labs in the early eighties, and now he was sitting in his new chair, preening himself on his appointment at the heart of British establishment science. He shuffled a few papers importantly as his administrator Takin came in and greeted him with a bland, vacuous expression. Takin was a tall, weaselly man with dishonest, shifty eyes. The two men had a natural affinity.

"One of our biggest headaches" Takin was saying "is the Research Fellow O'Malley, a bad-tempered bitch. They say she's very gifted, but all she does is make trouble. Professor MacFarlane offered her an excellent PhD student for the coming academic year, but she refused. Talks nonsense about keeping her options open about returning to Japan at the end of the year, about not being prepared to commit herself to the NPL for longer than that."

"I don't see the problem" said Milton, a smug grin plastered across his sallow face.

"The problem is about grants. Professor MacFarlane himself is going to explain the situation to you, in strictest confidence, of course. I'll be back shortly, Professor."

Takin came back a few minutes later with Professor MacFarlane.

Kenneth MacFarlane was Milton's deputy, the man who had chaired the committee that appointed him. Kenneth was pleased with his appointment; a 'safe pair of hands', as he put it.

"Ah, Kenneth, good to see you. Take a seat. I'll have Gillian bring in some coffee and biscuits."

"You can leave us now, Takin" said MacFarlane.

"Certainly, Professor" said Takin, oozing his way out of the door.

"How are you settling in, Jack?" asked MacFarlane.

"Fine thanks, Kenneth… Ah, thanks Gillian… Could you make sure we're not disturbed, Gillian… not disturbed for any reason, you understand?"

"Yes, professor" said Gillian, who shot a contemptuous look at the new man as she left his spacious office.

"Now, Kenneth, what's all this cloak and dagger stuff about a research fellow, what's her name?"

"O'Malley" said MacFarlane.

"From what Takin was saying, sounds straightforward enough to me. Girl's a pain in the arse, wants to leave. We should let her go."

"It's about grants" said MacFarlane.

"Yes, so Takin was saying. Well, fire away."

"The following is in strictest confidence, of course" said MacFarlane.

"Of course" said Milton, who was well used to underhand dealings.

"Well, incredible though it may seem for such an ill-mannered slut, it seems that O'Malley has friends in high places."

"Who, and what committees are they on?" asked Milton, taking out his propeller pencil from his top jacket pocket and preparing a lead for the pad in front of him.

"No notes, Jack… and it's not that straightforward, anyway. It's not that O'Malley has real friends in high places… bolshie girl like that, it's doubtful she's got any friends at all… might be better to say she's got admirers in high places… very high places. Someone has been talking too much, and a rumour has got around that she may become the first British scientist to win a Nobel Prize in Physics for over a generation. Of course, that Salem chap won one a few years ago, but that doesn't count because he's a Paki, really."

"Come on, Kenneth, I don't think we need bother ourselves with some wild rumours. Doesn't every junior research fellow think they're on the road to Stockholm?"

"It's not what O'Malley thinks that's important, Jack. It's what the Cabinet Office thinks."

"Cabinet Office?"

MacFarlane took an envelope bearing the prime minister's office's massive portcullis seal out of his briefcase.

"This, Jack, is the nature of the problem" he said as melodramatically as he could.

Milton was a master of disguise, and picked up the heavy looking folio as if he got mail from the Cabinet Office every day. The envelope was addressed to MacFarlane and the letter it contained was a simple one.

Dear Professor MacFarlane,

It has been brought to our attention that Dr G. O'Malley of your department is engaged in work of outstanding merit. Our chief scientific adviser has assured us that Dr O'Malley will win major international prizes for her work. We support outstanding work.

You are therefore requested and required to offer Dr O'Malley *whatever* support she requires to further her research work.

Yours sincerely

The Rt. Hon. Margaret Thatcher MP

And there it was, Thatcher's signature.

"Ah" said Milton.

"I've spoken to Smythe at SERC and he's received a similar letter… a direct order to rubber stamp any research proposal O'Malley makes… the bugger of it is, she now refuses to make research proposals. Says she's fed up with having her work trashed by talentless scum and leaving, as she puts it, 'for a first world job'."

"Ah" said Milton. This was his favourite response to anything unexpected. It reflected the profundity of his thought.

"Well?" said MacFarlane.

"Well" said Milton, "what could they do if O'Malley did leave? We could explain the situation, we could…"

"Have you ever seen the prime minister when she's crossed?"

"I have never had the honour of meeting the prime minister" said Milton grandiosely.

"Nor will you" said MacFarlane, "if O'Malley disappears to Japan in a huff. You have to understand how serious the situation is, Jack.

8

Smythe is shitting hot bricks. He told me bluntly that if O'Malley leaves Britain, and we can hardly prevent her, we can forget about anyone in this lab getting another research grant for years. The place will be ruined."

"Why don't we just tell O'Malley outright that SERC say she can have anything she wants?"

"You haven't met O'Malley, have you Jack?"

Back in Martina's flat off the Iffley Road, O'Malley gingerly took one of the aspirin that Martina offered her in her open hand and swigged it down with a glass of water. She motioned as if to get up.

"Take it easy, Grace" said Martina. "The dentist said you should take a complete rest for at least twenty-four hours."

"The dentist?"

"Yes, don't you remember? We took you to see her after they'd cleared you at the hospital."

"The hospital?"

"Yes, at first they thought you had a fractured collarbone, but it's only severe bruising on your shoulder. You've lost a tooth and got four stitches in a cut on the side of your face. Don't touch!" Martina continued as O'Malley raised her left hand slightly, then let out an awful groan.

"Stitches?"

"Yes, stitches."

"God, how long was I out for?"

"About six hours."

"What time is it now?"

"About five-thirty."

"And Julian, Tegid, Emily...?"

"I am not sure about Tegid and the other Welshmen. I think one or two of them were quite badly injured. Emily is still at the Radcliffe. She was lucky not to get a fractured skull, but she has severe concussion. She is being kept in overnight, at least. Julian was badly winded, but is basically OK. Richard is in prison."

"What?"

"Yes, apparently, their coach went round the back way from the beginning and Richard's group managed to prevent a few small coal deliveries from entering the power station. When the police saw that they had managed to persuade a few drivers they tried to move them on and Richard was arrested as one of a small party who staged a sit-down on the concourse. I think the rest were later dispersed by an attack similar to the one on our group."

"How do you know all this?"

"I went down to St Aldates Police Station where they are holding Richard."

"God" said O'Malley, "do you think it will be on the six o'clock news?"

"As you say in English, there's only one way to find out" said Martina, crossing the room and switching on. "Do you need anything?"

"Yeah" said O'Malley, "a whiskey."

"No problem" said Martina, "there's some Glenlivet on the fridge."

O'Malley motioned to get up a second time, but slumped back into her chair with a look of intense pain on her face. Martina fetched the whiskey. O'Malley was just getting into a first slug when the bell went. Martina went into the narrow hallway and answered the intercom.

"It's Richard" she said, and buzzed him up.

"But isn't he…?" started O'Malley.

The pain and whiskey weren't helping Grace to think clearly, but she definitely remembered that Richard was in prison. The six o'clock news had started.

"Hi, Grace. God, you look awful" said Richard.

"Thanks" said Grace, making a kind of wry smile with the good half of her mouth.

"Wow, that's Didcot" Richard said, looking at the scenes of mayhem on the telly.

The broadcast was cleverly done. Richard had been a witness to the first assaults by the policemen on the pickets. The miners had responded to the violence and this scene was shown first, creating the impression that the Welshmen had started the trouble.

"The bastards have got the media completely under their thumb" said Martina.

"Sshhh" said Richard, enthralled by the gory scenes.

On the telly, the policemen were curiously without the long staves they had used in the attack on the minibus.

"God" said Richard, "I wondered why they used the ordinary truncheons in one of the fights, the one when they suddenly retreated for no obvious reason. It must have been for the benefit of the cameras. The bastards…"

Grace slumped back into her chair, looking confused and depressed. She said

"Anyway, how did you get out of prison?"

and Richard replied

"Tom Bobbin bailed me out. He's a good bloke."

Tom Bobbin was a brilliant but erratic scientist who had spent his whole life at Oxford University, man and boy. Ever since Professor Bryant's arrival in 1980, he had been relentlessly bullied by the management. He had a small, gloomy office at the end of the long ground floor corridor of the Nuclear Physics Laboratory. It was 10.45 and the deeply ingrained ritual of coffee time was approaching. Tom was still tapping away at his computer when his post-doc Fyodor and Ph.D. student Judith arrived at his open office door. He stopped typing, looked up and said, with his usual jolly demeanour

"Fancy a coffee?"

"Just for a change" said Judith, with a grin.

"Is Grace in yet?"

"No" said Fyodor, dourly. "Just for a change."

The serious Russian post-doc, who was always in the lab by 8.30, disapproved of O'Malley's disorderly hours.

Taking the two flights of stairs up to the NPL coffee room was calming Tom Bobbin's nerves. He wasn't looking forward to introducing John Parker, his new PhD student, to Grace. Kenneth had seemed to think that the plan was a foolproof one. Tom would supervise John on a project that was, in all but name, one of Grace's rejected proposals from the Bryant days. Later, when Grace had been offered some sweeteners by the lab and had agreed to stay on for the full term of her fellowship, Grace would take over with Tom dropping into the background as second supervisor. The plan had the merit that if Grace did agree to take over John's project she would certainly stay on till '87. Grace had a lot of faults, but she'd certainly be loyal to a student. It was also immediately clear that, in addition to being a brilliant student, John was a very nice, if painfully shy, young man. It wasn't unlikely that Grace would take a shine to him. But a couple of things were worrying Tom.

First, there was Grace herself. Since the summer, Grace had gone into her shell and seemed to have developed a new morose, introspective streak to her character. Although Tom had never liked Grace's wild, polemical arguments with Fyodor and Judith, not to mention anyone else who raised a political topic, he now felt more worried by their absence. Grace was simply letting comments pass, even ones that annoyed Tom himself with their racist and misogynist undertones, which would have had Grace boiling up with arguments a few months ago. Grace also seemed to have lost interest in her amazing work on gluons, and had only been persuaded to take on a couple of new master's students with great reluctance. Even then, even though he and Kenneth had convinced her that she could take the pick of the bunch, she'd gratuitously taken on two of the weakest students of the year, Helen and Freddy, who would probably prove to be liabilities rather than assets in her research. She'd also missed the August deadline for CERN proposals, the first time she'd ever let slip the opportunity to fill her boots with instrument time. No, just when she seemed to be at the peak of her intellectual power, and with the department and SERC offering her opportunities at last, Grace seemed to be turning her back on it all.

The other thing that was worrying Tom was Milton's appointment. Tom had seen quite a lot of Milton through his joint projects with the Rutherford lab. Milton had alienated most of the staff there, who were happy to see the back of him. Len Hopper's words "We've sold you a real kipper there, Tom" were echoing through his brain, followed by Grace's gloomy prophesy that the NPL would replace Bryant with another such. Yes, Milton was indecisive and shifty, and definitely not up to the job. The prospects of him being able to handle Grace, even the subdued Grace of the past couple of months, seemed remote. The nagging doubt that Grace might be right after all, that British science in general and the NPL in particular were on the slippery slope downhill, wouldn't go away. He had to put a brave face on it, try to cheer Grace up.

"Tom Bobbin bailed me out. He's a good bloke."

"He certainly is" said Grace with feeling. "It's a pity he won't come off the fence and support the lefties, but I guess he's at home now believing every word of the BBC Six O'Clock Propaganda. Let's switch it off. It's getting on my wick."

13

Richard leaned over to switch off.

"The enemy within" continued O'Malley, musing to herself. Then to Martina and Richard she said "Look at Tegid and the blokes from Maerdy, then look at scum like Thatcher and the Tories. It's pretty bloody clear who the real enemy within are."

"It could be worse" said Martina. "Look at the decades we've had under Franco."

"Franco, Thatcher, Hitler, it's all the same bunch" said Richard. He was about to continue, but Martina cut him short by saying

"Come on, Richard, you're losing a sense of perspective in comparing Thatcher with Franco and Hitler. Those guys were evil by a different order of magnitude."

"Did one thousand Argies die?" asked O'Malley rhetorically, crushing a cigarette into the ashtray, which was a rather macabre little metal rectangular dish bearing a portrait of the pope. Martina had been brought up a Catholic.

"You need a rest, Grace" said Martina, looking worriedly at the research fellow's face. The combination of the beating up, the anaesthetics and the whiskey were clearly taking their effect. O'Malley's skin was as pale as it could become, and her eyes were clouding over.

"Bollocks" said Grace. "Let's pop down the Cricketers for a pint."

"They're not open yet" said Richard.

"Well, let's have another whiskey then" said O'Malley.

She poured herself a real stonker. At 6.30, Grace crashed out in her chair, and Richard and Martina quietly left the flat.

O'Malley arose in the middle of a terrible nightmare. In the bizarre fashion of dreams, she knew it was the future. She was in the office of a Milton lookalike. The sickening feeling that her beautiful new theory of gluon interactions had never been accepted, that Thatcherism was entrenched in Britain, and that this malicious grey haired dwarf was in a position of power over her quickly faded. This vision was replaced by even more horrible images of tens of thousands of charred corpses in the Arabian desert, fronted by a gloating Japanese-American face proclaiming the end of history – the ultimate triumph of capitalism. As the nightmare unfolded, the consciousness that the Eastern European peoples had been re-enslaved by the capitalists, the UN reduced to a rubber stamp for American imperialism, the British Labour party taken over by a bunch of upper-middle class freeloaders as right wing as the Thatcherites themselves, the…

The telephone was ringing and a sweaty, shaken O'Malley answered it.

"Is that you, Grace?"

"Yes, oh, Hiroshi, it's so good to hear your voice."

"I heard you were at Martina's. I was worried about you. I have been waiting in the King's Arms since eight o'clock."

"What time is it?"

"Eight-thirty."

"O, God, sorry Hiroshi. It's a long story, but I've got a good excuse. I've been in hospital and…"

"Hospital?"

"Don't worry, I'm OK, sort of. Look, I feel a bit out of it. Could you make it down the Iffley Road to the Cricketers Arms? I'll pay the taxi."

"O, Grace, are you OK? I will come as soon as I can."

"I'm OK. I'll see you down there nine-ish. I need a shower."

When O'Malley entered the bathroom, she was shocked at quite how bad she looked. Not exactly the dashing belle out to impress a lovely young Japanese man on a date – looked more like she'd gone a few rounds with Joe Frazier and lost badly. The first blast of the shower brought intense shards of pain raking through her skull, but then relief. In the end, she'd still be meeting Hiroshi, and things couldn't turn out as badly as in the dream, so why worry.

She was in the pub by 8.45. Hippy Pru and her boyfriend Paul were sitting at the window table. O'Malley stood three pints of bitter.

"God, you look awful" said Pru. "What happened?"

"I was at Didcot Power Station and…"

"…and you got beaten up by the police" interrupted Paul. "You realize, of course, that Scargill's tactics are all wrong. The miners need to broaden the revolutionary struggle and…"

"…and the armchair communists who sit around in pubs will overthrow capitalism for them" interrupted Grace. "Couldn't make it down to the picket lines this morning, Paul? Too busy wanking?"

"Calm down, Grace" said Pru. "Paul has been working very hard on his thesis. Haven't you, Paul?"

"Yes, I…"

"Yeah, I heard you'd been working with that git Trevor Beagleton. I guess post-modernist deconstructivism is a lot easier than actually doing something about our real situation."

"O, reality sucks" said Paul.

"Yeah, I noticed" said Grace, "and it's going to suck a lot worse if the miners get beaten."

"If?" asked Paul provocatively.

"Wow, who's that?" asked Pru.

Several heads in the pub had turned as an apparition with the full beauty of a film star had entered and was standing uncertainly in the doorway.

"Hiroshi" shouted Grace across the bar and the man turned and smiled shyly.

"Wow" said Pru, "you certainly know how to pick them."

16

"Sshhh" said Grace, "Hiroshi's different."

Grace got up and crossed the room, stopping a couple of yards from Hiroshi, who was still smiling until he caught sight of her face at close quarters.

"O, Grace, what happened to you?"

"It's a long story, Hiroshi. I'm so sorry not to have met you in the King's Arms. I was asleep after taking some painkillers. Would you like a drink?"

"Thank you. I will have a mineral water."

"I'm over by the window there with a couple of friends. Well, a friend and her boyfriend anyway."

Hiroshi looked puzzled. Although his spoken English sounded excellent – the only thing that gave him away as a foreigner was that he pronounced everything too perfectly – he still found it difficult to pick up O'Malley's banter, and looked vaguely uneasy in the smoky, tatty pub. O'Malley paid an exorbitant amount for a small bottle of mineral water without blinking and led Hiroshi across the room.

"Hiroshi, this is Pru and Paul. Pru and Paul, Hiroshi."

"Hi, Hiroshi, take a seat" said Pru. "We were just having an interesting political discussion weren't we, Grace?"

"Let's let it go" said Grace.

"How did you get that terrible blow?" asked Hiroshi.

"I was struck in the face by a police baton this morning" replied Grace.

"Grace is more used to giving blows then receiving them" said Paul, who had heard about O'Malley's date with Marco the previous week, and was preparing to enjoy himself.

"Sorry?" said Hiroshi.

"Yeah, I also hit a policeman" said Grace, giving Paul a meaningful gaze. "Just a moment, Hiroshi. Paul and I have something to discuss in private. See you in a minute, Pru" she said, taking both her own glass and Paul's over to the bar. Paul followed her.

"Oh, fallen for the little Japanese prince, have we, Grace? Well, I'm going to…"

"I'm going to give you just one warning, Paul. I got a perfect view of the rozzer who bashed my face in this morning and if I ever see him again, I'm going to kill him. If you screw up my date with Hiroshi tonight, I'm going to kill you, too."

Paul gave a little nervous laugh and downed his pint. He went over to the table and said

"We're going, Pru."

"But Hiroshi and I were just…"

"I said we're going."

Left just the two of them at the table, Grace gave Hiroshi an only slightly embellished version of events at Didcot earlier in the day. They both seemed surprised when last orders were called.

"Would you like a coffee?" asked Grace.

"Do they serve them here?" asked Hiroshi.

"I don't think so" said Grace, "but Martina's flat is just around the corner. I've got the keys."

Hiroshi looked worried and said "I think I should be getting back to college now."

"What time do they close the gates?"

"At midnight."

"There's still plenty of time. I'll pay for your taxi."

"Oh, please" said Grace, "I've had such a horrible day. It would be so nice to end on a pleasant note… and Martina's got an espresso machine."

Hiroshi hadn't had a real coffee since arriving in England several weeks ago.

"OK" he said.

Back at Martina's flat, Hiroshi's heart missed a beat when Grace declared her love for him.

"I was very jealous when you went out with my friend Marco" he said, "but I know you have many boyfriends and… and, I'm not sure…"

Hiroshi paused, seemed to have lost his way, and finished his coffee with a gulp.

"I have to be going."

It was 11.15.

"Hiroshi, if you would be my boyfriend, I would give up the others. Really."

"I have never had a girlfriend" said Hiroshi.

"You're kidding" said Grace, then bit her tongue. It was clear that Hiroshi was not kidding, and was very embarrassed.

"I am dying to kiss you, Hiroshi, but I can call a taxi if you want."

"I should go" said Hiroshi, "but I want to kiss you, too."

Grace rose from her chair and took two paces across to Hiroshi's chair. She leant down and kissed him very gently on the lips, then placed her hands under his armpits and lifted him to his feet. The second kiss was longer, harder and mutual.

"You haven't met O'Malley, have you Jack?"

"No" said Milton, "but I've just moved such a meeting to the top of my list of priorities. I'll think the situation over, and call her in tomorrow."

"Jack, I know you're head of department now, but I have to warn you that if you do any such thing, our chance will have come and gone."

"Any what thing?" asked Milton, genuinely puzzled.

"Call her in, as you put it. If you do that, she's likely to snub you, like she did Professor Bryant."

"Ah" said Milton.

"Even if you ask her politely to come in for a chat she might say no. She's a mad commie bastard, Jack, prides herself on 'not taking orders from anyone'."

"Does she come in for morning coffee?" asked Milton.

"Usually" said MacFarlane.

"What time is it?" asked Milton.

MacFarlane looked at his watch.

"About 10.45" he said.

John Parker followed Tom slowly into the coffee lounge, stooping and shuffling, always a pace behind. Tom bought them both coffees and chocolate biscuits, and seemed to get less change than he expected. Inflation was getting out of hand, too. Grace was already at their usual table with Helen and Freddy. She sounded more animated than recently. As Tom sat down, Grace turned to reveal the left side of her face.

"God, Grace, what happened?"

"I got in the way of the Thatcher juggernaut at Didcot Power Station yesterday."

Tom let out a groan and, with what he realized was a false smile on his face, said

"Anyway, Grace. I'd like you to meet my new PhD student, John."

"Oh, hi, John, pleased to meet you."

John had a bad stutter and couldn't seem to get a word out. There was an embarrassed silence, until John, still standing, produced a rush of words.

"Errr... pleased-to-meet-you-Doctor-O-Malley-I've-heard-so-much-about-you."

"Take it easy, John, and take a seat. And please call me Grace. We don't stand on ceremony in the elementary particle group, do we Tom?"

"Not at all" said Tom, his smile now looking and feeling more relaxed.

"John, I'd like you to meet Helen and Freddy, my two high-flying masters students..."

Helen and Freddy snorted in unison.

"Hi, John."

"Hi, John."

"...and here's Fyodor, our resident post-doctoral Stalinist and gamma ray expert."

"Thank you for your charming introduction, Grace. Pleased to meet you, John" said Fyodor.

John missed his cue again, then blurted out

"Pleased-to-meet-you-Fyodor-Freddy-Helen..."

and left the words hanging in the air.

"Well" said Tom, "it's always nice to feel..."

He was interrupted by a stagy cough from behind his right shoulder. It was Kenneth.

"Good morning, Tom" Kenneth said with forced joviality. "Professor Milton here is doing the rounds meeting all the groups... team spirit and all that... could you introduce your chaps to him?"

Helen gave a derisive snort and pushed her tits out. Jack Milton leered at them for a moment, then said

"Good to see you again, Tom. May I sit down?"

and without pausing, he squeezed himself in next to Helen, who visibly recoiled. Kenneth stood hovering and was rescued by Richard's genuinely cheerful arrival, dragging two chairs, which he plonked down between Freddy and Grace.

"To what do we owe the honour of your esteemed visit to our humble group, Professor?" Richard asked Kenneth as the two of them sat down.

Tom Bobbin shot him a filthy look, but Kenneth didn't seem bothered by the heavy irony, and said

"I was just doing the rounds with Professor Milton, our new head of department..."

At this point he inclined his head towards Jack Milton

"...Tom was about to make the introductions."

"Yes" said Tom, "Jack, I'd like you to meet Helen, Freddy, Richard, Fyodor and Grace."

"Pleased to meet you all" said Milton, suavely.

He ignored the younger members of the group, turned straight towards O'Malley and said

"You must be Dr O'Malley."

Grace turned her head slowly in Milton's direction and finally fixed him with a gaze. After a short pause, she said

"I am indeed. I think we met once at the Rutherford labs, when you were chairing a beam users' meeting... beam time for the boys on the new neutron source, if I remember rightly."

Tom groaned internally and puffed his cheeks, but Milton didn't seem fazed.

"Not at all, Grace... may I call you Grace?... all the proposals at the new ISIS source have been, and will be, treated strictly on merit... isn't that right, Tom?"

"Yes, of course, Jack. It's all perfectly fair and above board, Grace."

"Yeah, sure" said Grace.

"Just as it will be in the allocation of resources here... by the way, Grace, one of the first changes I'm planning to make here is to upgrade the status of all SERC and Royal Society Fellows to be more or less on a par with the permanent staff…"

"More or less?" O'Malley interrupted with a snort.

Milton continued suavely, as if his sentence hadn't been broken at all, by saying

"…and I'd like you to join us at the full staff meeting I'm calling next Monday afternoon."

"Wow, an outbreak of common sense in UK science management" said O'Malley petulantly, by way of reply.

"Well, I'll be leaving you now" said Milton, "lots of people to meet, you see."

Milton and MacFarlane got up and left. Their places were taken by Judith and Tom's new masters student, who had been waiting awkwardly in the wings. When they were safely out of earshot, MacFarlane said to Milton

"You see what I mean, Jack?"

And Milton replied

"Don't worry, Kenneth, I've cracked tougher nuts than that."

Chapter 2

A CERN Experiment

Since falling as madly and completely in love as Marvell with his coy mistress and taking Hiroshi's long-preserved virginity, O'Malley had turned back to analytic field theory, and armed only with a pencil and paper was having an *annus mirabilis* with her theoretical work on the gluons. One morning, she was sitting with Tom's group on the opposite side of the coffee room. She looked happy and relaxed.

"So" Judith was saying, "I hear you've moved out into the sticks near Bibbleton."

"Yup" said O'Malley, "Hiroshi and I wanted to live together. We've rented a cottage till the end of the academic year."

"Hiroshi and you?"

"Yup, we've moved in together. We…"

"My God, what's all this 'we, we, we' stuff. You're not settling down are you, Grace?"

Grace gave a radiant smile.

"Well, I don't know about settling down. We'll see how it goes when we've been living together for a year or so."

"A year? What about your fan club of toy boy admirers?" asked Judith, with a hint of needle in her voice.

"I'm monogamous" replied Grace blandly.

"Wow" said Richard. "Are you having a housewarming party?"

"We sure are" said Grace. "You'll all be invited, of course. I hope you and Pat will be able to come, Tom."

"We'd love to, Grace" Tom replied.

It was a remarkably warm day for late October and Hiroshi and Grace had decided to hold their party in the garden. People were starting to get quite pissed already, although it was only three o'clock in the afternoon.

"Hi, Martina" said Grace. "Long time, no see."

"Hi, Grace" said Martina, handing over a very expensive looking bottle of '76 Rioja, "I've brought you and Hiroshi a housewarming present."

Tom Bobbin came up cheerfully.

"What a lovely place, Grace. Isn't it, Pat?"

"Yes, darling" said Pat.

"Good to see you again, Martina. How are things in the world of trans-uranium elements?" Tom asked.

Martina seemed to come to with a start.

"Oh, fine, Tom. It's not like elementary particle physics though. I'm starting to find it too empirical."

"Sounds a bit like school physics, Martina. How are you doing, love?" asked Colin. "Fancy a Pimms?"

Colin had been O'Malley's best friend in their undergraduate days and, after bumming round China for a year in the late seventies, had taken a PGCE and gone into teaching at an average comprehensive school in Abingdon in south Oxfordshire, just down the road from Bibbleton. Colin had a momentary uncanny feeling that O'Malley could control the weather. It had been cold and pissing down all autumn. Now, out of nowhere, it was an Indian summer.

"Isn't Pimms a little bourgeois for you, Grace?" asked Tom, who liked to rag his protégé about her working-class attitudes.

"I don't see why the upper-class twits should bogart all the good things in life, Tom. We've got buck's fizz for good measure, if the Pimms isn't bourgeois enough."

"What does 'bogart' mean?" asked Pat.

"It means to hog something" said Richard, detaching himself from a small group that included Freddy and Helen. "The expression comes from the film *Easy Rider* as in the phrase 'Don't bogart that joint my friend'…"

"…pass it over to me" chorused Grace.

"Talking of which" said Richard, "I see the Iffley Road hippies have arrived."

A dilapidated multicoloured van had pulled up and was disgorging four outlandish-looking individuals, two women and two blokes.

"Ben" called Grace across the garden.

"Far out, man."

"Far out."

There weren't many hippy communes left by the mid-eighties but Oxford being Oxford, there was still a huge squat going on in a massive house on some prime real estate at the town end of the Iffley Road.

"So how's boring monogamous more or less married life treating you, Grace?" asked Ben.

"Well, we've only been at it for a few weeks, man, and we don't have a monogamy clause in our relationship."

Pat looked a bit shocked.

"Good for you" said Ben. "Is it cool to skin one up?"

Grace looked across at Pat, who was looking whiter by the minute in spite of the bright sunshine.

"Maybe down the end of the garden, by the shed. Fancy a drink?"

"Mineral water only. I've taken the precepts."

"I though the precepts were about intoxication of any kind" said Grace.

26

"Come off it, Grace, this is a party after all. Let's party!"

The youngest of the hippies, Maya, who had brought a four pack of canned cider, was already on her third buck's fizz.

"Ooh, Grace, this stuff is lovely, and my skin goes such a lovely colour in the sunshine."

Grace thought that the half-Black, half-Mediterranean olive brown of Maya's bared arms was quite lovely enough with or without sunshine, and said so.

"Ooh, flattery will get you everywhere... Hang about, Ben's lit one up."

So saying, Maya headed off towards the shed, where the sweet smell of cannabis was drifting across the air.

Tom Bobbin came up to Grace and said

"I say, Grace, is that smell what I think it is?"

"...hmm, yes, I guess so, Tom. Hippies will be hippies, you know."

"Grace. Cannabis is an illegal drug and..."

"...cool it" said Arne, the eldest of the hippies, who had replaced Maya at O'Malley's side.

"Aren't you going to introduce me, Grace?" he said, giving Tom an appreciative look. Pat was giving him a rather less appreciative look in return.

"Arne. This is my former PhD supervisor and current nuclear physics guru, Tom. Tom, this is Arne."

"Don't I get some kind of description, too, Grace? Something like... This is Arne, the man who time forgot, or... This is Arne, also known as Ron Tripper for his exploits on acid, or..."

"I think we'd better leave, Tom" said Pat.

"Yes, I think you're right, Pat" said Tom.

"Goodbye, Grace" said Pat a little frostily as she huffed off to the huge bourgemobile parked incongruously next to the hippy van.

"What a pity" said Arne. "He was kind of cute. Wife seemed a bit freaked out, though. Any of your other colleagues here I could freak out?"

"Nah, Tom's the only one I'd invite from the NPL, apart from the students of course. There are plenty of them around, but I don't think you'll freak them out with tales of exploits on acid."

"Guess what" said Arne.

"What?" said Grace.

"I've got some acid with me."

"Wow" said Grace, "I haven't done any acid since '82 when I tripped with Ben in Paris."

"Look" Arne said, "let me give you these. When there's a right time for you and Hiroshi…" So saying he opened up a little box with yin and yang symbols on the front and slipped a couple of tabs into O'Malley's shirt pocket.

"God, thanks Arne. That's really kind of you."

"It's good stuff" said Arne. "The best I've had since the late sixties. Make sure you've got a whole day spare."

"I will" said Grace. "Oh, Colin, hi…"

Colin joined them with a half-pint of Pimms in one hand and a buck's fizz in the other.

"Wow, looks like you mean business, Colin."

"Sure do" Colin replied, with a hazy smile. "This is a great party, Grace."

"Just a moment" Grace said. "We've got more guests."

Grace got up and mouthed a question across to Hiroshi. "Do you know these people?"

He shook his head.

They were plain-clothed policemen.

Tony Woodbridge unlocked the double security locks on his huge basement flat in Pimlico and flicked the switch in the hallway. The 60 watt bulb hardly lifted the gloom, which matched his spirits. This wasn't a job he was going to enjoy.

The flat must have been fully four hundred square metres of prime real estate, less than five minutes' walk from the Thames. Four generations of Woodbridges had been commanders in the British Army, and Tony had broken the sequence. But he was batting for Britain in a more subtle way. He'd been recruited by MI5 in his early postgraduate days and had cut his teeth working against the NUM under the Heath government, a problem that had been solved by brute force by the present administration. None of the careful traps in the hallway had been tampered with and he relaxed slightly as he played through the taped messages on the phone in the main living room. Nothing important there, he thought, taking out the file on O'Malley.

Tony had been a postgraduate at Oxford when he met O'Malley in the mid-seventies, just after Grace had taken her starred first in physics. By then, Tony was already in his seventh year of working on a strange thesis about the Silk Route, about overland connections between India and China in the days when Europeans were living in mud huts. Tony could speak Chinese, Urdu, Arabic, Russian, German and French, and had visited over half the countries in the UN whilst playing the eternal student. The long drawn-out PhD had proved to be perfect cover for his first foreign forays and it had been a clever move to arrange for his own failure, thereby pushing him out of his natural field in academia into the Foreign Office and the civil service. He'd especially enjoyed his work against the Sendero Luminoso in Peru and prided himself on being one of Britain's top operators. The present job seemed way below his capabilities, but then again, his masters knew best, and he would set himself diligently to the task.

It was getting on for two o'clock in the morning, his favourite time for work. All the early stuff he knew already, up to Grace's brilliant first in '75, and there didn't seem to be anything exceptional about her PhD studies at Oxford, her first post-doc in Germany, her brief return to Oxford, or her JSPS Fellowship in Japan. He didn't need to be told that Grace was intellectually brilliant and capable of working both at a high level of abstraction and in practical applications of science. Any contemporary of Grace's at Oxford could have told you that. Nor did he need to be told that the woman was a rabid communist, though for such an intense individualist it was maybe mildly surprising that she had joined mainstream socialist parties in both Germany and Japan. Like Tony, Grace had principles. Misguided ones to be sure, but she deserved respect for the way she stuck to them when the tide of the times was clearly flowing against her. It was hard to imagine Grace, with all her woolly academic and hippy friends, as a dangerous individual.

But Tony had to admit to himself that economic and scientific espionage was the coming trend. The commie threat was for the suckers who believed the newspapers and TV, and the straight Cold War stuff would soon be over. From his extensive knowledge of world affairs, Tony couldn't imagine the Eastern bloc holding out for another five years, maybe less. Behind the rhetoric, all the top people in Britain and the States knew that they had the Soviets by the balls, and that all that remained was the mopping up operation. Their work in Poland had been particularly successful and the re-enslavement of the Eastern European peoples by the capitalists was a foregone conclusion. But the Japanese and the Chinese were a different matter. The Chinese were majestic, Tony thought – pity about their government, but a great people. They would be the greatest long-term threat. He'd just started learning Japanese as part of his present job, and didn't rate them so highly. However, in the short term, it would be difficult to ignore them and anything that strengthened the Japanese economically and scientifically against the British and their American friends had to be regarded as a genuine threat.

Tony flicked to the final section of O'Malley's folder, to the chief scientific adviser's report on the commercial possibilities of the polymer work. This was new material for him, and his interest was piqued. Companies like the soap and detergent giants Unilever, the paint people ICI, the oilfield drilling company Schlumberger and, of course, the oil companies themselves like BP, accounted for a significant proportion of the British gross domestic product, not the hot silly money that exchanged hands in the City, but the real stuff of production and exporting. If these people were outflanked by scientific advances in polymer science – if the Japanese did to these companies what they'd already done to the British shipbuilding, car, steel and electronics industries – well, it didn't bear thinking about. The report got technical, started talking about something called SSK theory. Tony skipped the mathematics.

The report made it clear that the British academic polymer establishment thought O'Malley was wrong, that the Yamato theory she had been pursuing was fundamentally flawed. But then, they would, wouldn't they? Tony understood full well the vanities and stupidities of the academic world from his own decade at Oxford and he knew that the oldies wouldn't give up their cherished ideas, particularly not when the established theory had a solid, reliable European base – the 1940s work of Sokolnikov and Smetternich in Russia and of Klaarenbeek in the Netherlands – and the challenger was an unknown from an obscure private university in Japan. The prejudice that the Japanese could only copy, never produce original thought, was deeply ingrained, and probably shared by Tony himself. But he'd played O'Malley at go, and lost. Tony was very proud of his go, a skill he had honed during a year spent at the University of Shanghai. He had had many private games with the British go champion and had won the vast majority. But Grace had beaten him within a year of learning the rules, a defeat that still rankled with him. Without knowing any of the scientific details, Tony's intuition told him that Grace was probably right.

At the back of the folder were copies of letters from the prime minister's office to O'Malley's head of department and the head of the Science and Engineering Research Council, together with an

31

internal NPL report prepared by Professor MacFarlane about the difficulties the NPL were having in managing O'Malley.

His first thought in dealing with the case when he'd been briefed verbally last week had been to take a simple line – arrange a drugs bust of Grace's place in Bibbleton. They could easily plant some cannabis in her cottage for the police to find. The Japanese were very touchy about criminal records, especially for drugs offences, and would then refuse Grace a visa. Blocked from returning to Japan, the sweeteners they were prepared to offer her for staying in the UK would seem a lot more palatable and, even if she went somewhere else abroad, at least she wouldn't be working for a main economic rival.

Tony perused his cuttings of a murder case being sensationalized in the national press. Two weeks earlier, an off-duty policeman had been murdered in Abingdon. Although the incident had taken place in the early evening on a fairly busy road, there had been no witnesses. The case was still unsolved as Tony considered his options. Arranging a drugs bust seemed much too crude. It was sure to alienate Grace, and they didn't want her to run away anywhere. She was a bright girl and, if correctly handled, a lot of potentially big profits for UK plc could be squeezed out of her. Tony thought his superior's 'carrot and stick' approach to the problem was misguided. Grace didn't like carrots and wasn't frightened of sticks. What they needed was to get some really compromising shit on her. An implication in a murder case, no matter how vague or ill-founded, could be exactly what they needed. O'Malley was a smartarse, but everyone has their weak points. Tony was a master at exploiting these, both in life and across the go board. He took a sip from a large glass of Chivas Regal and lit a Dunhill. The police records of the Abingdon case could wait till morning.

"Excuse me, madam" said the first of the two officers, who was looking very uncomfortable in his dark jacket. "Are you Grace O'Malley?"

"I am indeed" said O'Malley, putting a brave face on it. The acid tabs in her shirt pocket seemed to have become larger. She was in possession of a class A drug.

"We are involved in a murder investigation, and would like to ask you a few questions."

"Murder?" said O'Malley, looking nonplussed. "Please come this way" she continued, and showed them into the cottage, which was cool and deserted. Hiroshi followed them in.

"What's it all about?" O'Malley asked.

"We're investigating a murder that took place in Abingdon recently" the second officer said. "It's just a routine enquiry. Won't take a minute."

O'Malley looked calmly at the two men.

"Take a seat" she said. "Would you like some coffee?... a tea, perhaps?"

"No, thank you, madam" the two men replied together.

Hiroshi said "I'll make a coffee, anyway" and disappeared into the kitchen.

One of the policemen was a huge man, the other short and wiry.

"We'll be brief, madam" said the little one. "It's about the murder of a PC Lofthouse... as you can imagine, we are eager to follow up any clue in such a case, and to eliminate certain possibilities from our enquiries ..."

He left the sentence hanging in the air. O'Malley didn't say anything. The sounds of an espresso machine bubbling up came from the kitchen.

"...and we've received information that your car, or a similar one, a turquoise Fiat, was seen in the neighbourhood of the crime at about the time..."

Again, he allowed his words to hang in the air in mid-sentence. Again O'Malley said nothing. There were clunking sounds of cups and saucers from the kitchen.

"…of the murder. We're terribly sorry to bother you, Dr O'Malley, but you do understand that we have to follow up every lead in such a case."

"Yes" said Grace.

"And, well, madam, were you in the area at the time? We'd be happy to eliminate you from our enquiries…"

"When was it?" asked Grace.

"About five-thirty, madam."

"It's a while ago" said O'Malley. "What day did you say it was?"

"The ninth, madam."

"I'll have to check my diary" Grace said, and disappeared into the kitchen.

She returned to the living room with her briefcase. After rummaging around and producing her diary, she said

"Ah, yes, I see, yes, that's it, the day I came back from CERN…"

Ici l'halle de conduit de neutrons
Neutronleiterhalle
Neutron Guide Hall

Freddy looked up at the trilingual notice above his head and prepared to follow O'Malley across the little bridge that led to the instrument area. Freddy had never been so tired in his life. It was day five of the six-day electroweak decay experiment and he felt he had hardly slept since their beamtime had started at nine o'clock on the Wednesday morning. He counted the days off in his head – yes, he had crossed the hundred-hour barrier – only two more nights to go. He started to yawn stupidly as he reached the top of the stairs, but suppressed it immediately when he saw O'Malley turn on the gangway.

Normally Freddy wouldn't have bothered what anyone thought about him. He had the typical air of self-confidence of the ex-public schoolboy with wealthy parents. He was perfectly happy whiling away his time at Oxford, heading for a gentleman's third-class honours degree – time spent in the library was really too boring when one could be out with one's friends drinking Pimms or champagne. Without being very conscious of politics, he knew that the Thatcher victories meant that the world belonged to his sort of people. In fact, he knew he would be earning more than O'Malley next year and would normally have treated the scruffy academic with the same contempt that he treated all poor people.

But respect for O'Malley had come sneaking up on him over the weeks of his research project and it had rocketed to a kind of hero-worship over the past few days. Freddy rather prided himself on his excellent French, which was much better than his physics owing to summers spent at daddy's chateau in the Rhone Valley. He had been well impressed with O'Malley's fluency when they had arrived in Geneva on the Monday night. When they had signed in on the Tuesday morning to get their site passes and film badges, O'Malley had joked and chatted effortlessly with the admin staff and the technical support team. When Freddy was introduced to the German instrument responsible Hans, Hans had addressed him in perfect colloquial English, then had started chatting to O'Malley in German. Although he could only understand a few words of German and didn't frankly understand much about the experiment he was about to perform (beyond the importance of his preparing good samples that O'Malley had impressed upon him with unusual urgency), it was clear that Grace and Hans were discussing complicated problems and that Grace's German was as perfect as her French. But what had really bowled Freddy over was the evening when they had gone out with Toshiro Kamakura, one of O'Malley's co-workers from his two years in Osaka, who had come out for an experiment on neutron decay on the NIB instrument. Slipping from using English with him and Helen, French with the waiter and German with Hans, O'Malley had started emitting a stream of light pattering syllables that Freddy rightly took to be Japanese. Later on, when he went back for the late night sample change with O'Malley and Kamakura, he thought that even O'Malley's face looked different when she spoke Japanese, and her whole body language changed such that she seemed exactly like Kamakura, right down to the slight inclination of the head that seemed to show attentiveness in the passive partner in the conversation. Freddy had a good friend studying Japanese at Trinity, and he knew it was an incredibly difficult language.

The deep respect that the other professional scientists at CERN, both in-house staff and other visitors alike, showed for O'Malley had also had an impact on Freddy. He was vaguely puzzled and disturbed when he contrasted this in his mind with the way that Milton and Takin always approached O'Malley in the NPL. Perhaps even the concept of injustice flickered in his socially raw brain. Certainly he now began to understand O'Malley's contempt for such men.

But the most amazing thing of all was O'Malley's stamina, the way she constantly led from the front without sparing herself. At the beginning of the experiment he had been surprised by the urgency with which O'Malley had transmitted the 'unwritten rule' that no one work alone on the instrument at night. Freddy and Helen had alternated the night shifts, but O'Malley had always been there, day and night. She couldn't have got more than three hours' sleep a day since they had arrived. How did she manage that, Freddy had asked the previous afternoon. Yoga and meditation on a good day, caffeine and nicotine on a bad day, O'Malley had replied with a laugh. Did she speak other languages? Only a little Italian and Chinese, O'Malley had replied. Freddy wasn't going to be seen to be yawning by this woman, not when he'd enjoyed eight hours' sleep the night before. He'd give it everything he'd got for this lass until the beams shut down on Tuesday morning.

As O'Malley turned on the gangway, she saw Freddy suppress a yawn, and she smiled quietly to herself. It was a four-person experiment even for experienced scientists and she was quite exhausted by effectively running the instrument on her own for four nights on the trot, but Freddy and Helen had done their best and had been good company. She remembered her own first CERN experiment as a PhD student with Tom Bobbin, many moons ago, and how knackered she had been in the last two days. She'd have to take it very easy on the students from now on, especially in the sample preparation laboratories. Freddy's eyes looked glazed over and he was breathing heavily.

"How's it going, Freddy?"

"Fine, thanks."

"Let's check the instrument together this time. There's plenty of time to sort out the samples later."

"Great" said Freddy, with a relieved air.

"Fancy a coffee?"

"Yeah" said Freddy, with enthusiasm. "I'll get them in."

From the gangway, O'Malley's practised eye had already taken in the fact that the multidetector was out at as wide an angle as it could go. They'd timed it perfectly. The diffuse scattering scan was coming to an end and it was time to get down to the really hard low-angle work with the cobalt samples. As O'Malley entered the cabin, the printer went into a burst of activity as the run finished. The CAMAC crates stopped blinking for a minute as O'Malley took the 'director's chair' between the four computer consoles that ran the instrument, the data acquisition program, the data reduction program and the graphics displays. She was busily but unhurriedly typing into the first of these when Freddy returned from the coffee machine.

"Cheers, Freddy, that's great" said Grace, taking a sip.

"Mmm, yes" said Freddy. "I feel like a new man."

"Good" said Grace, "because we've got four or five hours' hard work ahead of us. Are you up for it?"

"You bet" said Freddy.

"OK, let's go and get the methacrylate gels out of the fridge and load up. Hand steady after that caffeine rush?"

"Excellent, yosh…"

By seven, a sample that Freddy had been truly proud of had been crushed in the pressure cell and Grace was looking very excited.

"Great sample, Freddy. We're on our way to Stockholm…"

"*Le Prix Nobel!*" exclaimed Freddy.

"At the very least" replied O'Malley. "Let's set up a diffuse scattering scan. Seven-ish now… Let it run through to midnight… Then I can come back with Helen for four or five hours' squeezing…"

"I wouldn't mind four or five hours' squeezing with Helen myself" said Freddy with a high-spirited laugh.

"Five hours squeezing gels, Freddy" Grace said.

"Yeah, I know" said Freddy. "God, I'm starving."

"Yeah, me, too. I could murder a serieux. If I set up the run, could you give Helen a bell. I fancy the Monte Cassino tonight. Let's suggest meeting Helen in Place Grenette, at that big café that sells the Belgian beers."

As O'Malley set up the command file, Freddy got through to the hotel reception and gave Helen's room number. The phone rang several times, and was finally answered by a very groggy sounding young woman.

"Oh, hi Freddy, what time is it?"

"About seven."

"God, I've been asleep for hours."

"Sweet dreams?"

"None of your business, Freddy. How's the experiment going?"

"Great. We're nearly through here and heading off down to Place Grenette. Next bus is at seven-twenty. Meet you there at eight?"

"Fine" said Helen. "I'll grab a shower. Wait a minute. Where in Place Grenette?"

"The Café Lux."

"Fine. See you later."

Freddy and O'Malley were at one of the outside tables, bullshitting away wildly. O'Malley was obviously in a high mood and Freddy was well lit up.

"Hi, Helen. Wow, you look great."

"Thank you, Freddy" said Helen with a little blush. "You look pissed."

"Rubbish" said Freddy. "This is only my second Leffe, isn't it, Grace?"

"What can I get you, Helen?" asked Grace.

"Oh, I'll have a Leffe, too" said Helen, "just a demi."

"I'll have another serious Leffe" said Freddy.

"Take it easy, Freddy" said Grace. "You'll be back in action at eight o'clock tomorrow morning. Don't forget that. By the way, if I don't make it in, you can start some runs going with Hans... *Excusex-moi monsieur, trios Leffes s'il vous plait, un demi et deux serieux...* I'll give him a call at home this evening. Maybe I should do that now, before we head down to the Monte Cassino... *Excusez-moi, monsieur, est-ce qu'il est une telephone ici?... Merci...* I'll be back in a minute."

"Hi, Hans, sorry to disturb you at home, but..."

"Ah, Grace, so you've heard the bad news already."

"Bad news?"

"About the beams."

"What? No."

"They've had to end the cycle prematurely. I don't know the details…"

"But we were there just an hour ago. Everything was running fine."

"There was some kind of power surge in the multipole wigglers about half an hour ago, and they had to shut down immediately. There may be no more beams for weeks…"

"Shit, we had our best ever sample in the beam. *Scheisse, scheisse, scheisse…*"

"I'm sorry, Grace, there's nothing to be done about it."

"Yeah, sorry, Hans. *So ist das leben, kurz aber brutal.* Anyway, I'll see you tomorrow eight-ish. At least I'll get a decent night's sleep tonight."

"Yes, sleep well, Grace. See you tomorrow morning."

"Good night, Hans."

Freddy and Helen were already tucking into their beers when Grace returned to the table.

"The experiment's over" said Grace.

"What?" they chorused.

"I just spoke to Hans. Apparently there was a power surge in the wigglers about half an hour ago. There wasn't really a safety problem, but they've had to shut down as a precaution. As the cycle was due to end Tuesday morning, they've already decided to end the cycle early."

"But…"

"No buts, I'm afraid. The only thing we have to decide is whether to kick our heels here tomorrow, or fly back tomorrow afternoon… Don't look so worried, there's plenty of data in the bag for your master's theses already… How about it?"

"Tomorrow" said Freddy, echoed by Helen.

"Fine" said Grace, "I'm quite missing Hiroshi and heading back tomorrow's fine by me. Anyway, I'm starving. Let's go and eat."

Their flight from Geneva touched down at Heathrow at noon. O'Malley had had a lot to sort out with Hans and Toshiro, and she hadn't even had time to phone Hiroshi to tell him she'd be coming back a day early. When they got back to Oxford bus station, it was early afternoon and there were not many cars, especially compared with the traffic in O'Malley's home town of London, but it only needed a few for everything to come to a more or less complete standstill. From two to two-thirty the bus crawled down the Abingdon Road. O'Malley tried to distract her attention from visions of having it off with Hiroshi by getting into Murakami Haruki's latest novel *Hitsuji o meguru booken*, but the characters just flapped and danced before her eyes.

"Excuse me" asked a plummy voice over her shoulder, "is that Chinese?"

"No" replied O'Malley. "It's Japanese. I'm reading."

Three o'clock and still two miles left to Bibbleton. O'Malley thought about giving Hiroshi a bell and asking him to come and pick her up in Abingdon. Mindful of the extra delay this would cause in consummating her mounting desire, she got into the only taxi and they set off. It was the final leg of her return trip, and she could put it down on expenses, anyway.

"Travelled far?" asked the driver.

"From Geneva" replied O'Malley.

"Where's that, then?"

"In Switzerland. In the Alps."

"Good holiday?"

"I was working. Working my arse off, in fact."

"What kind of work was that?" asked the inquisitive taxi driver.

"Neutron scattering experiment" replied O'Malley without further elaboration.

"Oh" said the driver.

"It's the next left" said O'Malley. "The cottage down the end of the lane."

"Oh, I know it" said the driver. "I dropped a ride off there the other day."

"Beautiful Japanese bloke?" asked O'Malley.

"No, Spanish looking lass" replied the driver.

O'Malley's heart gave a dull thump. The taxi pulled up outside and O'Malley paid the driver off with a hugely generous tip. There were two cars parked out the front of the cottage, Grace's Fiat 127 and a battered blue Volvo. It was Martina's car.

O'Malley stood rooted to the spot, with her suitcase and holdall bag on either side of her. The curtains of the big bedroom at the front of the cottage were drawn, but the windows were open. O'Malley just couldn't bring herself to stick the key into the front door lock. She didn't want to know. It was too late. She heard the unmistakeable sound of Hiroshi's groaning orgasm beginning from a few feet above her head.

The idea of going in and confronting Martina and Hiroshi, perhaps even of attacking Martina, seemed too gross. She suddenly felt exhausted and deflated. She went over to the little turquoise Fiat 127 and rooted around in her holdall. Yes, she had a key. She opened the boot and chucked her luggage in. Hurriedly, with a bizarre guilty feeling, almost as if she didn't want to be discovered by Martina and Hiroshi, she got into the driver's seat and backed quietly out of the drive. She didn't know where she was going or why, but she had to get away.

A burn up the motorway did O'Malley good...

...and yet she still felt angry and jealous and mad at Martina and Hiroshi. What was she going to say to Hiroshi when she got back?

Different possible conversations with Hiroshi started to take place in her head. Abingdon was only a couple of miles away now. She needed another detour for a few minutes while she composed herself. Of course, it would be a good idea to cruise past Martina's place to see if the car was back. She definitely didn't want to bump into Martina back at Bibbleton. She couldn't face that. So she turned towards North Abingdon. The blue Volvo was sitting on the suburban driveway. As O'Malley slowed down involuntarily as she drove past, she thought she recognized the rozzer who had bashed her face in. For a split second, O'Malley was tempted to mount the curve, speed up and simply mow the bastard down. But it could be a mistake… the civilian clothes, the orange streetlighting that had just come on… God, it might be an innocent bystander. Grace realized she was being assailed by dark thoughts, did some deep yoga breathing, and sped off. Ten minutes later, Hiroshi opened the door of their little cottage in Bibbleton. The pink-washed walls, the thatched roof, the climbing rose, the smell of flowers in the evening air… Grace breathed it in. The sex with Martina didn't matter. She was in love with Hiroshi.

"Well, madam?"

The bigger man had his pen poised.

"Dr O'Malley, I want you to think very carefully. Anything, and I mean anything, you may have seen that afternoon might be of importance to us."

"I remember the witness appeal" said O'Malley. "I would have come forward earlier if I'd seen anything suspicious."

"Anything at all, madam."

"I'm sorry, I don't think I can help you. Look…"

O'Malley looked down at her watch.

"…I'm in the middle of a party…"

"Very well, madam" the smaller officer replied, standing up. The bigger man closed his notebook and also stood.

"If anything does occur to you, please could you contact me right away."

He handed O'Malley his name card.

"Sure, no problem" said O'Malley. "Are we done… I've got a party to get back to, you see."

"Just one other thing, madam."

"What's that?"

"Possession of cannabis is a criminal offence. We haven't got a warrant, but we could come back with one."

"Yes. I see."

"You could try being a little more discreet, Dr O'Malley. Then I'd be free to concentrate on more serious matters."

"Yes, I see."

"Very well, madam, thanks for your co-operation, and I wish you a pleasant afternoon."

The unmarked brown Austin trundled back off down the lane. O'Malley had completely lost any sense of time. She went out into the garden and was amazed that it was still sunny, warm and drunken. She rejoined the hippies and said

"Hey, you guys. That was the rozzers. I got a warning about the ganja smoking. Let's be careful, OK… O, hi Pru, haven't seen you for ages…"

"Hello, Grace. I'm so happy you are being open and cool about what happened between Martina and Hiroshi. It will be good for your relationship long term. We all think Hiroshi's lovely. And we think you're lovely, too" she added.

"You're too kind" said Grace.

"I want to talk to Martina. Do you know where she is?"

"No idea" Grace replied. "She was here a while ago, but I got distracted by the police…"

"Don't worry about it" said Pru.

"I've had a weird month" Grace said. "Let's get really pissed."

Chapter 3

Discovery

Sunday morning, Grace woke up at five-thirty. She did not have a hangover. She was starting to boil with calculations, and started to mull over the strange idea she'd had when she and Ben had been on the all-night vigil outside the American Embassy after the Tripoli bombing. Surely the four-dimensional mean-field theory that had been used in so many renormalization group calculations, including her own on gluon interactions, could be applied to space-time itself... Grace was self-consciously cleverer than most, but realized that there were lots of other clever people around and somebody else would surely have thought of it... But then again, by the mid-eighties, most of the clever people were turning into dour computer bores, spending all their time writing programs and running jobs. She was one of the last who could sit down for hours on end with nothing more than a pile of scrap paper and a biro. Maybe you could expand space-time itself in its own epsilon neighbourhood. Maybe the twistor theory of Dirac could be applied. Maybe...

She decided to drop the acid. Hiroshi was still asleep. Would he trip with her? She tried to control her emotions and different possible conversations with Hiroshi were starting to take place in her head. In one version he was looking very worried and saying

"O, Grace, LSD... I'm not sure... I don't think I could..."

and in another he was being a lot braver, his face was lighting up with that dimpled smile that drove Grace off her rocker and he was saying

"O, Grace, how exciting... Let's do it."

She decided to drop the acid at lunchtime with or without Hiroshi. If he wasn't prepared to trip with her, maybe their relationship didn't have a long-term future, she thought.

46

Ten minutes later, Grace woke Hiroshi up, then popped him the question about hippy Arne's acid. He agreed without hesitation, and she felt guilty about ever having mistrusted his reaction. She explained to him that it might last eight hours, and how they should make arrangements – the supermarket in the morning, the light brunch, the phone off the hook, everything secure so that they'd have the whole day to themselves, to spend indoors or outdoors as the mood took them.

They were lucky that it was a lovely day, the last of the Indian summer. As planned, they dropped the acid around noon. The LSD that hippy Arne had given Grace was the last of the great acid ever to hit the streets in the UK, a real blast from the past.

... purple, green and brown interleaving patterns of coloured lights around the edge of her vision on a pure white ground whilst listening to what could not have been more than ten seconds of Larks Tongues in Aspic but which seemed at least a thousand years as she hit the peak... the debris of the half-eaten apples and chocolates (the quintessential apple, man, it really was)... Hiroshi's face as he looked into a rose and she saw his hallucination, with the flower opening up to football size, the intense smells walking across the fields, the madness of people sitting in little metal and glass boxes – yeah, cars, that's what they were called – the spiritual harmony with all things...

As Grace was coming down, she thought that it's not hard to understand why establishments everywhere have outlawed LSD and why the Operation Julie people got such savage sentences. Nobody who's had an experience like that would even dream of putting up with the relentlessly aggressive and abusive management style that characterizes our system, no one would give up a sunny day for the good of their mortgage or pension or whatever other myth they're deluding themselves into wasting their lives for.

By ten, Hiroshi was down too, then suddenly out like a light. Grace watched him sleep on the sofa, as his long slow breaths drew in space, in time, in space, in time, in space...

Then she began to calculate.

When the first wave of calculations hit her, she felt physically sick and was unable to write, but when she'd smoked a cigarette to calm down, the biro grew wings and started to fly across the pages. You can't imagine the four-dimensional integrals she took on, the way the four-dimensional second-rank tensors gave way to higher-order tensors, to completely ripping away the veil that surrounds reality, to seeing it raw, in its pure, pristine mathematical completeness. If you could do that, you'd have climbed K2 and Everest in one night, like she did. Maybe instead imagine being on a Pacific beach and huge rollers crashing in, leaving you gasping for breath, certain that you're going to drown, then suddenly receding and you come up for air, amazed to be alive… and that happening for hours on end.

She handwrote over a hundred pages in one night, always scribbling, scribbling, the arcane symbols piling up on the floor, the calculation following its own logic and her body locked into a simple rhythm – fifty minutes writing, ten minutes cigarette break – hour after hour. By about four o'clock in the morning she'd already done enough to pull out all the main features of the unified field theory, but she was driven on and on and didn't really feel she'd resolved the tension racking her body until around six. Hiroshi was then stirring fitfully, and she put on a little pot of espresso. The espresso machine was one of those primitive but stylish ones with two parts of decagonal cross section. Grace was so tired and nervous that she was hardly able to unscrew the upper part.

"I'll do it" said Hiroshi.

"O, Hiroshi, hi, you're awake" Grace said stupidly.

"O, Grace, you look tired. Couldn't you sleep? What time is it?"

"Er, about six, I think."

The birds were twittering unnaturally noisily outside.

They wandered outside with their coffees. Grace's head was throbbing, but she was determined to apply the finishing touches and she said

"Hiroshi, I've been calculating all night. I need a couple more hours to finish."

And that's exactly what it took. By eight o'clock, she had finished writing the theory that Einstein sought in vain for thirty years. She had unified electromagnetism and gravity and the weak and strong forces had fallen out as natural consequences of this unification. The piecemeal efforts of Salam and Weinberg to unify the weak and electromagnetic forces had been a brave effort, but not in the right ballpark. She should have been very happy. But she wasn't, because she'd also discovered the epsilon twistor. Just as Einstein's 1905 paper '*Ist die Trägheit eines Körpers von seinem Energiegehalt abhangig?*' (Does the inertia of a body depend upon its energy content?) was the progenitor of the atom bomb, so her 1984 calculations would be the progenitor of a much more powerful device, one that would destroy a whole continent. At about seven o'clock in the morning Grace named this device the epsilon twistor because of the way she had applied mean-field calculations which make a perturbation of space-time in the epsilon neighbourhood of four dimensions with the twistor algebra that Dirac had developed.

According to her calculations, the energy released by such a device would be enough to destroy a continent in the time it took a light beam to cross a few thousand miles, let's say a hundredth of a second. Unless you've done physics, you wouldn't realize how bizarre such a result is. It's just like the way the half-life of a neutron is about fifteen minutes when *a priori* it could have been anything over fifty orders of magnitude from the immeasurably short to the immeasurably long. Here we had a device that could probably be built by a modern technologically advanced society that would destroy not the entire Earth, but about a continent at one go. The last calculation she did in that long, long night was at five to eight in the morning when she checked the energy release of the epsilon twistor by a different method of calculation.

The result agreed.

Her final scribbled note was 'Approximate devastation zone NY-LA'.

After Grace had washed up the coffee things, she collected the hundred or so pieces of paper strewn around the living room, put them in a folder and locked them away in her desk. She thought about destroying them immediately, but something, probably the idea of fame and power, held her back. No one was going to come snooping around the cottage of an obscure Oxford academic working on harmless projects in elementary particle physics. There was no need to be paranoid, yet. She asked Hiroshi if he fancied a stroll into Abingdon to pick up a morning paper. He said that he did. Most unusually for him, after popping upstairs, he came back down in Japanese clothing. It was on the tip of Grace's tongue to say something like

"Hiroshi, I've got something important to tell you."

and blurt it all out, but she loved him, and didn't want to compromise him with the knowledge. She realized that she was mentally, physically and emotionally exhausted after twenty-four hours of extreme nervous excitement and she had to bite her lip until she'd had a chance to sleep on it at least a couple of times, to think it over. Sleep still seemed a long way off, though. Her head was throbbing.

Hiroshi was in high good spirits. On the walk across the fields into Abingdon he kept springing off the path and twirling round like a whirling dervish, spinning so fast that his yukata would fan out horizontally. He was constantly laughing at nothing, and said

"God, Grace, why on Earth is that stuff illegal? I've never had a better day in my life. I've never felt better in my life than I do today."

'And I've never done a more amazing calculation in my life than I did last night. And I never will' Grace thought, with a touch of melancholy. At this moment she recognized the downside of having climbed Everest and K2 in one night. There were no bigger mountains left to climb, not in science anyway.

"It's illegal because, well, could you imagine going into a boring office or factory job today, after what we've been through yesterday?"

"Hmm…" Hiroshi hummed thoughtfully. "I see what you mean."

"Can you imagine having some talentless little prat who's been on a Thatcherite management course screaming military-style orders at you?"

"No" said Hiroshi. He never swore, and didn't like it when Grace did, so she was amazed when he said

"I would say 'Fuck off you talentless little prat, I am going to take some LSD and play in the fields'." His face lit up with a daring, brilliant smile.

They wandered into a copse, taking in the cool morning air. The smell of the world was fantastic. Grace's head stopped throbbing on the walk into Abingdon. Needless to say, although their world had changed inexorably in the past twenty-four hours, the papers were filled with more of the same. Hate for Gadaffi, worship for football players, hate for teachers, worship for film stars, hate for commies…

"I can't take any of this poisonous rubbish today" Grace said. "Let's not buy one."

When they returned home Grace slept blissfully through the afternoon. By the time she woke up, she'd already decided what she was going to do about the epsilon twistor, and it was a dangerous and lonely course. Grace desperately wanted to live together with Hiroshi, but it couldn't possibly be fair to ask him to come along for the ride unless he realized quite how long and bumpy it was going to be.

Jack Milton was nonplussed. The softly, softly approach with O'Malley wasn't working. Autumn was wearing on and the young upstart had just ignored him completely. She seemed perfectly happy working away in a shared office with the ordinary post-docs and in a ridiculously inadequate basement lab with two of the weakest masters students of the two hundred that had just taken finals. Jack Milton had to explain this to SERC. Smythe was putting on the pressure. Jack Milton prided himself on being a man of action. It was time to force the pace. If the carrot wasn't working, it must be worth trying the stick. He decided to call O'Malley into his office after coffee.

Tom Bobbin was a decent man and, though often cowed by the aggressive, abusive management style that had continued seamlessly from Bryant to Milton, he couldn't resist getting in a heavy blow to Milton's overweening pride every now and again. That morning he crossed the coffee lounge to the little table where Milton sat with his regular cronies in the NPL hierarchy. Christopher Vane was in full flow.

"I say, Professor, that was a splendid paper of yours on the t-J hopping model Hamiltonian that I saw in Topics in Nuclear Physics."

Topics in Nuclear Physics was the NPL house journal, the only place where Milton could get his work published.

"Talking of fine papers, Professor" said Tom Bobbin, "have a look at this latest masterpiece by O'Malley on scaling concepts in gluon interactions."

He passed it across the coffee table and Milton made an expression like someone had just stuck a particularly pungent dog turd just under his nose.

"She's already sent it off to PRL and let me have a preprint."

PRL was the academics' acronym for Physical Review Letters, the leading American journal where O'Malley published much of her work. Milton had never had a paper accepted by PRL.

"The way she's going, she's going to win a Nobel Prize in her thirties."

As Tom had hoped, Milton looked physically sick.

"I think you overestimate O'Malley's work, Tom. From what I've heard, she's merely developing Yamato's theory. I've been told that her work on gluons is unoriginal and unexceptional."

Tom Bobbin had been in elementary particle physics for more than a decade.

"Anyone who thinks Grace's work is unoriginal doesn't know their arse from their elbow" he said. "I believe the latest manuscript to be the greatest advance in understanding fundamental physics since Dirac's 1928 paper. It's that massive" he added, twisting in the knife.

Tom's group were at their usual table. Grace was in full flow.

"…that's the problem with having a dishonest, lazy, rude, intellectually incompetent head of department like Jack Milton" she was saying. "What a talentless little Thatcherite prat."

"Calm down, Grace" said Tom, who had just returned from Milton's table.

"Look, Grace" Tom continued, "Professor Milton hasn't done you any harm. In fact, he wants to meet you in his office after coffee to discuss your future research plans."

"He knows I'm leaving at the end of the year" said Grace. "It's none of his business."

"Grace, he's your head of department. You are still employed here and your contract stipulates that you must carry out your duties to the satisfaction of your departmental head."

The other conversation around Tom's group's table had withered away.

"I see" Grace said.

At 11.15, O'Malley knocked on the door of the professorial office and walked straight in. Milton was seated at his vast desk, and Takin was standing slightly behind his chair. Milton rose from his chair with a smug smile on his face, and said

"It's time we had a chat about your research plans, O'Malley. I..."

O'Malley cut him short. She didn't even look at Takin. She was staring intently, like a woman capable of murder, at Milton.

"I don't allow people to use my unadorned surname. You previously addressed me informally as Grace. I prefer that. If you use my surname, you have to call me Doctor O'Malley."

"Have to?..."

Milton stammered, the superficial smile wiped from his face. His mouth was working in its usual downward turn. It was one of his standard methods for establishing the pecking order, to dismissively use the plain surname of subordinates.

"What do you mean by..."

started Takin, but Milton cut him short. He was staring intently at O'Malley, like a man who had already broken the spirit of several junior academics. He recovered his composure quickly, and the smug smile returned like a mask. He said

"I don't think there's any 'have to' about it, O'Malley."

There followed a short silence.

O'Malley looked straight at Milton and her tranquil facial expression did not even ripple at the second use of her unadorned surname. However, she moved with lightning speed to deliver a resounding slap to Milton's face before Milton or Takin could react. She was already back standing upright opposite the professor when she said

"Never use my unadorned surname again. Do you understand?"

"What the hell do..."

began Takin, but O'Malley cut him short.

"I asked you a question. Do you understand me?"

The tears were welling up in Milton's eyes and rage was contorting his face. He replied

"I hope you understand what this means for you and your career, *Doctor* O'Malley."

"I rather think I do" said O'Malley.

"*Kangaete oite kudasai*" she continued in Japanese, closing the door quietly behind her.

Tom was fiddling with his filing cabinet when Grace arrived at his open office door. He turned round and said

"Hello, Grace. How was it with the professor?"

"Could have been better, Tom. I slapped his face."

Tom Bobbin's genial expression immediately clouded over. As Grace's former PhD supervisor, he was well used to his protégé's bizarre sense of humour, so he wasn't unduly fazed and replied

"Come off it, Grace. What really happened?"

"He called me plain O'Malley. I warned him and he repeated it deliberately, so I slapped him."

There was something about Grace's delivery that made it clear that this was not a joke.

"My God" said Tom. "There'll be disciplinary hearings. You may lose your fellowship."

"...mmm, could be. Sorry, Tom, I've got to go."

Colin was waiting outside the town hall. It wasn't like O'Malley to be late for anything, but for a political rally...

"Hi, Colin, sorry I'm late..."

"It's OK, Grace. I don't think Purvis is speaking till two. Couldn't tear yourself away from the port and cigars after college luncheon?"

"Come off it, Colin, in fact..." said O'Malley with a feigned air of righteous indignation "I have just been discussing sample preparation with one of my research students and haven't had college lunch at all... apart from a bite of roast swan washed down with a '61 Pauillac, of course. It's still only one-thirty. Do you fancy a quick pint before we go in?"

"Yeah, why not" said Colin.

Colin had enjoyed his work as a school physics teacher when he first started, but since they'd got the new headmaster and deputy head things had taken a rapid turn for the worse. By the mid-eighties Colin had been hardened by his years in school, and his recent troubles soon came pouring out.

"You won't believe what I got from those wankers Runner and Bishop yesterday."

"Try me" said Grace.

"I got a direct military-style order to take over the sixth form careers advice stuff. It's a huge job and they're offering me nothing – just do it."

"I can believe you all too easily, Colin" said Grace, "sounds just like the management style in our lab."

Grace had heard Colin complain many times how the two new men had been parachuted in by the head of the board of governors, who was in the Tory party. The holidays were being eroded; the pay, frozen against a background of galloping inflation, was becoming worthless, the tasks and initiatives were mindlessly multiplying as yet madder and weirder ideas were dreamed up by Keith Joseph and his cronies in Whitehall. Colin's rants went on and on. More or less all the good people he'd been with on the PGCE course had already left the profession, leaving behind a crushed dispirited rabble who couldn't get better jobs and just had to put up with the shit. The timid, hopeless teachers who stayed in 'professional' unions like PAT, AMMA and NASUWT were black-legging the decent, spirited teachers to defeat. A pall of oppression was descending on school life everywhere...

"Anyway" said Colin, "it's not the first time. I got the bottom set second and third years, and the non-examinable core science fifth years on a Friday afternoon. An absolute nightmare timetable, no sweeteners, no promotion on offer, just do it. The only guy who's been promoted in the past couple of years is an arrogant, incompetent prat who's, guess what, a big fan of Thatcher's and into 'efficiency'. Now that he's senior tutor, he's part of an unholy triumvirate with Runner and Bishop, turning Rivermead into a 'leaner, fitter team'. My best mate Fred has buggered off to Brazil and the only other physics teacher in the school buggered off to the, all hail, wonderful privatized world of BT."

"My brother works for BT" said O'Malley.

"Wow" said Colin, "I never knew you had a brother."

"Well, I guess he's more into football and domestic blissification than into science and politics, so we don't see much of each other. Poor Francis, he joined the Post Office after he left school as an easy way out of the capitalist rat-race and now that they've been privatized, he's right in it. They've cut the staff in the Sheffield area from eight thousand to five thousand in the past five years, you know. He's worried about his job."

"Shit" said Colin, "and I thought teaching was bad."

"Well, it is" said Grace, laughing.

"You don't know the half of it" said Colin. "Apart from Bishop, who wouldn't lift a bloody finger in a classroom because he's too busy doing 'timetabling', I was the only qualified physics teacher in the school until a few weeks ago. The new bloke Andrew's a probationer – seems a bit straight, but OK. Doesn't know his arse from his elbow…"

"Hey, man, that's a pretty good moan you've got going there…"

"And guess how much our budget is for teaching physics in a school of one thousand children?"

"No idea" said Grace.

"Go on, have a guess."

"Well, the squeeze on public spending has been pretty vicious, so I'll guess low. Ten thousand quid?"

"In my dreams."

"Lower, really?"

"Just by an order of magnitude."

"One thousand quid?"

"Yup."

"But mending an oscilloscope costs at least fifty quid."

"Yup."

"Shit."

"Too right it's shit" said Colin. "Halfway through the year you tend to run out of interesting experiments to do with a piece of string."

O'Malley looked at her watch.

"Bollocks" she said. "It's gone two. Let's go."

Grace and Colin walked up the imposing steps between the NUT rally posters, one of which was flapping appropriately in a school notice board kind of way.

A uniformed commissionaire barred their way in.

"We're going to the NUT meeting" said Grace.

"O, no, you're not, madam" said the commissionaire confidently. "The room's already full and it's against fire regulations."

Colin's last lesson, between morning break and lunch, had been a double period with twelve lit Bunsen burners distributed among thirty-four adolescents including a boy in a wheelchair, whose presence blocked the aisle down one side of the lab. He was at the end of his tether.

"Look" Colin spluttered, "I've just given up my bleeding lunch to get here, and I'm going in."

So saying, he attempted to brush past the commissionaire, who was a much larger man than him. The commissionaire stuck his arm out to block Colin. He then looked at Grace. With the violence of her confrontation with Milton still coursing through her veins, the six-foot tall O'Malley was clenching her fist and it was obvious that she was about to lash out. The commissionaire hurriedly lowered his arm. His job wasn't worth aggro like that.

"I was only concerned for your safety, madam" he said. "It's very crowded in there."

The hall was indeed packed and, contrary to council fire regulations, there were dozens of people standing at the back and in the aisles. A feisty young woman was giving a fiery speech about protecting our children's future from the Thatcherite onslaught.

As the speaker banged on, Colin floated off into an uncomfortable dream in which a minister of state was lecturing him about something called 'political correctness' or 'PC'. In the insidious way of dreams, Colin somehow knew that this phenomenon meant the disguising of their sexism and racism by sexist and racist people, and with a sinking heart he felt that the sanctimonious politician was the kind of middle-class do-gooder who would continue the Tories work in keeping the teaching profession down even after the Tories had finally been routed. A loud round of applause brought Colin back to the hall, and Frank Purvis was announced. Both Colin and Grace were disappointed with this timid little man, who appeared like a frightened rabbit staring into the headlights of the oncoming juggernaut. The effects of the beer were wearing off. Grace whispered

"Let's go."

They slipped out the back of the hall into the vestibule and started down the steps.

"Did you know Martina and Darren have moved to Abingdon?" asked Colin.

"Sort of" said O'Malley. "Richard mentioned something about it a while back. I guess we're nearly neighbours. Bibbleton is just down the road."

"Great" said Colin. "Anyway, let's get some go together. Talking of which, how are you fixed for this afternoon?"

"I've got to go back to the lab, I'm afraid. I'm meeting up with my masters students at teatime. I'm sorry. I can't skip it. We've got some CERN data to analyze."

"Still firing beams of neutrons at little pieces of cobalt?"

"That sort of thing. Sorry, Colin, I've got to go. It's half three already."

"OK, Grace. It was good to see you again. Thanks for coming to the rally. I'm sorry I moaned on and on…"

"No problem. There's plenty to moan about. I'll let you catch up on my moans when I get back from the Sakamoto conference the week after next."

When O'Malley got back to the lab, she went straight up to the coffee room, where she knew she would find Helen and Freddy. Afternoon tea was as deeply ingrained a ritual in the NPL as morning coffee. Tom Bobbin was in the queue at the hatch. He turned to Grace with an almost awestruck expression and said

"You didn't really hit the professor, did you?"

"…mmm, but not hard, only a slap. Things have gone downhill here really badly since the seventies, haven't they?"

Tom looked over his shoulder at the lengthening queue, which did not include Milton or Takin.

"Well, not that badly" he replied, uncertainly.

"O, come off it, Tom. This new regime looks like an absolute disaster zone. I guess they really fancy themselves since Thatcher got back in."

Tom sat down at the same table his group always sat down at, and said

"It's no use being confrontational, Grace. There's going to be trouble enough as it is. I think you should head things off at the pass by making a full apology to Professor Milton, and by laying off the politics."

"Actually, I've just come back from the NUT rally in the town hall, and I'm joining the miners' picket line at Didcot Power Station again tomorrow morning."

"O, God…"

"… and as for Milton, he's just a talentless little prat… hasn't produced a research paper in ages, and Fyodor already told me that his lectures are a complete disaster zone."

Fyodor had just sat down next to them and the students in the group were on their way.

"…but he's head of department, Grace."

"Look, Tom, Jack Milton's just one of the talentless scum that's floated to the top under Thatcherism. They're not going to sack me for slapping a little arsehole like him."

"What" exclaimed Fyodor. "You struck the professor. That's outrageous."

"Well, it might be outrageous in a Stalinist second-world hole like Russia…" began O'Malley.

"Calm down, Grace" said Tom.

"Far out" said Richard. "Did I hear you say you were going down to the picket lines at Didcot tomorrow?"

"Yeah, we've got a minibus going from St Aldates at five."

"Five?"

"Yeah, they're starting the deliveries early to try to avoid the pickets. Julian was tipped off."

"Well, one thing I'm sure of" said Judith, giggling, "is that Richard will not be up at five in the morning."

"Says who?" said Richard. "I bet Martina will come, too. Her dad fought with the anarchists in the Spanish Civil War."

"Wow" said O'Malley, "I didn't know that."

"Yeah, he was in the last group cut off by the fascists down by the harbour in Barcelona in thirty-eight."

"Far out" said O'Malley.

"So she says" said Helen. "Martina is such a bullshitter."

Richard was about to reply, but was cut short by the appearance of Professor Milton at their table. Studiously avoiding looking in O'Malley's direction, he said

"Tom, I'd like a word with you in my office, after tea."

"Certainly, Professor" said Tom, to Milton's retreating back.

"Well, at least he used your Christian name" said Grace. "Maybe he's catching on."

"Don't be flippant, Grace. This is serious."

"Isn't everything fucking serious in Britain these days? I've hardly seen a smile in here since I got back from Japan."

There was an awkward silence, broken by Tom.

"Well" said Tom, turning to Freddy and Helen. "Did you enjoy your first CERN experiment?"

"Oh, yes" said Freddy.

"They're dead envious of me at St Angela's" said Helen, "going to Geneva and all."

It was 4.15 and people were starting to drift downstairs.

"Could I have a word with you after I've seen the professor, Grace?" asked Tom.

"Sure" said Grace.

Later, when Grace sat down in Tom's office, Tom got up and closed the door behind them, the first time Grace had ever seen him do this. Tom looked very worried.

"Grace, I realize that advice is a double-edged sword, but I really think you should make an official apology to Professor Milton and the university authorities. It's going to look bad enough for the department anyway if word gets around that a Royal Society research fellow has struck the professor. You could say you were suffering from delayed shock from that terrible bash you got on your head a few weeks ago. You could..."

"It's not worth it" said Grace. "Hiroshi and I are planning to emigrate next year, anyway, when he's finished his course."

Tom let out an involuntary groan.

"Emigrate?" he said.

"Come on, Tom. There's nothing going on for me here. You can see that for yourself. Now that they've crushed the miners, steel workers and car workers, the professionals will be next in line. I see only the winding-up operation for UK science. The Miltons and Takins of this world have won in Britain. I'll be at my peak in my thirties. I can't afford to spend them in the economic and scientific second world."

"Where...?"

"We haven't decided yet... probably back to Japan... we're going together for the Sakamoto conference next week so we can check things out..."

"Anyway" Grace continued, "I've got to prepare my lecture for the conference."

She got up and left Tom's office with a rather desolate expression.

Professor Yamato was nervously greeting guests in the entrance hall of the Kyoto University Conference Centre. He wasn't normally a nervous man. In fact, he usually exuded an air of Buddha-like calm, as befits a man who could calculate at the highest level of abstraction. He was an elementary particle physicist and was at his happiest engrossed in his work on the mass of the elusive Higgs boson. That summer, his paper on flavour changing neutral currents with his PhD student Shinoda had been submitted to Physical Review Letters and he was still awaiting the outcome of the long drawn-out reviewing process. But he was used to that. It was over a quarter of a century ago that he had done his own PhD with the great Yukawa at Kyoto University, and he had learned patience. No, there were two other things that had rattled his usually serene cage.

First, there was this polymer business. Until the previous evening, 5th November 1984, the four-day conference of which he was a reluctant co-host had been the only significant cloud on the horizon of Yamato's largely unruffled, peaceful life. Then he had read an envelope full of scruffy, chaotic calculations that O'Malley-san had passed to him in his office the same afternoon.

"Would you like a coffee?" Yamato had asked.

"O, yes, please, Kimio" Grace had replied.

"That would be nice, Professor Yamato" Hiroshi had said. "It is so beautiful here, the only place I have visited as lovely as my native Fukuoka."

"Ah, thank you very much" Yamato had replied.

And so the small talk had continued. Just when Grace and Hiroshi were preparing to return to their hotel, Grace had said

"Err… Kimio, I've got something I'd like you to take a look at."

"Certainly" Professor Yamato had replied blandly.

"It's very important that you don't copy it. Sorry… I would be very grateful if you could read it, then pass it on to Professor Kamakura… I am very sorry, but I have to ask you to ask him also not to take any copy of the material, but to write to me in England saying he has read and understood my paper. I am very sorry to make these strange requests, but later I think you will understand me…"

Professor Yamato had smiled indulgently. Part of Grace's character flaw was a kind of paranoia about anyone stealing her ideas. Doubtless the brown envelope that Grace was taking out of her briefcase contained some new work on what now, Professor Yamato was forced to admit to himself with a sense of embarrassment, was becoming known as the Yamato theory.

Yamato and Kamakura had looked upon Grace as a gift from the gods – a Westerner at a prestigious university who understood their work immediately, had developed its elementary particle physics version, and was prepared to fight for it, even at the cost of being regarded as a maverick in her own community. The two years she had spent in Osaka had endeared O'Malley to her Japanese hosts by her willingness to learn Japanese, her open, questioning mind and her sense of fun and excitement in her work, despite her propensity for tempestuous arguments, which Yamato regarded as a character flaw. The new O'Malley looked over-excited and tired. She had arrived with her Japanese partner, who seemed to fulfil all the Japanese concepts of beauty and grace, at the weekend. She would be an important player in the conference – only she and the American Ron Green would support the new theory, and both were giving invited lectures.

"Yes, Grace-san" Yamato said, "I understand."

"It would probably be better... very sorry... but it may be better for your peace of mind if you read it after the conference. I'm only giving it to you now because I'm worried about leaving it in my hotel room and I'm not enjoying carrying it around."

Professor Yamato frowned, not so much at the request as at the fact that Grace's paranoia seemed to be a worsening trait.

"Yes, Grace-san" he said, "I understand."

It was better for Grace not to get upset when her performance in the coming days was likely to be so important.

"Well" said Grace, "Hiroshi and I should be going now."

"Yes" said Hiroshi. "Thank you so much for the delicious coffee, Professor Yamato."

"Ah, to meet you has been a great pleasure" Professor Yamato said. "I look forward to your company at the conference dinner. Please enjoy Kyoto. If you wish, one of my graduate students can take you sightseeing while we are busy with our boring science. Kyoto has many beautiful temples."

"That's very kind of you, Professor Yamato" Hiroshi replied. "I will be coming to the opening ceremony tomorrow morning and perhaps I could meet your student then."

"Excellent" said Professor Yamato.

"Well, bye Kimio, and please accept my apologies for the trouble I am going to cause you" Grace said enigmatically.

Professor Yamato frowned again.

"Ah, no problem, Grace-san" he said, not sure what the problem was.

At eleven o'clock in the evening, after his wife and son had gone to bed, Yamato took the envelope out. He was afraid Grace might have found some flaw in the new theory on the very eve of the conference. She had certainly seemed unusually agitated. Yamato started reading with puzzlement. The manuscript wasn't about polymers at all. By three o'clock in the morning, he had become the second person to understand the physics of the epsilon twistor, and the third to know of its possibilities. The hundred and twenty or so pages of scribbled calculations were all in the same ink. On to the final sheet a note had been added in a different ink, in a different, less frantic, handwriting. It was in Japanese, not bad Japanese for a foreigner. It said:

Dear Kimio,
When you have come this far, you will be the third person to know of the epsilon twistor, along with Hiroshi and myself. I see

in its development possibilities for an end to the yoke of American imperialism under which the world groans and suffers. I see also great dangers for humanity. I have never made a copy of these calculations, though they are etched on my mind. Please, I beseech you, do not make a copy of any page, but pass the document on to Professor Kamakura. He has many contacts in the Japanese government and will know what to do with this terrible material better than either of us.

Please accept my apologies for the trouble I am going to cause you. If you feel you cannot pass the knowledge on, please destroy the manuscript thoroughly. If you ever refer to it in correspondence with me, please call it my work on extremum thermodynamics.

Take care, Grace

Chapter 4

Two Go Games

Kamakura had already badgered Yamato and O'Malley into meeting him in Shugakuin in the evening. His choice of the American-style Speakeasy bar was typically idiosyncratic and not to Yamato's liking. O'Malley had laughed and insisted on bringing Hiroshi along. It had been a favourite bar of hers in the days of her JSPS Fellowship, when she had lived for a few weeks in the International House just round the corner.

There weren't many people in the bar – the clientele and staff had changed completely since O'Malley had been there last. There was no sign of the friendly bikers. Kamakura ordered a bottle of Jim Bean bourbon and poured three stiff ones on ice, Yamato taking a mineral water. To the surprise of the three scientists, it was Hiroshi who spoke first.

"Grace told me on the way here that she was afraid you'd think in terms of using the device against the Chinese rather than the Americans."

Kamakura gave a little start. So did O'Malley. Yamato continued to look gloomy.

"I wish Grace had never discovered the thing and I wish she'd never given it to you, but…"

"Wait a minute" said Kamakura.

"Don't interrupt me" said Hiroshi.

Kamakura lapsed into a shocked silence.

"I know you are a very powerful man" Hiroshi continued, "and I appreciate your hospitality here, but please hear me out. The device is a doomsday weapon and should only be used to protect the Eurasian peoples…"

"Eighty percent of the world's population" interjected O'Malley.

Hiroshi gave her an exasperated glance. O'Malley said

"Sorry"

and stared into her bourbon.

"It should only be used to protect the Eurasian peoples against American domination. We are not occupied by Chinese troops here. We are occupied by Americans."

"As are the British" he added as an afterthought.

"Have you finished?" asked Kamakura.

"Yes, I have" Hiroshi replied.

The three whiskey drinkers took a long slug. Yamato said

"Shouldn't we be holding this conversation somewhere safer?"

"Nonsense" Kamakura replied. "If you want to hide something, you should leave it out in the open." As if to emphasize the point, he took the brown envelope out of his briefcase and slapped it down in the middle of the table.

"I think you are missing the main point, Mr Fujimoto…" Kamakura said.

"Hiroshi" Hiroshi said.

"Hiroshi" Kamakura echoed, giving Hiroshi an exasperated look. "Anyway, the point is that it is by no means certain that such a device could be built…"

"The calculations are definitely right" said O'Malley.

"Yes, they are" said Yamato, with a depressed air.

"Yes, yes" said Kamakura impatiently, "but the American Manhattan Project…"

"The project that led to Hiroshima and Nagasaki…" O'Malley interrupted.

"The American Manhattan Project" Kamakura repeated testily, "took years of work of the greatest Western scientists. There were thousands of man-years of work of many top scientists in between Einstein's letter to Roosevelt and, yes… Hiroshima and Nagasaki. It is ridiculously premature to think about how the device might be used…"

"No, it isn't" Hiroshi interrupted.

"Surely" said O'Malley, "a journey of a thousand steps must start with a correct one in the right direction."

"Very well" said Kamakura, "but this still leaves the question of how we set out. You must all be aware that if I pass this document…"

Here he tapped the brown envelope with the base of his whiskey glass, and the ice made a little tinkling sound.

"…on to the Japanese government… and, as Grace guessed, I do have the contacts to start, shall we say, the Japanese Manhattan Project, the control will pass out of our hands anyway. We will be powerless to control how it is used in, let us say, twenty years' time."

"I am still planning to be around in 2004" said Hiroshi.

"So am I" said O'Malley.

"Yes, yes, so am I" said Kamakura, "but we will not be the ones with our hands 'on the button'."

"Hmm…" chorused Grace and Hiroshi.

"It is also highly unlikely that such a 'Manhattan Project' could be kept secret right up to its fulfilment" Kamakura continued, "and we will all be in great danger."

Yamato looked nervously around, as if expecting a CIA agent to open fire on them at any moment. He was a timid man, and he knew that his life had changed irreversibly for the worse.

"Grace" Kamakura continued, "and, of course, you too Mr Fujimoto… Hiroshi… I have an important question. Do you want to come to Japan to work on developing the idea of extremum thermodynamics?"

He tapped the envelope again.

"Hiroshi?" Grace said.

"I think we have to, don't we?" Hiroshi asked.

"Yes, I think we do" Grace replied.

"That is unfortunate" said Kamakura, "as it was going to be my suggestion that you return to Britain."

Grace and Hiroshi looked flabbergasted.

"If you stay here" Kamakura continued, "you will attract attention. My suggestion, Grace, is that you go back, and only work on SSK theory in connection with the polymer revolution. We can find ways to contact you about the extremum thermodynamics project that we set up here… I am assuming that I will get support from the government… and the Japanese bureaucracy moves very slowly, so its development will be painfully slow… What do you think?"

"Well, I think Hiroshi and I would be in danger" Grace said. "The police were already on to us…"

"Look" said Kamakura, "our secret service has been investigating the murder they were trying to intimidate you with. They will find out who did it. You would be safe back home."

"Yes, I suppose so" said Grace. "But what if they know something about the twistor?"

"How could they?" Kamakura replied. "But as soon as I pass the information on…"

"When do you intend to do that, Toshiro?" Yamato asked, shifting uncomfortably in his seat.

"Tomorrow" said Kamakura decisively. "…as soon as I pass the information on, the chances of a 'leak' increase with every day and you will not be safe in Japan."

"Wait a minute" said Grace. "I'd like to think it over. Can we leave that open as a possibility?"

"Of course" Kamakura replied. He was immediately confident that he would get his way.

Yamato said

"I do not think I am needed here any longer. Why did you use me as an intermediary, Grace-san, why?"

He had perhaps meant the question to be rhetorical, more of a lament than a request for information, but O'Malley immediately replied.

"Because Toshiro couldn't have checked the calculations on his own. I needed you to convince him. And because… and this is why I hope you will stay with us a little longer this evening, Kimio… because there are ramifications for the polymer revolution, too."

"Eh?" chorused Yamato and Kamakura.

"Look" said Grace, "we've decided already to go ahead, haven't we?"

"Yes" said Kamakura decisively.

"So we're going to be principal players in a Japanese Manhattan Project, aren't we?"

"Yes" said Kamakura again.

"So do you think it's a good idea to be also high-profile scientific revolutionaries in another area?"

There was a short silence, before O'Malley continued

"I think we should take our foot off the accelerator of the polymer revolution. Let the establishment bores believe what they like for a few years… otherwise… well, I'm not sure, but I don't like the idea of attracting a lot of attention for our polymer work. There's big commercial interests at stake there, and people may spy on us for the wrong reasons."

There was another short silence, then Kamakura said

"I see what you mean, Grace. I hadn't thought of that. Replacing the SSK theory has long been a cherished hope of mine, but perhaps companies like du Pont and Proctor & Gamble may get interested…"

"…and Exxon and the other oil companies… don't forget the Yamato theory applies to rubbers, too" said Grace.

Yamato gave a little start at the mention of his name, and said

"Ah, Grace, so you are going to deprive me of my scientific breakthrough in this field, too… o, my…"

"I'm sorry, Kimio" Grace said. "I didn't mean we have to give the work up. That would look even more suspicious. I just meant that we should probably keep a lower profile… not so many conferences drumming up support, for example…"

"Hmm…" said Kamakura, draining his glass and re-filling it with another large shot. "Perhaps we could feed things to Ron. We'll see… Anyway, we don't have to decide tonight."

As if chairing a session at the conference, he went on

"Do we have any more business to decide on the matter at hand?"

He again tapped the fateful envelope.

"No" said Grace, Hiroshi and Yamato together.

"Then let us celebrate the greatest scientific breakthrough of the twentieth century in as relaxed a manner as possible."

He re-filled Grace's and Hiroshi's glasses and poured a bourbon for the reluctant looking Yamato, too.

"Grace, it is a tragedy of modern times" he said pompously, as if addressing a hundred delegates, that your unified field theory calculations cannot be published immediately. I promise you that you will be given precedence in this field at a later date. I drink to your good health and your long life. And to yours, Mr Fujimoto. And to yours, Kimio."

"Kanpai" the four said in unison, and crashed their glasses together.

They all downed their drinks in one, and Yamato came up spluttering.

"I really have to go now" Yamato said, a pale orange colour already suffusing his face.

"Hi, Ben" said Grace.

"Hi, Grace, good to see you, come in" said Ben. "I'm glad you could make it. You seem to have been so wrapped up in your work recently…"

They were still standing in the dimly lit porchway at Iffley Road. It was black, cold and drizzling.

"…come in, come in…"

They embraced briefly in the doorway and went into Ben's room on the ground floor. The only furniture was a couple of mattresses. The floor was covered with Afghani rugs on bare boards.

"It's ages since we chilled out together, Grace. Have you got the whole evening free? Promise me…"

"Sure, Ben. Hiroshi knows I might be staying out tonight."

"Great. You look as stiff as a board, you need to relax. Would you like me to give your shoulders a rub?"

Grace started. She said

"Err… yes, that would be nice. I've just completely lost track of my yoga practice recently… I just haven't seemed to have the time…"

"You're obsessed with time, Grace. You should take time *out.*"

Ben almost shouted the final word. He knelt behind Grace and began to gently massage her shoulders. Grace craned her neck backward and tried to allow her neck and shoulder muscles to relax.

"mmm…thanks. I might ask Arne for a massage later on."

Ben withdrew from behind Grace's back and pottered around, bringing out his go board and go stones, a couple of bowls for the prisoners, some radishes with salt, a bowl of houmous, assorted seeds and a bottle of red wine. He sat cross-legged opposite Grace in the upright way of a yoga devotee of many years.

Grace seemed eager to get on with the go, fiddling with a few of the white stones.

"Relax, Grace" Ben said. "I haven't seen you on your own in ages. Let's talk before we get sucked in by the stones."

"Yeah, sorry, Ben. I've had so much science whizzing round my brain this year. Eighty-four has just come and gone. Apart from parties, it must be February since we got together…"

"Forget about time, Grace. Let it go."

"It's not an obsession about time… I promise you I'm not going to bring it up again… it's just that I feel I'm a completely different person since when we last met, not properly, just the two of us…"

"But you're still in love with Hiroshi, aren't you?"

"O, yes. That's about the only thing that's been constant in my life for the last few months."

"So what's the big change, Grace?"

"It's difficult to talk about. It's science stuff. I thought we weren't going to talk about that this evening… Do you mind if we start the go, Ben. I need to get absorbed for a while. Maybe play for an hour or two then have something to eat?"

"Sure" said Ben. "I'll put on a pot of coffee."

Grace seemed to compose herself, and they sat down opposite each other in cross-legged positions, with the board between them. It was a handmade wooden board, with four designs etched into the corners including a yin and yang symbol and a snake eating its own tail. Ben took a handful of black stones.

"Even or odd?"

"Even" Grace replied.

Ben emptied his hand into the centre of the board and separated the stones into pairs. There were eight stones.

"White is right" said Ben.

Ben scooped the eight stones back into his bowl and, without hesitation, played on O'Malley's left-hand three-four point, closest to his partner.

An hour later Arne came in to find the two of them engrossed over the board, their faces lost to the world.

"Hi, Grace. Am I interrupting?"

Grace slowly re-surfaced and sat up straight.

"Oh, Arne, hi…"

"I just popped in to say that I'll give you a massage anytime you like, Grace… Is this a good time?"

Grace couldn't help glancing back at the board, wondering how she was going to rescue the invasion in her right-hand corner. It looked as if she could throw it into ko.

"Grace?"

Grace sat up with a start.

"O, sorry, Arne, what was that?"

"Ben'll tell you, Grace" Arne said, striding out of the room and closing the door firmly behind him.

"Let's take a break, Grace. I think this has breathed enough. He poured two big glasses of burgundy and filled two beakers with mineral water. Grace took a big swig of the wine, and said

"O, Ben, that's lovely… thanks…"

"A pleasure, Grace."

Grace was still looking at the board.

"Come on, Grace. There's only forty moves played. Another couple of hundred to go later on. We've got all night… Relax… Why don't you go up to Arne's for a quick massage while I do a bit of cooking…"

Grace took her gaze away from the board.

"Yeah, sorry, Ben, I have to stop looking at this…"

O'Malley couldn't find the light switch in the hall, and tottered up the stairs in the dark. It was cold and damp on the landing. A little patch of yellow light showed the way to Arne's ill-fitting door. O'Malley groped for the knob and finally succeeded in turning it. She nearly fell into the room, where Arne was kneeling on the bed.

"Hi, Grace, come in…"

Arne gave a beatific smile. He loved working with his hands. Grace still had an absorbed self-conscious look.

"Shall I close the door?" she said, with a catch in her throat.

"Sure, Grace" said Arne. "Anything you feel comfortable with."

Grace turned and pushed the door to, but couldn't turn the handle. Arne stood up and nimbly crossed the room. He stood next to Grace and put his hand on her shoulder.

"Calm down, Grace" he said.

He reached round her and turned the handle easily. He took Grace by the hand and led her over to the centre of the room.

"You look so stiff, Grace. You really need a massage. Would you like it on the table or the bed?"

Grace looked at the precarious looking orthopaedic massage table and the warm comfortable looking bed over by the electric bar heater.

"On the bed" she said.

Arne worked his way right down to the tips of her toes, and worked his way gradually back up. He then did her face, and knelt back beaming, because she looked ten years younger. She was no oil painting, but she was an undergraduate again, taking a brilliant first, full of hope about the world.

"O, Arne, that was brilliant" she said, without opening her eyes.

"Would you like an aftercourse?" Arne asked.

Grace opened her eyes wide, and said

"I'm dying for one."

Arne got up, crossed the room, and locked the door.

"You're in for a long and bumpy ride, Grace" he said.

"Promises, promises" said Grace.

Dinner was in Maya's room. Ben, Arne and Grace were joined by Pru. Grace had brought a one-and-a-half litre bottle of saké back from Japan, together with her little saké set of two flasks and five cups.

"Perfect Japanese dinner party" Grace said. "All the saké sets and sets of bowls come in fives…"

She filled the five cups with the warm saké, and they sat cross-legged about the cloth on the floor laden with vegan munchies.

"*Kanpai*" said Grace.

"Cheers" chorused the Iffley Roaders.

"You should come here more often, Grace" Maya said, with a meaningful look at Arne.

"Yes, I really should" said Grace. "Here's to your very good health." She raised her cup again.

"*Itadakimasu*" said Ben, helping himself to some houmous.

Grace helped with the washing up. The epsilon twistor, the polymer revolution, even Hiroshi, had all evaporated. Even the go game had evaporated.

"Hey, Grace, that's enough… thanks… let's play go…"

They headed back downstairs with a pot of jasmine tea, and re-installed themselves cross-legged across the go board. The situation in the bottom right-hand corner didn't look any more promising, and O'Malley launched a counter-attack in the top left-hand corner. She seemed to be playing an unusually risky game.

When they finished the game at one o'clock, Grace was looking very tired, and Ben wound up with the seventy points to Grace's fifty-five.

"Well played, Ben" said Grace.

"*Onegaishimasu…*" Ben replied "Thanks, Grace, that was a great game. We should do this more often…"

"More often than nine monthly…"

"Forget about time…"

There was a short silence, then Grace scrabbled around with go stones, putting the white ones back in their bowl. Ben did the same with the black stones.

"You're welcome to crash here…"

Ben gestured to the mattress in the corner.

"Yeah, why not?… I don't think I could face Hiroshi, tonight."

"Too fucked?"

"Exactly."

Grace had an ear-to-ear smile on her face and lay back full length on the floor looking up at the ceiling. Then she said something she hadn't meant to.

"You know, Ben, I've made an amazing scientific discovery…"

"I thought we had a moratorium on science, man" Ben replied.

"It's not the boring old gluon stuff" said Grace. "It's a field theory. Maxwell would have been proud of me. It's…"

She suddenly stopped herself.

"I'm talking too much" she said.

"Nah, you go on, Grace, get it off your chest."

"No, we agreed to let science go this evening. I should have stuck to that…"

Grace trailed off, and looked deeply self-absorbed.

O'Malley's birthday was on Friday 30th November, and she had hired the college Middle Common Room for the big event. It was a beautiful room, just like you imagine in an Oxford college, high ceiling, oak beams, panelled walls. It was packed with about eighty people. Grace was really going to town in marking the end of her youth, as she put it.

Grace had actually been going to town since about four o'clock in the afternoon when she'd knocked off early from the lab with Richard and Judith. They'd soon been joined by Helen, Freddy and the first contingent of the Iffley Road hippies, Arne and Maya. By half four Grace had already downed a couple of pints and a couple of vodkas and was lit up like a Christmas tree, when Hiroshi arrived.

"Hiroshi, hi, you look great" said Grace.

"Thank you" said Hiroshi, blushing modestly. "Grace, could we go outside for a moment?"

Grace nodded, and floated out of the King's Arms into Broad Street. Somehow it had got to be dark and had started raining. The streetlights cast astounding multicoloured rays into the dripping gloom.

"O, Grace, you look drunk…"

"O, Hiroshi, do I? Well, I must confess I have had a few drinks. God, you look incredibly beautiful tonight."

Hiroshi looked into her sparkling eyes and his face went very serious. He said

"Grace, you're very lit up… please be careful not to tell anyone about that thing… you know…"

He looked up and down the street, at the gleaming windows of the King's Arms.

"…you know… the extremum thermodynamics."

Grace suddenly went serious, too.

"Yeah, sure, Hiroshi. I'll be careful…"

Hiroshi gave her a big hug, and they stood there motionless for a moment in the thickening rain.

"Let's go in" said Hiroshi, giving a little shiver. "I'm soaking."

The party was already about thirty strong when they all crossed the high street around seven, a motley and noisy crew even by Oxford standards. Fred, the studious porter, and Ed, his tough young assistant, heard the row coming from a hundred yards away down the cobbled back street of O'Malley's ancient and hallowed college. Pru, wearing a seventies full-length crushed velvet dress and a headscarf and Maya, wearing multicoloured rags, were the first to arrive at the porter's lodge. Fred and Ed barred their way.

"And where might you young ladies be heading?" asked Fred.

"To the party" said Maya happily.

The crowd was now pressing up against the college gates and O'Malley half staggered, half threaded her way through it.

"Ah, it's you Dr O'Malley" said Fred. "Are these young ladies with your party?"

"They certainly are, Fred. So are these other miscreants. May we come in?"

"Of course, Dr O'Malley" said Fred, stepping aside with the kind of gesture that had, outside Oxford, gone out of fashion since Walter Raleigh had spread his cloak out for Queen Elizabeth.

Ed was giving Maya a rather more modern look.

"Hi, Ed" said Grace. "Is the MCR locked?"

"No, Dr O'Malley" said Ed.

O'Malley suddenly remembered that it was a condition of the party that it be open to all college MCR members, so there were likely to be some boring straights hanging around up there in the armchairs.

"Ah, yes, of course" said Grace.

Fred had retreated to his cozy room behind the pigeonholes. Grace turned to Richard and said

"Hey, Richard, could you show everyone up to the MCR… the cases of booze in the corner are ours… I'll be up in a minute."

Then she turned to Ed, and said in a conspiratorial tone

"Ed, can I have a word with you?"

"Certainly, Dr O'Malley" said Ed. They were still within Fred's earshot.

As the noisy party followed Richard across the front quadrangle, Grace took Ed to one side and said

"Ed, I've got some pretty hippy friends coming along this evening and… well, there might be a bit of smoking later on in the MCR. If anyone complains, could you head Fred off and come up and pretend to deal with it yourself."

"I understand, Dr O'Malley" said Ed. "Don't worry. I'll look after everything. I'll direct any of your friends who come later up to the MCR."

And come and come they did, including Freddy and Helen, Tom Bobbin, on this occasion without his wife Pat, and even Fyodor. A second wave of hippies, including Ben and assorted friends, arrived about nine. By ten o'clock the air was blue with smoke, the music was pumping away and some people had started dancing. Maya made a beeline for Tom Bobbin and said

"Would you like a dance?"

"Er, no, I should be going really" said Tom.

"Oh, please" said Maya, "just one."

"Go on, Tom, go for it" said Grace. "She doesn't bite!"

"Oh, all right then" said Tom, who finally set off like a marionette on very jerky strings.

"Wow" said Richard, heading over to where Grace and Hiroshi were enjoying a moment of peace and a mineral water in the corner. "Look at that, man, Tom Bobbin's dancing with one of the hippies… hope Pat never finds out… she'd go ballistic… this has got to be the party to end them all."

As Grace took a deep breath, a voice from a decade ago drifted into her left ear, an unexpected voice from a man she hadn't invited.

"Dr O'Malley, I presume" this deep and beautifully modulated voice said.

"Tony" Grace said, and turned.

"Tony" she repeated. "What a pleasure… Hiroshi, I want you to meet a very good old friend of mine, Tony Woodbridge… Tony, where have you been all these years?"

"It's a long story" Tony said.

Tony was working for the Foreign Commonwealth Office, or so he said.

Tony was chain smoking Benson & Hedges, and looked exactly as he had back in the seventies, middle-aged, balding, mysterious.

"Whatever happened to that strange thesis, Tony?" O'Malley asked.

"It was rejected. The external examiner described it as pure dilettantism" Tony replied calmly.

"Oh…" said O'Malley. There didn't seem anything appropriate to say.

"Well…" she continued, "What have you been doing with yourself? Still visiting weird and wonderful places? Still playing go?"

"Oh, this and that" Tony replied noncommittally. "I haven't played go with a human being for quite a long time."

Fragments of an amazing life unfolded against the backdrop of a party that was becoming more and more animated, but in which Grace and Tony seemed to have disappeared in a bubble of quiet conversation. Tony had joined the Foreign Office, worked in the Middle East, moved on to the National Audit Office and worked in South America… there was something about a year's computer course in San Francisco somewhere along the line in the early eighties… and now he was in the Foreign Commonwealth Office, working part time on his pet project, writing a computer program capable of beating a Chinese one-dan go player.

"So what's this FCO job all about?" O'Malley asked.

"Oh, this and that" said Tony.

He seemed to have moved seamlessly from one Whitehall department to another. He'd obviously signed the Official Secrets Act, and was keen to turn the conversation to his go programming.

"Did you hear about the million-dollar prize offered by a Taiwanese businessman to anyone who could write a go program to play at the one-dan standard?"

"No" said O'Malley.

"The prize was offered in '81" Tony said, "and no one has come even close to collecting. It's not like chess programming" he said. "Chess is a trivial game" he continued disdainfully. "Do you play go these days, Grace?"

"Yeah, mainly with Ben" Grace said. "Did you ever meet Ben, Tony?"

"No, I don't think I did" said Tony. "Is he here?"

Grace pointed Ben out, and said

"He's the guy wearing the orange jacket and tartan kilt in the corner… I must introduce you two sometime… Ben spent a year in the Soviet Union, in Moscow… you could practise your Russian, play go maybe."

"Maybe" said Tony noncommittally, opening a second can of cheap lager.

"Yeah" said Grace. "I've got a few go partners... try to get in at least one game every month... we should get a game together sometime soon, Tony... I'd really like that."

"Yes" said Tony. "Let's do that. I'll check my diary when I get back to London and give you a call."

Tony had taught Grace how to play go and had slaughtered her on the first few occasions, even giving Grace a seven-stone handicap. But Grace had learned how to play phenomenally quickly and had reduced the handicap to three stones in a matter of months. They had spent many a long night locked in a struggle of wills over Tony's beautiful go-ban, sometimes hardly speaking for hours on end. Within a year of learning the rules, Tony had finally had to concede an unhandicapped game to Grace as a pale dawn came over the college chapel tower in the summer of '77, the last time they'd met.

"Yeah, it'd be a lot more fun than playing a computer, Tony. Let's go for it."

"Yes" said Tony, "but I'm keeping you from your guests. I have to go now."

"But you've only just arrived, man. It's early days yet."

It was about eleven o'clock.

"Do you need crashing space?"

"No, thanks, Grace. I have to head back to London... Early meeting tomorrow morning... I don't want to miss the last train..."

There was still an hour and a half left before the last train was due.

"...well, a pleasure to meet you, Hiroshi. I hope we'll meet again... You're a lucky man."

So saying, Tony disappeared. Grace hadn't even got his address.

"Wow, that was a blast from the past, Hiroshi" Grace said, giving Hiroshi a bleary look.

"I don't trust that man" Hiroshi said.

The college gates closed at midnight, and people were starting to drift away. The dancing had stopped. By 11.30 they were down to the hard core of drinkers. Ed was starting to rattle the MCR keys ostentatiously. He had his job to do. Grace switched the music off and the murmur of voices sounded suddenly very loud.

"Hi, everybody" said Grace, using her lecture theatre voice. "We're going to have to move on in ten minutes... there's a post-party party down at 49 Iffley Road starting at midnight..."

By ten to midnight, the last stragglers were being ushered down the stairs by Ed and chattering their way across the echoing Front Quad of the college. The party was over.

Back in Pimlico, Tony checked some dates. Grace had been away at a CERN experiment in the week before PC Lofthouse's murder. She had flown back from Geneva on the day of the murder, and had arrived at Heathrow in the early afternoon. Grace hadn't denied it when she had been questioned at her party in Bibbleton, nor had she denied her car being in the vicinity of the crime around the time that PC Lofthouse had been murdered. Her exact movements were unclear, but she must had been driving from Didcot to Bibbleton at four or five in the afternoon. There was nothing else of interest in the police report.

The last thing Tony envisaged was an actual prosecution of O'Malley. It would be much better to use the case to gradually undermine her self-confidence, to put the frighteners on her if she refused to co-operate. Yes, O'Malley had plenty of weak points, and Tony had all the back-up he needed to press the buttons. He decided to put Grace and Hiroshi under high intensity quiet surveillance from now on. Getting some shit on Hiroshi Fujimoto might prove useful, too.

Tony checked Grace's itinerary for December. There was a neutron scattering experiment at the Rutherford labs from the 13th to the 17th, when O'Malley was scheduled to work on the new ISIS source with her two masters students. She certainly wouldn't miss that. O'Malley never spared herself during the experiments... by the final morning she would certainly be deeply preoccupied and at a very low ebb physically. He would arrange for two officers of his own unit to pay O'Malley a visit that morning and begin the process of bringing the young Bolshevik to heel. The next move would surely be to arrange a go game with her. The birthday party had been a gift – know thine enemy, as the old biblical saying goes. Not that Tony thought of Grace as an enemy, more as a rival in a game.

He closed the file, poured himself a Chivas Regal, wandered over to one of his many well-stocked bookcases and took out a book on go openings. He was as determined to win the game as he was to crack the case.

The doorbell went. With O'Malley's physicist's sense of timing, she rang the bell at exactly eight o'clock, the time of her invitation. Tony put a book away in a leisurely fashion and went to the intercom. Grace was uncomfortably aware that she was under a video camera in the doorway. They exchanged crackling voices, and Tony climbed the narrow stairs to the lobby. At the top, he undid the bolts and the two double locks.

"Sorry for all the security stuff, Grace" Tony said. "Central London, you know, can't be too careful..."

"No, sure..." said Grace, hesitantly.

Tony suddenly extended a hand, and Grace shook it.

"It's good to see you again, Grace, please, come in..."

Tony stepped aside and Grace went down the stairs first. Tony assiduously double-locked everything behind him and joined Grace in the dimly lit hallway. The corridor seemed to stretch on for ever.

"Would you like a drink?"

"O, yes, please, Tony. How about a beer?"

"I've got a few Stella in the fridge" said Tony.

An amateur would have got some Kirin, O'Malley's favourite beer in Japan, and given away suspicious clues that showed he knew too much about the client. Tony wasn't an amateur and he had his usual boring Belgian beer, the stuff he liked. They stood rather awkwardly in the kitchen while Tony cracked two tubes. He knew O'Malley preferred bottled beer to can beer, but Grace was too good a guest to let any disappointment show.

"…hmm… thanks, Tony… that's lovely" she said, taking her first big swig directly from the can.

"I'm looking forward to the go tonight" she continued.

There was a brief pause, then Tony said

"So am I."

There was another longer pause, which O'Malley broke lamely by saying

"Well, Tony, how have you been?"

"Fine" Tony replied. "Shall we go through to the living room?"

Tony's long, gloomy hallway looked like an ancient tomb. The living room was vast, too, but not cavernous because of the books and incredible variety of junk, Afghani swords, a Chinese globe… O'Malley was surprised by the clutter and stood gawping in the doorway. Tony came in and rummaged around for his go stones. The board was a huge slab of jet black Welsh slate, cut into a perfect, sharp-edged rectangle. You could have killed a man with a blow from that board, even without using the corner as an axe-head. The lines had been ruled white into it, and they looked perfectly rectilinear. The stones were large glass pieces, ideally suited for a clean, objective view of the game. They drew their armchairs up on either side of the small table and Tony laid the slate on it. He took a handful of black stones and said

"Even or odd?"

"Even" O'Malley replied, without hesitation.

There were eight stones.

"So I get the whites" O'Malley said.

Tony looked displeased. He was unused to playing with the black stones.

"Boum, Shivah" Grace said, lighting her first cigarette.

"What's that you said?" asked Tony.

"Boum, Shivah. It's an Indian way of thanking the gods. A bit like saying grace. Well, that's what Ben told me anyway…"

"Ah, Ben, that outlandish-looking chap I saw at your birthday party… you were saying he was a go player, too…"

Tony left the sentence hanging in the air.

"Yeah" said Grace, "and a pretty mean go player, too. We had a game recently, our first in ages, and Ben beat me by about fifteen points."

Tony smiled inwardly to himself. If O'Malley had lost to a bombed out hippy like de Montfort, her go must certainly have slipped over the years. He placed a stone confidently on his own right-hand four-four point. Grace played peacefully on her own right-hand three-four point, closest to herself. An hour later, with just twenty-five stones on the board, O'Malley made the unorthodox play of a stone exactly in the centre of the board. Tony looked very displeased.

"Fancy another beer, Grace?" he asked.

"Ooh, yes please, Tony. What do you think of my last move?"

"In China" Tony replied, "it is regarded as an insult to play on the centre point in the opening."

O'Malley was flabbergasted. "But we've both got groups extending out from opposite corners. It's a natural linking play" she said.

"Highly speculative" said Tony.

"Well, we'll see" Grace said, sounding hot under the collar.

There was a short pause.

"Yes, we will" said Tony, turning and disappearing into the corridor.

He came back with two more beers.

"I've got a bit of re-thinking to do now I've got this unexpected *sente…*" said Tony, before attacking in Grace's bottom left-hand corner.

The two of them were completely engrossed for two hours. By eleven o'clock, still only eighty stones had been played.

"God, this is a titanic struggle" said Grace, standing up and stretching her neck and shoulder muscles.

"Do you fancy a break, Tony? How about a whiskey, or something…"

Tony was still staring intently at the board. His best laid plans had been blocked, and that ridiculous stone in the centre was providing a stepping stone for two one-eyed groups. O'Malley was definitely ahead in the game, perhaps by ten points or so.

"Good idea" said Tony, sitting up suddenly. "I've got some Chivas Regal. Or would you prefer a single malt?"

"What have you got?" asked Grace, her eyes lighting up.

"Glenlivet, Glenmorangie, Laphroaig…" Tony started intoning.

"Whoa, man, that's plenty to be going on with. I'll have a Laphroaig, thanks…"

Tony poured two stiff ones, a Chivas Regal for himself. He lit another Dunhill, maybe his tenth during the game.

"Shall we have a mid-game break?" he asked.

They chatted desultorily about the weather, about how much nicer it would be if they could shift the game to the autumn sunshine of Kyoto or the perpetual steamy heat of Hong Kong. They tried to be jolly about old times they'd had together at dinner parties and punt trips in college days, but something had come between them, a decade of divergence too extreme for friendship to survive it.

"You seem very happy with Hiroshi" Tony said. "He seems charming."

"Yes, he's a lovely man" O'Malley replied in a way that did not excite further comment.

"Shall we go on?"

Tony's attention had already been sucked back into the board. He knew he should be pumping Grace, but he was more worried by his weak position on line C than he was about sordid details of O'Malley's private life. O'Malley struck just where he feared, dividing his position into two weak encampments. Even with Grace getting pissed, it was going to be an uphill middle game and Tony wasn't used to defending. By one o'clock in the morning, Tony's position had collapsed. O'Malley was twenty to thirty points ahead. It was Tony's heaviest go defeat ever by a non-Chinese player. Instead of responding to the move, he simply said

"Well played, Grace. I concede a deserved victory."

"Thanks, Tony... that was a great game. I still think you could have swung it if you'd persisted in that attack in the left centre. I was very worried about this group..."

She wafted her hand over a group on the lower edge that had ended up with three eyes.

"There are always might-have-beens in a go game" said Tony. "I thought you always had eyes for that group... anyway, fancy a nightcap?" he asked, starting to gather up the stones.

O'Malley looked at her watch. Tony's flat had a vaguely unhealthy air to it and she was longing for the foggy night air.

"I've got to be going, Tony" she said.

"So soon?" responded Tony. "I thought there was plenty of time before the bus left."

"I've got to go" said Grace, standing up and staggering into the corridor.

Tony realized calmly that the present chance had gone. He helped Grace up the stairs.

"Take care, Grace" he said.

Grace gave him a bleary look.

"Take care, Tony" she said. "Thanks for the game."

"A pleasure" Tony said, through gritted teeth.

It looked as if, once again, O'Malley was going to be under-staffed for a neutron scattering experiment. Four days on the ARES instrument with only two raw masters students to help her was a nightmare scenario. It wasn't that Helen and Freddy wouldn't do their best – she knew that from the CERN experiment – it was just that she needed another experienced scientist on board. Martina would have been one of her least favourite choices in the world, but she hadn't had any choices. Putting aside an uncomfortable vision of Martina and Hiroshi in bed together, Grace had swallowed her pride and phoned her. They were meeting at the instrument the following morning.

Grace and Hiroshi were spending a rare quiet evening at the cottage in Bibbleton on the eve of the experiment.

"Hiroshi, I've got something to tell you" Grace said.

"Yes, Grace" Hiroshi replied with a dimpled smile.

"Well, you know about that thing you had with Martina…"

"Yes, Grace" Hiroshi said. The smile had gone from his face.

"And you know I didn't make a fuss about it…"

"Yes, Grace" Hiroshi said. It wasn't hard to guess what was coming next.

"Well, you know I've been monogamous since we started going out…"

"Yes, Grace" Hiroshi said.

"Well, that was until a couple of weeks ago…"

"The night you spent at Iffley Road?" Hiroshi said.

"Yes…"

"I don't want to hear any more about it" Hiroshi said. "No confessional details… I'm happy about it, Grace, I really am."

"Happy?"

"Yes, because I didn't know how I was going to tell you about how I saw Martina again that evening."

Grace's jaw dropped. The thought of meeting Martina at the instrument at nine o'clock tomorrow morning suddenly looked even less promising.

"You always said we shouldn't have a monogamy clause in our relationship, didn't you?… That we should be monogamous by choice…"

Grace was silent and staring down at the carpet. Yes, she'd screwed Arne. It was perfectly fair.

"O, Grace, you're not angry, are you?" said Hiroshi with a frown.

"No. I had a great time with Arne… Are you going to do it during the experiment?"

"I want to" said Hiroshi. "Her skin is so beautiful…"

Grace had a painful vision of Hiroshi and Martina doing it on the carpet in front of the fire, while she and Helen and Freddy were slogging it out in the ARES cabin.

Chapter 5

Nightshift

Martina was already in the cabin when Grace arrived with Helen and Freddy. Len Hopper, the scientist responsible for the ARES instrument, was also in the cabin, fiddling about with the CAMAC for the temperature controller. Len had worked with Grace before many times and had been Martina's local contact for an ARES experiment earlier in the year, on Grace's recommendation. They needed no introductions.

"Hi, Grace" Len said. "We've been having a bit of trouble with the Lauda bath, so I'm switching over to the Julabo… Software doesn't seem to like it, though" he added, frowning.

"Hi, Grace" said Martina, "good to see you again…"

"Another fivesome" O'Malley said, while Martina was computing up the data from the first run.

"Fivesome?" echoed Len.

"Well, five is the Japanese ideal for a group, dinner parties, scientific project workers, you name it, and here we are…"

"A fivesome" Helen said.

She didn't like Martina, but she liked men, and wasn't unhappy about being in the small cabin with two blokes, especially Freddy. Freddy was a better football player than a scientist, but he was trying hard to follow Martina's manipulations of the data.

The first scattering pattern was promising.

"Let's get a coffee" said Helen.

"You'll be disappointed with the coffee here after CERN, Helen" Len said.

At eleven o'clock they turned up in the coffee lounge at R70 and beheld the new management cult at ISIS. There was talk of 'tickets' being used to extend bureaucratic control of beam-time on the instruments, an air of insecurity, no hint of laughter over the fifty or so people in the square, unstylish lounge.

"Hmm" said Helen, after imbibing a disgusting sip of oily, tasteless coffee. "I see what you mean, Len…"

"There's a machine in the guide hall…" said Len.

"…which makes even worse coffee…" interjected O'Malley.

"Worse than this?" said Helen, with a grimace.

"We have to put up with four days of this?" said Freddy.

"Let's get an espresso in a café somewhere" said Helen.

Grace and Len snorted with laughter.

"You won't get a decent cup of coffee within fifteen miles of here" Len said. "You'd have to go all the way back to Oxford."

Helen looked dumbfounded.

"We have to put up with four days of this?" she said.

Martina didn't have time to get away on her own until the afternoon of the following day. Things had panned out ideally of their own accord. After doing the early morning shift, Len had headed off for a sleep at his home in Lower Womble, and Grace was with Helen in the cabin. Things were going surprisingly smoothly, and Martina could see at least one paper coming out of the experiment already. Freddy had done the night shift, and was out running after waking up at two in the afternoon. As usual during an experiment, after most of thirty hours under fluorescent lights, Martina had completely forgotten about the outside world. She was pleased to notice that the dull, grey sky that she vaguely remembered from yesterday morning had broken up, and there was plenty of light in the crisp air. She drove down at exactly the regulation 20 mph to the perimeter fence and chatted briefly with the gatekeeper. She also kept assiduously to the 30 mph speed limit up to the main road, when she was still within sight of the guards lookout. As soon as she hit the main road, she climbed to a dangerously high speed. She had to get to Bibbleton as soon as the engine would take her there. Her yearning for Hiroshi was very strong and she was sure he would be there, waiting for her. She was right. Back in the cabin, O'Malley was thinking that she'd survived the first thirty or so of the hundred hours duration of the experiment. The ear-to-ear smile over Martina's face when she came back in the early evening told her that the next sixty to seventy hours were going to be an uphill struggle.

At eight o'clock in the morning on the last day of the experiment, Grace and Hiroshi were in bed. There was a loud knock at the door.

"Let's leave it" said Grace.

The knocking was repeated. Hiroshi hurriedly put on a sweatshirt and tracksuit bottoms, and went downstairs. There were two men in the porch. When he opened the door, the larger of the two men pushed a police badge towards his face. Grace heard the unfamiliar voices and came downstairs.

"Ah, good morning, Dr O'Malley" the first man said. "We are pursuing a murder investigation. May we come in?"

Grace didn't move from the doorway, and said

"Look, I've already spoken to the police about this. There's nothing I can say to help you."

"In that case, madam, we will return shortly with a warrant" the second man said. "The murder of a police officer is a serious business, and your car was seen in the vicinity at the time. We need to investigate."

O'Malley sighed. "I suppose you'd better come in" she said.

The four of them sat down in the living room, and O'Malley said

"I'm very busy at the moment… I'm in the middle of an experiment…"

"What kind of experiment is that, madam?" asked the smaller officer. The bigger one had taken out a notebook and was ready with his pen.

"A neutron scattering experiment" said O'Malley, "at the Rutherford labs."

She didn't offer any further explanation.

"Ah, I see, madam" said the little one. "Well, we'll be brief…"

The two policemen laboriously went over the details of Grace's return trip from Heathrow, and pressed her about her movements in the fatal hours.

"So you drove back through Abingdon between five and six in the evening?"

"Yes" Grace said, "I already told you. Look, I'm in a hurry."

"We understand, madam. Just one last question. May I ask what route you took back to Bibbleton that evening?"

"I can't remember how I came back."

"Please try, madam."

"I'm afraid I can't remember."

"Up the Northcourt Road would be the obvious way, wouldn't it, madam?"

"I suppose so" O'Malley replied.

The two men looked at each other. They were under strict orders not to press too far, too soon.

"Very well, madam" the smaller officer replied, standing up. "Please keep yourself available for further enquiries."

O'Malley prided herself on the loyalty she showed her co-workers by never being late for a sample change. She was late already by the time she passed the Milton roundabout and headed up the gentle hill into Harwell. She was driving the little turquoise blue Fiat 127.

O'Malley prided herself on her chronological memory, too, but she just couldn't remember what she'd done that November afternoon. Everything was jumbled up; the twistor, Martina and Hiroshi, Arne, the parties, the go games... What had happened when? She couldn't concentrate on the driving, and pulled into a lay-by opposite the gates of the Atomic Energy Research Establishment at Harwell. Even at a time of intense personal stress, O'Malley couldn't help noticing another sign of the times. The AERE Harwell sign had been replaced by a posh new logo with the title Harwell Business Centre. She killed the ignition and rested her head on the wheel. She could remember the day up to seeing Martina's car on the drive... her usual chronometer had been ticking, and she'd set off from Oxford bus station around three. Over a confused and chaotic month, she even remembered the crawl down the Abingdon Road till 3.30. She must have got back at about a quarter to four. But everything after the shattering sound of Hiroshi's orgasm was a blank until her second homecoming. She remembered the twilight then, the orange street lights being on. Around six, maybe a quarter to six? But the two hours in between were a blank. O'Malley jerked her head back from the wheel. She fell into a noisome sleep against the headrest.

"No" Grace groaned out loud.

"I didn't do it..."

Some dribble was coming out of the corner of her mouth as she came to, sweaty and shaken.

It was a very dishevelled looking O'Malley who arrived in the cabin shortly after ten o'clock. Len and Helen were the only two occupants. Len had never known Grace be late for her shift, and said so. Helen knew Grace's striking boyfriend, and thought she could guess the reason.

"Sleep well, Grace?" she asked with a laugh.

"O, fine" said Grace vacantly.

"We've been looking at the overnight scans, Grace" Len said with excitement. "That diffuse scattering you predicted is definitely there. Here, have a look…"

Len seemed disappointed that Grace showed no enthusiasm for the beautiful ripples of diffuse scattering in the high angle detector, and left as soon as Martina and Freddy arrived in the late morning. Martina looked disappointed when Grace said

"Martina, could you run things here for a while. I've got to pop back home for an hour or two. I'll see you after lunch."

"But…" Martina replied.

"No buts, Martina… it's important. Helen, why don't you take a break?… I'll meet you here around three…"

  Back at the cottage, Grace embraced Hiroshi strongly, crushing her body against his.

"Something's happened" she said. "How come the police are taking such an unnatural interest in me? Those blokes sounded like they had something up their sleeves. I'm so confused, Hiroshi. I can't remember what happened."

"What if I did it?" Grace added, anguish in her voice.

"Don't be ridiculous, Grace. Of course, you didn't. You're a good person, you're not capable of it."

"But I remember seeing him. That definitely happened. I told you when I got back to Bibbleton."

"You also told me that when you recognized him, you realized you were having bad thoughts, and drove home."

"But I had a horrible nightmare in the car this morning."

"That wasn't reality, Grace. The police had just come… you were highly stressed…"

"No" Grace said, "I was kicking him on the ground. It must have been a memory."

"Nonsense, Grace. You have been reading about the case. It was auto-suggestion."

"So, it's a coincidence, then, that the very same bloke who beat me up on the picket lines gets killed around the time I recognized him?"

"Yes, Grace. Trust yourself. You didn't do it."

"Thank you, Hiroshi" Grace said. "I love you. But I was scared when those rozzers came. Do you think they know about the twistor?"

"How could they?" Hiroshi replied.

"I don't know" Grace said, "but I think we should get out while we've got the chance. Let's leave tonight."

Hiroshi's eyes opened wide.

"Tonight? Where?"

"To Japan" Grace replied.

"But Grace..."

"No buts, Hiroshi. I'm not spending the next twenty to thirty years of my life in prison. We have to get out now... we were planning to go there at Christmas anyway, weren't we? What difference does a week make?"

Hiroshi continued to look doubtful.

"For God's sake, Hiroshi, let's do it" she almost shouted. "I'm afraid" she said, more quietly.

"Me, too" said Hiroshi.

"Will you come with me tonight, Hiroshi?" she asked, desperately.

"Of course, Grace" he replied, without hesitation. "What do you want me to do?"

"It'll look odd if I take too much time out from the experiment. I want you to go straight to a travel agent's, buy two tickets to Japan tonight... Tokyo... Osaka... anywhere... it doesn't matter... pack a couple of bags... don't forget your passport... and meet me at the security fence at nine o'clock tonight… I'm on the nightshift with Martina… I'll have her do it alone… she owes me one anyway… after you've got the tickets and the bags sorted… lock the place up and wait round at Iffley Road… there's bound to be someone there… they'll look after you… don't say anything to anyone… I've got to get back to ARES. Ring me there."

Grace got into the car, and disappeared down the lane, back towards Abingdon and Didcot.

The simple bugging device that the bigger officer had fixed to the underside of the coffee table in the middle of the living room had picked the conversation up very well, and Tony was listening to it with a grim smile of satisfaction by the time Grace and Helen had got the next run going. So, Doctor-Cool-Grace-O-Smartarse-Malley had panicked at the first gentle squeeze of pressure. Tony knew that PC Lofthouse had been clubbed, not kicked, to death. He smirked at Grace's paranoia. How wrong his superiors had been about this weakling. No need to hurry. No need to panic like Grace had done. He had all the back-up he needed. It would be so much more deflating for O'Malley to think she was escaping, then get caught at the airport. Tony checked his clock. There was no evidence at all, but he would get a special warrant for O'Malley's arrest issued later in the afternoon, and delivered to her at Heathrow. For Heathrow it was. Fujimoto's every move to the travel agent's and back had been followed, and the travel agent had already been bullied into releasing the information that two seats were booked in the names of O'Malley and Fujimoto on the midnight flight to Narita. Tony recalled his favourite Sun headline, when they had sorted out those Argie bastards. Gotcha, he thought.

At four, Martina tried to sneak out of the cabin.

"Hang on a moment, Martina" said O'Malley. "Could I have a word with you? It's about the nightshift."

"Sure" said Martina, uncertainly.

"Let's grab a coffee" O'Malley said, ushering Martina out of the cabin.

Down by the coffee machine, O'Malley got straight to the point.

"Look, Martina" she said, "I know you're trying to sneak off to give Hiroshi one, but I've had enough. If you do… in fact, if you leave my sight before nine o'clock this evening… I'm going to thump you one. Understand?"

In order to make the point more forcibly, O'Malley closed her hand into a fist, her knuckles white with tension.

"I'll smack you one if you try to leave. Understand?"

Martina gawped.

"I asked you a question, Martina. Do you understand me?"

There was an otherworldly, stony stare in O'Malley's eyes. Hiroshi was great in bed, but…

"I understand" Martina replied. "Calm down, Grace" she continued. "It was only a bit of fun."

"Yeah, well, the fun's over."

O'Malley's whole demeanour changed suddenly. There was almost a friendly look in her eyes.

"Experiment's going well, isn't it?" she said.

"Better than the coffee" Martina replied, with a hesitant laugh.

"Let's go back to the cabin" Grace said.

Grace and Martina explained the change of plan to Len and the two masters students. They were going to run the instrument for the rest of the beamtime, like in the old days on NIB at CERN… no, they didn't need any help…

Len Hopper had been very put out by 'that bighead' Martina's arrival in the first place and stomped off at the regulation five o'clock. Helen and Freddy were punch drunk with exhaustion, and only too happy to be put into a taxi back to Oxford around six. Grace and Martina had a dreadful canteen dinner at 6.30, and worked feverishly until 8.30, setting up the final overnight scans. As the preliminary data came in, Grace sat back in the rotating director's chair, and finally unburdened herself.

"Martina, I'm going on a trip tonight" she said.

"Eh?"

"Your penance for screwing Hiroshi is to run the instrument on your own tonight…"

"What are you talking about, Grace?"

"Hiroshi and I are going away on a trip, tonight…"

"Where?"

"I'll fax you when I get there."

O'Malley suddenly stood up and left. An hour later, Martina realized she hadn't been joking.

Hiroshi was down at the perimeter fence, chatting nervously to one of the guards.

"Ah, here's Dr O'Malley" the guard said. "We could have arranged for a taxi for you, Doctor…"

"No problem" said Grace. "You've got to admit I've got a nicer driver this way."

Hiroshi looked particularly striking in the orange half-light, wearing a long coat and boots, smoking a Camel.

"I see what you mean, Doctor" said the guard with a wink.

Hiroshi looked surprised when Grace clambered into the driver's seat.

"Aren't you tired, Grace?"

"I'm OK… get in… sorry… let's go…"

When Hiroshi had closed the passenger door, and they were on their way up the slip road, Grace thought a black Ford Grenada was tailing them.

"What time is it?"

"Nine" Hiroshi replied.

"Check in?"

"Ten" Hiroshi replied. "O, Grace, there's no hurry…"

As they got to the roadworks, where the dual carriageway was reduced to a single lane, Grace undertook a dangerous overtaking manoeuvre, and only just nipped in front of a big lorry before the road narrowed down. She then really stepped on it, the little 1000 cc engine gasping as she gunned it up to 90 mph.

The man and the woman in the black Grenada weren't unduly fazed about losing the Fiat. They just radioed ahead to their contact at the airport.

"We've lost our clients. ETA at Heathrow ten o'clock."

"Roger" said the tough-looking man, who was ready with a squad of four armed men. "Will intercept at JAL desk."

"O, Grace, please slow down…"

When Grace hit the slip road to the motorway, she roared on.

"O, Grace, we've missed the turning" Hiroshi moaned, as they ripped past the Heathrow intersection.

"We're not going to the airport" Grace said, stonily.

"But…"

"No buts… something's happened. There's a midnight ferry from Dover to Ostend… I know, I caught it often enough when I was a post-doc in Germany… We can buy tickets at the port… We can make it…"

"O, Grace, why?"

"Something's happened. Trust me…"

At ten-thirty, Grace eased back down to seventy on the A road to Dover. She didn't want to get stopped for speeding.

"I'm sorry I couldn't explain, Hiroshi" she said. "I found an electronic bug under our coffee table. It was planted by one of those policemen who came this morning. Someone was listening to our every word. They'll probably be waiting at the airport for us."

"O, Grace, I'm afraid."

"Me, too. This is our last chance."

At eleven o'clock, the clients hadn't checked in for their long-haul flight. The squad leader phoned Woodbridge. A nasty feeling of how O'Malley had frustrated all his plans over the go board started to churn in Woodbridge's stomach. He was now regretting not having informed his superiors about the special warrant. He could hardly close the ports to O'Malley with no official police warrant in place. It was too late anyway. O'Malley and Fujimoto were already in the car loading bay of the ferry.

Grace and Hiroshi were still in a state of high tension when they settled down in their cabin. Every other passenger had looked like a secret agent, and they feared a knock on the door at any moment. None came.

At four in the morning, they docked in Ostend and passed into continental Europe without incident. It was foggy and freezing cold. Shivering with exhaustion, they drove across Belgium with just one coffee stop for sustenance at an all-night garage. A grey dawn greeted them in Aachen. They'd crossed the German border, and O'Malley had a strange feeling of relief. She'd worked a lot at the KFA in Jülich, and felt on home ground. She checked into her favourite hotel.

"Now our troubles are beginning" she said with an attempt at a smile.

Woodbridge's superiors were furious.

"You mean to tell me, Woodbridge, that you authorized a special warrant and mobilized an armed squad for some obscure academic who may or may not have something to do with an ordinary police matter… and then you missed the woman, anyway."

"Yes, sir" said Woodbridge.

"As I understand it, Woodbridge" M said, tapping the file, "you were supposed to keep this O'Malley character under gentle surveillance, the important thing being to keep her in Britain for her scientific work."

"Yes, sir."

"And now you've panicked the bitch and she's fled to Japan."

"Maybe, sir…"

"No maybe about it, Woodbridge." He tapped the folder again. "She was on a Lufthansa flight from Frankfurt to Tokyo yesterday afternoon."

Kamakura had a hard time persuading Grace and Hiroshi to stick to the original plan. He assured them that the Japanese Secret Service were dealing with the murder case in Abingdon, that Grace was in no danger of being framed for a crime she had not committed. They had cracked MI5 codes and knew that Grace was being pressurized solely because of her work on the polymers. The British knew nothing about the epsilon twistor and the best way to keep it secret was for her to return to her work there, with the project leadership in Japan left to a frontman. He was already working on possible candidates. He had less difficulty in persuading Grace that, if she did return, she should move her fellowship from Oxford and make a fresh start at another university, severing her connections with the elementary particle physics group there. After a heart-rending discussion, Grace and Hiroshi decided that they would return to Britain in the New Year.

It fell to Tom Bobbin to announce the bad news to Helen and Freddy. It was a cold day in early January, and O'Malley had been AWOL for three weeks. O'Malley had faxed him from the

Department of Condensed Matter Physics at QEC. He re-read the fax now, with a feeling of deep dejection.

Dear Tom,

I am terribly sorry to have to tell you that I have resigned my fellowship in Oxford. I have just written to Professor Milton to that effect.

I have a huge favour to ask you. Could you take over Helen and Freddy's projects for me? That, or get someone else competent (not Christopher Vane) to do the job. I feel terrible about letting them down in the middle of their masters, but at least we have some great data in the bag from the last ARES experiment and Martina and Len can help them with the data analysis. I'm writing faxes to them, too, today.

It's impossible for me to explain my sudden decision to you. Suffice it to say that reaching thirty focussed my mind on the fact that I badly wanted to work in more practical science. I think I have reached the end of the road with the gluons, and have decided to concentrate on the polymer applications of SSK/Yamato theory. When Professor Cuthbertson offered me a permanent lectureship here to work on polymer gels, I decided to accept. There's no point me continuing in Oxford on work I no longer believe in – with Milton as head of department, I had to leave sooner or later anyway.

Anyway, I guess you have worked hard behind the scenes on my behalf and I have let you down. I offer my unreserved apologies.

I'll write a longer letter soon.

Best wishes to Pat and all the group

Take care

Grace

There wasn't anything controversial or private in the single page, so Tom had already decided to show it to them directly. It was eleven o'clock. For once, the whole group was together around their usual table in the NPL coffee lounge.

"What a bastard" said Helen, passing the fax on to Freddy.

Freddy was disappointed, but not too bothered. His mind was already on the 2.30 kick-off against Teddy Hall later in the day. Richard, Fyodor and Judith were very subdued, as the enormity of their loss sank in. The funereal quiet of his own group allowed Milton's plaintive whine to penetrate Tom's consciousness. Milton also had a fax with him, and was showing it to Christopher Vane and a couple of other cronies. Milton's fax was much shorter and to the point than Tom's. It read

Dear Professor Milton,

I am writing to you to resign my fellowship in the NPL with immediate effect.

May I take this opportunity to tell you that I (and most of the rest of the staff at the NPL) regard you as a talentless little prat?

Yours sincerely

G. O'Malley

"What a bitch" said Milton.

"Don't worry, Professor" said Christopher Vane. "O'Malley was overrated anyway. Professor Marmotville told me a couple of weeks ago that this Yamato theory business is all nonsense. We're better off without her. By the way, Professor, my own group is a little under strength this year. I could take over Freddy Richardson's masters if you like."

"Talk to Tom about it" said Milton, snappily.

Normally, he liked having his arse kissed by Christopher Vane, but this morning he just wasn't in the mood for it.

The other recipients of O'Malley's faxes that cold January day were genuinely upset. Unlike the old crusties, any of Grace's peers who had worked with her knew she was a great scientist and felt themselves privileged to be her co-workers. Len Hopper's feelings were purely professional and unmixed. He had had visions of a long and fruitful collaboration with O'Malley on the ARES instrument, leading to a stream of brilliant papers for them both and a promotion to senior instrument scientist, or higher, for himself. At first he thought the fax from Cuthbertson's lab had been some strange kind of hoax... although Grace had always been very straight with him, she was reputed to have a bizarre sense of humour... but his call to Tom Bobbin in Oxford had confirmed the bad news. Now he knew he'd just get landed with helping those two hopeless masters students, with no real rewards at the end of the day. Len cursed O'Malley out loud.

"What a bitch" he said.

The word immediately brought Martina to his mind. Perhaps that bighead could be conned into doing most of the donkey work on the data analysis for Helen and Freddy.

Martina's feelings were more mixed, not least because Hiroshi would now be leaving Oxford. In spite of Grace's threats, she'd still had visions of re-igniting the affair at a later date. That final afternoon, the day before their disappearance, when he'd had her from behind, replayed before her eyes. She had given him the spurts, well and truly. Still, London's not too far way, she thought. She'd miss Grace, too. The woman was a mad bugger, but a lot of fun. CERN would be a duller place without her visits. Still, the important thing at the moment was not to get roped in to doing all the data analysis for those two hopeless masters students. She felt sure that that boor Len Hopper could be conned into doing the donkey work on the papers.

O'Malley's letters started to arrive the following week, and the first recipient was Ben.

Dear Ben,

Thanks so much for looking after Hiroshi on the day of our flight. He really appreciated your company at what was a very fraught time. Knowing Hiroshi, he'll be writing to you himself shortly.

I'm so sorry I never had the chance to say goodbye. Our decision to split was a sudden one, driven by forces beyond our control. I wish I could explain it to you properly, but I can't. Suffice it to say that there was some heavy shit going down at the lab, and we had to get out as soon as we could.... I'm involved in some pretty strange science... there's some big issues at stake... Anyway, I won't be back in Oxford for a while and the fact that I didn't say goodbye doesn't mean I don't love you. I do.

Maybe we could play a long range go game. If you're up for it, my first move is

1. c4

I hope you don't mind me bogarting the black stones... seems fair enough as you won the last game, anyway.

I'll miss you and everybody else at 49... please say hi to everyone for me and let them know they'll all be welcome to crash with me and Hiroshi if they can make it down to London. I hope it goes without saying, that we've always got crashing space for you.

At the moment we're staying in an eccentric place in Harrow just under the hill. We're living in half of a traditional farmhouse owned by an eighty-year-old called Mrs Roberts who likes foreigners... She's taken a shine to Hiroshi, and keeps bringing us baskets of apples. The garden's great... totally overgrown, a little adventure paradise... the little instamatic pictures don't do it justice, I'm afraid.

The piccies of the inside aren't much good either... they don't show the weird curves and warps in the walls... or give you any idea of quite how the wind whistles in around the ill-fitting windows. It's really freezing at the moment and I'm sitting under Hiroshi's kotatsu... a queer little square table with a heating element underneath and a quilt trailing out from the four sides... my legs are warm, anyway... Hiroshi's down at the launderette, which is a lot warmer. The kitchen's totally primitive and the bathroom is outside, across some wooden slats that lead around a quiet inner courtyard with a Celtic statue in the middle... strange ornament, but it has a lovely serene face.

It's pretty uncomfortable here, but we'll probably be moving on early in the spring to somewhere closer to the lab... we've put in an offer on a three-bed semi in Kenton... by the way the best way to contact me is...

Dept of Condensed Matter Physics
Queen Elizabeth's College
Gooch Street
London

I've got a big favour to ask you... really sorry to bother you with this boring shit, man... but could you sort out one or two things for us vis-à-vis the cottage in Bibbleton?

I really don't want to go back there. I've written to the landlord and paid off three months rent... what a bummer... so there's no problems there, but we left a lot of gear... clothes, papers, books etc... and I'd be very, very grateful if you could get our personal effects together into a couple of trunks and send them on to my work address. I've enclosed a cheque for a grand (It won't bounce!) to cover the expenses. There's no hurry... but the coats would be much appreciated... It snowed here yesterday... As Hiroshi left you a key... he's just got back, and sends his love... and the landlord's expecting you, there shouldn't be any problem... apart from the hassle... sorry about that.

Anyway, I'm rambling on and there's a million and one things to do... estate agents, solicitors, helping Hiroshi to find a masters position in London, blah, blah, etc.

I'd really appreciate a line from you... just a postcard... would make it feel more real that we're here somehow.

Love, Grace

Ben put the letter down, let out a big sigh, and rolled a joint. He hadn't seen much of Grace last year, but he knew he'd miss her, badly. He regretted being out of touch for so long when Grace was just down the road. When he lit up, he even forgot his usual ritual incantation of 'Boum, Shivah', deep in recollection of the Japanese

111

proverb Grace had taught him on her last visit... 'ichigo-ichie'... a once-in-a-lifetime meeting. Originally part of the teaching of the tea ceremony, it meant that every occasion of extending hospitality to another person is a particular opportunity never to recur in one's lifetime, so one should try to make the occasion perfect. Well, at least that evening last month had lived up to it, he mused, taking a second deep toke. Arne had been asking him when he was next going to invite Grace round for another go game... he'd be disappointed, too. As he took his third toke, he suddenly stood up, rummaged around in a pile of papers in the corner and found a few blank postcards. The one to send stood out immediately. The whole card, orange ground in the upper half, a pair of staring eyes in the lower half, conveyed the simple message

The most
potent weapon in
the hands of the
oppressor is
the mind of the
oppressed.

It was a quote from Steve Biko.

He flipped the card over, took a fourth deep toke, and wrote

Dear Grace,
Great to get your letter.
2. q16
love to you and Hiroshi
take care
Ben

It had seemed natural to play on a star point, his favourite method. After finishing the spliff, he floated straight off down to the post office on his magic carpet. The together stuff could wait.

In Kamakura's lab it was business as usual and, as usual, Kamakura was still working at eight o'clock in the evening. He was feeling pretty pleased with himself. He'd got the go ahead for dual ERATO projects, a 'front' project on magnetic multilayers and the epsilon twistor project in a 'super-lab' next door, to be sited in a science complex in Kamakura's home city of Hiroshima. Kamakura smirked to himself. A decade or two from now, Japan would be the most powerful country in the world, and the woman who was going to make it possible would be slogging away in Britain for a fraction of Kamakura's own salary.

He took out a bottle of saké and a beaker from his briefcase. The publishers were pressing for a spring deadline for the Sakamoto Conference Proceedings. He hated writing in English, and the introduction was giving him a lot of pain. His mind went back to his teenage days and a story about an American helicopter over the Ryoanji, then to O'Malley's note to Yamato at the back of the scruffy calculations

"…an end to the yoke of American imperialism under which we all suffer…"

But it could be used for different purposes, too, Kamakura thought.

He started again with his anecdote about the American helicopter, the first fuel of alcohol of the day driving him into it.

Kamakura soon put the pen down, unable to concentrate on the task. He took another deep draft of saké and pulled O'Malley's file out of his briefcase. He had read it thoroughly at home already, but the international politics of the project was on his mind. The Japanese Secret Service had done a meticulous job. He flicked ahead to the 'politics' section of the O'Malley file. O'Malley was clearly a frustrated rebel, who couldn't make her mind up between the anarchists, the communists and the ecologists. Everything Kamakura himself had heard Grace say had expressed disgust at the politics of the eighties in Britain, the USA and Germany, where Thatcher, Reagan and Kohl reigned supreme. She'd been in the mainstream British Labour party for a short while, and drifted in and out of various far left groups. Kamakura thought the idealistic socialism of Grace and Yamato to be nonsense, but had been careful not to air this opinion.

Kamakura re-filled his beaker and went on to the recent friendships section of the folder. The two outstanding meetings were with two Englishmen, a Ben de Montfort in Oxford and a Tony Woodbridge in London. Kamakura took a deep draught of saké and flicked through the attached memo on Ben. He was much more interested in the attached file on Woodbridge.

The file on Woodbridge was on a top British secret service agent. He was implicated in the deaths of up to seventeen people, mainly in Northern Ireland, and had commanded SAS squads. He was fluently polylingual, including Chinese and Arabic, and a very gifted computer expert. He came from a family of British Army commanders and worked under cover of civil service jobs in Whitehall. He was a capable, if unenthusiastic, administrator. His CV ran on and on… the work in Libya… the work in Peru… recently he'd been in Kuwait and Iraq… now back in London… resident in Pimlico in strongly armed flat block.

It seemed hard to imagine that Grace had made friends with such a man… but college days were different…

…Kamakura wandered off into a reverie of his own college days, and poured himself another beaker of saké. It was ten in the evening and time for him to prepare his own report for the ministry. He shooed away the last remaining students and locked the lab.

His report identified a potential major hazard on the horizon… the work of Woodbridge and the British Secret Service. The circumstances surrounding O'Malley's abrupt departure in December had been cleared up by cracking British electronic codes, and it was possible that Woodbridge had discovered something about the twistor in the time O'Malley was under surveillance. She was most likely under some kind of surveillance now. On the plus side, there was no evidence that O'Malley had registered on the consciousness of the CIA and no evidence that the British interest ran much beyond that dangerous man Woodbridge. Kamakura signed off. He poured himself a fourth beaker of saké.

Ben believed in synchronicity, morphic resonance, call it what you like, so he wasn't in the least surprised when, the same day as he had received a letter from Grace, he received a call from Tony, that Maya conveyed to him from the freezing hallway.

"Who is it?" called Ben, from the proximity of his little bar heater.

"Someone called Tony" Maya said. "I think it's that bloke I fell over at Grace's party."

"I'm coming" said Ben to Maya. "Hello" he said into the receiver.

"Is that Ben de Montfort?" the upper-class voice enquired.

"Sure is" said Ben. "What can I do for you?"

"My name's Tony, Tony Woodbridge… old friend of Grace's… we had an excellent go game recently and Grace suggested the two of us might get together for some go…"

He let the sentence hang in anticipation.

"Oh, hi, Tony" Ben said. "Did you know Grace has moved to London?"

"No, really?"

"Yeah, got a letter from her this morning…"

"Really?" said Tony, with interest.

"Yeah… she's holed up in Harrow, some trouble with the lab here…" He checked himself. "Anyway, Grace told me you were a mean go player… It would be great to get together… Do you fancy coming up here?… How are you fixed?"

"That's very kind" said Tony. "I'd love to come around. Any time in the next week or two would be fine… How about Wednesday?"

"Sorry, man, that's my yoga class."

"Thursday?"

"Piano lesson."

"Friday?" suggested Tony, with a touch of exasperation in his voice.

"Friday would be cool. Would you like to come for dinner?"

Tony had visions of a group of boring hippies sitting around eating beansprouts and millet, and declined, fairly gracefully.

"It may take me a while to get off work on Friday" he said. "I think I'll grab a bite in London and set off later, if you don't mind."

"Sure, man. When do you think you can make it?"

"Shall we say nine?"

"…hmm… late start, but why not?… Do you want to crash?"

Tony had visions of uncomfortable hippy mats on cold, draughty floors, and again declined.

"No, I'll be fine, thanks. I'll be coming by car…"

"Out of London on a Friday?"

"The traffic's not that bad…"

"Get the bus, man… think ecologically…"

"Yes, well" Tony said. "Next Friday at nine, then…"

"Great, man…"

"One last thing."

"Yeah"

"What's your address?… Grace only gave me your phone number."

"49, Iffley Road."

"Ah, just off the Plain."

"That's the one."

"See you then."

"Ciao, man."

Tony felt pleased, but uneasy. He'd be off to Tripoli in March, and should have been preparing for his new mission. But he'd been thwarted by Grace, and just couldn't get the case out of his mind. He liked to be in control of situations, and hated it when people had a secret he couldn't fathom. In particular, there was something on that tape that had really got under his skin. As soon as he had hung up on Ben, he pressed re-wind, stop and play for the dozenth time that evening.

O'Malley   …don't say anything to anyone.
Fujimoto   O, Grace, I'm afraid. Do you think they know anything about the twister?
O'Malley   I'm not sure. I'm afraid, too, Hiroshi…

Tony poured himself a big slug of Chivas Regal, hesitated for a moment between the Benson & Hedges and the Dunhill, lit a Dunhill, crossed the dimly lit room and pulled out a dictionary.

twister…n. one who, or that which, twists: a sophistical, slippery, shuffling, or dishonest person: a ball sent with a twist.

The transcript on his desk was definitely correct, but the reference just didn't make sense.

You don't get to Tony's level in the secret service by battering away like a blockhead. Tony was a big fan of de Bono's lateral thinking. It must be a physics term… Tony was nothing if not well read, and he started thumbing through his science collection. The only reference he found was in a book he'd bought in the late seventies when he was trying to keep abreast of modern developments in quantum mechanics. In the index of this daunting book on field theoretic techniques there were two mentions. Tony thumbed up

p.84… nothing much there…

p.215… last chance… just some strange pictures of Feynman diagrams labelled 'Twisted' and 'Anomalous' and the forbidding comment that 'The actual proof of these rules is extremely complicated and tedious…'

I can imagine, thought Tony, but doubtless Grace would be clever enough to understand the topological properties of twister diagrams, or twisters. Tony's instinct told him he was on the right track. His first thought was to get a subordinate to do the rest of the donkey work in the British Library, but his superiors had been angry enough about the O'Malley case to dissuade him from using official means. On second thoughts, he'd make some excuse about background reading on the Libya case, and go there himself tomorrow afternoon.

By early the following evening, he was acquainting himself with the recent work of Penrose and Hawking. He didn't understand the technical details, of course, but he got the gist. Twisters were mathematical entities and twistors were some kind of little knots in space-time, somehow connected with the fundamental stability of matter at its most elementary level. Tony was still puzzled. This stuff had nothing to do with O'Malley's work... He returned the reference books to the desk and walked pensively back to his basement flat, unaware of the bustle of the commuters thronging the pavements. He had a lot of work to do in brushing up his Arabic, but the O'Malley file sucked him in again. Ben de Montfort had an amateurish interest in quantum mechanics, too.

Chapter 6

A Dinner Party in Cuddleton

"Hi, Tony" said Ben.

"Hello, Ben" said Tony, "pleased to meet you properly at last…"

They were standing in the dimly lit porchway at Iffley Road. It was black, cold and sleeting.

"…come in, man, come in…"

Tony suddenly extended a hand and Ben shook it. To Tony's relief, they went straight into Ben's room on the ground floor without meeting any of the other occupants. Tony professionally hid his distaste at the bare, dank room.

"Do you have any chairs?" he asked, politely.

"Don't use them myself" said Ben. "Bad for the posture… but I'll fetch one from upstairs if you like."

"That would be nice" said Tony.

His sharp eyes had already picked out the envelope lying next to the mattresses in the corner, with Grace's unmistakeable big, printy, almost childish handwriting. He didn't comment. An amateur would have tried to sneak a look while Ben was away upstairs in Rory Grungy's room, borrowing a chair. Tony wasn't an amateur. Plenty of time to have the place burgled later… windows looked pretty insecure… and a discreet photocopy taken.

"Here you go, man" said Ben, returning a few minutes later. "Take a seat… Mind if I stay on the floor… I feel better grounded that way… Have you eaten?… Fancy a spliff?"

"I have eaten, thanks" said Tony, "and I gave up smoking cannabis a long time ago. You go ahead."

'It'll be much easier to pump this boring hippy if he gets stoned' Tony thought.

Ben brought out his little tray of smoking paraphernalia, his go board and go stones, and a couple of bowls for the prisoners.

"Would you prefer to sit up to play, Tony?" he asked.

"I would, rather" Tony replied. "Bad back, you see…"

"That's because you don't sit on the floor, man" Ben replied with a laugh, sitting in his usual cross-legged position. "I'll fetch a coffee table."

Ben disappeared for a slightly longer time than before and came back with a peculiar low table. He settled it in front of Tony and put the go board onto it.

"This is the best I could do, man. You'll have to reach down a bit."

"That's fine" said Tony.

"Anyway, Boum Shivah" Ben said, lighting his spliff. "Shall we start?"

"Yes, I'm looking forward to it" said Tony.

"Me, too" said Ben, taking a handful of black stones. "Even or odd?"

"Odd" Tony replied.

There were seven stones.

"So, you get the whites" said Ben, plonking a stone down on his own left-hand four-four point.

"Grace said you had a bold style" said Tony, replying immediately with a more conservative stone on his right-hand three-four point, nearer the right-hand edge.

As is the way with go players, an hour or two drifted away as the first sixty or seventy stones were played. Tony was building up a commanding position.

"Shall we take a break?" Ben asked.

"Certainly" Tony replied.

"Wow, Grace wasn't kidding when she said you were a mean go player. I need some inspiration… I'll skin one up… Boum, Shivah…"

As Ben was crushing the joint out with a very spaced look on his face, Tony asked

"How do you usually get on with Grace, Ben?"

"O, Grace usually wins" said Ben, "but I won our last game. How about you?"

"O, I usually win" said Tony, "but Grace won our last game. She seemed to have a lot of mental energy…"

"Well, she usually does, man" said Ben with an unsteady laugh.

"I guess it must have been that twister theory she's been so worked up about…"

"Twister theory?" Ben replied, with total innocence. It looked as if the arrow had missed the target.

"Yes, you know, that field theory Grace has been so interested in. Didn't she mention it to you?"

"Oh, yeah" said Ben blearily. "I remember… said she'd made some kind of breakthrough… said Maxwell would have been proud of her… she's always been a big fan of Maxwell, hasn't she?"

"She certainly has" said Tony. "Right since college days. I remember her telling me that the Maxwell equations were one of the greatest human achievements ever… she's always been into field theory, hasn't she?"

"Yeah, I wish she'd talked more about it… said it had nothing to do with her gluon or polymer stuff, but then suddenly clammed up… what did she tell you about it?"

There was a hint of jealousy in Ben's question.

"O, nothing much" said Tony, "about the same as she told you, it sounds… not like Grace to be secretive about her science, is it?"

"No, it isn't" said Ben, doubtfully.

Tony suddenly looked different, more alert.

"Shall we resume?" he asked.

Two hours later he had crushed Ben, and made his farewells. He was smirking to himself when he got into his silver Lancia Beta, parked discreetly in a side road. He put on a Ry Cooder tape and slid quickly up through the gears. A very successful evening had been had. Spanking that hippy de Montfort at go had been a much-needed boost to his ego, and he'd hit the bull's eye with the field theory. So, Grace had made some kind of field theoretic breakthrough and her boyfriend was concerned enough about it to bring it up at a moment of extreme tension... maybe there was something to be salvaged from the O'Malley case after all. When Tony purred on to the motorway to London, he was humming along to the tape. At that moment, he was as happy as a man like that can be.

Grace and Hiroshi were having their first serious row. It was mid-February, and the heating had broken down, leaving their rooms in Harrow freezing cold. The sky was leaden and biting shafts of wind were penetrating under the ill-fitting doors.

"When are we going to be moving, Grace?"

"I don't know, Hiroshi. Professor Kamakura is trying his best."

"This is ridiculous. Think of all we've done for the Japanese, probably at great danger to ourselves... and this is the way we get treated... why don't they send us the money?"

"Look, we discussed this. Kamakura is right. If we start splashing money around and get a flashy house it will look suspicious. We've got to keep a low profile..."

"I'm not talking about a flashy house. I'm talking about an adequate one... this place is disgusting... and we haven't got any money at all have we?"

Grace looked crestfallen.

"No, we haven't" she said.

"Well, why not?" said Hiroshi, with exasperation. "Why don't they give you an advance on your salary here? We've been here for weeks now and they just keep us waiting for everything. I want to leave. You could get a decent science job anywhere in the world…"

There was a heavy silence. Grace recalled the way she'd been treated when she first arrived in Osaka on her JSPS Fellowship. She had been disappointed and angry that for the first two months she'd been in a crappy little thirty-five square metre bedsit with poor facilities, that her trunks had been held up at the airport, that it had taken ages for her first pay check to come through… yes, Kamakura was a control freak… O'Malley had seen that other foreign visitors to his lab were treated in the same way. It made them dependent on Kamakura's munificence. Sometime in the second month, everything would slot into place… a decent apartment would be found, the trunks would be released from bond, the money would come through and the visitors would be grateful.

"Well?" Hiroshi asked, impatiently.

"It's his way" Grace said, weakly.

"Well, his way isn't good enough" Hiroshi said with genuine heat. "I've given up my master's degree, we're poor, I'm cold… I can't even phone my mother…"

"Calm down, Hiroshi."

"I am not going to calm down. I've had enough. Unless we're in a decent house by the end of the month, I'm leaving. With or without you…"

Grace's jaw dropped. The idea of Hiroshi leaving her had simply not occurred to her from the moment they first made love. Bibbleton in the autumn seemed a long, long time ago.

"I'll fax Kamakura, tomorrow" Grace said.

"You better bloody well had" said Hiroshi. "I've given up my master's, I've got no friends. I hate it here…"

"But, but when we came here on holiday you said how amazing London was…"

"That was different. We were staying in a lovely comfortable hotel then…"

"…and you had Martina chasing you around…" Grace interrupted, bitterly.

"So what if I did. At least Martina was fun."

"And I'm not?"

"At the moment, Grace, no."

There was a long silence, broken finally by Grace.

"I'm sorry you feel like that, Hiroshi" she said, quietly.

"O, Grace, I'm sorry" said Hiroshi. "I didn't mean that, it's just…"

"No, it's true" said Grace. "I've landed us in a crock of shit here. Look, shall we go out somewhere warm, stay in a hotel tonight?"

"O, Grace, can we afford it?"

"I've still got my credit cards" said Grace. "Let's do it."

They were silent throughout the train journey into Euston, and during the walk down the Tottenham Court Road. The lights and the hustle and bustle of the shopping crowds seemed to lift their spirits, and they had an excellent meal in an Italian restaurant, but by the time they found a hotel near Leicester Square, Hiroshi was sagging again. As Hiroshi was falling asleep, Grace said

"I've booked the hotel for a week, Hiroshi. We've spent our last night in Harrow. I'll fax Kamakura and see Cuthbertson tomorrow."

Prof. Cuthbertson was an accountant. He looked like an accountant, with his wispy hair and circular glasses. He thought like an accountant. He prided himself on "running a tight ship" at QEC. He acted like an accountant. This included cutting down on the number of storemen, technicians and secretaries… he was into the new phase of "downsizing". He was also a terrible lecturer. His advanced statistical mechanics course had decimated the third year from eighty to three students. He knew O'Malley was a brilliant lecturer, and he didn't like her. O'Malley's sudden departure from Oxford had put her nicely in his power. Things couldn't have worked out better.

O'Malley arrived at nine, her brows knit with thunder. The people in the lab looked startled even before Grace strode across the main lab and banged on the door of Cuthbertson's office. She opened straight away and stepped in.

"Lee, I want a word with you."

"I'm rather busy at the moment, Grace…"

"Now!" O'Malley said, cutting him short and banging the door to behind her.

A look of fear passed across the faces of the students in the lab, and they nervously continued their tasks. Heated voices were scarcely muffled by the thin door.

"How dare you…" spluttered Cuthbertson, a man who was accustomed to being treated with obedience.

"Shut up, Lee, and do some listening for a change. Hiroshi and I have had enough of this fucking around in Harrow…"

"You'll do…"

"I told you to shut up and listen. Interrupt me one more time and I'll stick your teeth down the back of your throat. Unless we've got a decent house and a decent wad of cash in hand by the 28th, we're leaving and you can stick your polymer gels up your arse."

O'Malley stormed out, ignored the nervous calls of

"Good morning"

from her terrified new colleagues, and headed off to the fax machine.

At ten O'Malley's time, seven pm his time, Kamakura was on the phone to the Cabinet Office in Tokyo. The best solution was clearly to make O'Malley happy in London, and Kamakura received a sharp rebuke from the prime minister's personal secretary for not having ensured the bank transfer already. Even Japanese bureaucracy can be overridden in the interests of national security. By four o'clock in the afternoon, a transfer of ten million yen had been made to a new account established for O'Malley at the Harrow branch of the Royal Welsh Bank.

After an unpleasant conversation with the head administrator at QEC, Professor Cuthbertson had established that their new star academic from Oxford would receive an advance on her salary, and help from the newly established Human Resources Department with her house hunting. Cuthbertson suddenly realized he didn't know where Grace and Hiroshi were staying, in order to convey the good news about the new arrangements to them. Grace hadn't been back to the lab. Cuthbertson had a terrible sinking feeling in his guts. The young couple had fled England to Belgium a couple of months ago at a few hours' notice. They could be on a boat out of Dover on their way to the continent at this very moment. He needn't have worried. Grace and Hiroshi were downtown shopping.

At five-thirty, Grace re-entered the lab a little sheepishly and sat down at her desk. She felt curiously drawn by the twistor calculations, and started fiddling with the pieces of paper strewn untidily around her narrow space. Cuthbertson came out of his office and said

"Grace, I would like a word with you."

He was all smiles and charm. At six, Grace left Cuthbertson's office and headed straight back to her hotel. She was looking forward to telling Hiroshi the good news.

On March 3rd, the final day of the miner's strike, Grace and Hiroshi moved into their new house.

"I'm so happy" Hiroshi said.

"I'm not" said Grace.

Hiroshi gave a puzzled frown and Grace continued.

"We're in a cage" she said.

126

She looked around the big, well-heated living room, with its glowing gas fire.

"A beautifully gilded cage, to be sure, but a cage nonetheless. We're trapped by the… by the extremum thermodynamics thing."

"O, Grace, don't let's think about it like that."

Grace continued to look disconsolate.

"And the miners have been crushed."

"They've given us some money, too, haven't they?" Hiroshi said, trying to change the subject.

"Yes" said Grace, with an attempt at a smile, "about ten million yen…"

"Which is?"

"Somewhere between sixty and seventy thousand quid."

"Wow" said Hiroshi. It seemed the only appropriate thing to say.

"What's better than that is that I've been given the whole week off. I don't have to go back to the lab until the tenth…"

Martina had moved to the east side of Oxford, to the village of Cuddleton. Her main motivation had been its convenience for travelling to London. Not just that it might be useful for popping down to see Hiroshi – she had met another charming man, Tony, who lived in Pimlico. Although she wasn't any great friend of that boring hippy Ben, she was grateful to him for the introduction. Ben was also heading down to London a lot these days, courtesy of his new relationship with Catherine. Ben's new girlfriend Catherine was a professor at Oxford University, but often worked from her home in Brixton. She had had three books published, and had two children. How did she manage it, and how had Ben managed to snaffle her, she wondered. Then she recalled what Pru and Maya had told her about Ben's prowess in bed, and her mind turned back to Hiroshi, now settling down with Grace in a boring London suburb called

Kenton. When she had discovered that Grace knew Catherine (had actually snogged her and groped her tits at a drunken party, so the rumour went), and had known Tony for years, a classic dinner party for six, with an Oxford-London theme, had seemed a perfect way to celebrate her new contract. Martina, as she often did, had got exactly what she wanted – half her salary paid by CERN (a huge amount, in Swiss francs) and half by Oxford (a lesser amount, but a more relaxed lifestyle). She was humming a Madonna song away to herself in the kitchen of her new home, the former vicarage of Cuddleton, when the doorbell rang.

Hiroshi and Grace were the first arrivals.

"Martina, hi" said Hiroshi, giving her a little peck on the cheek.

Martina greeted Grace rather awkwardly, but Grace suddenly embraced her and greeted her as cordially as she could.

Ben arrived next, with Catherine's two children. He was a frequent, and loving, child-minder.

"This is Roberta" said Ben, introducing Catherine's seven-year-old daughter, "and this is Carlo" he said, introducing her three-year-old son to Hiroshi and Grace.

"I didn't know you were bringing the children" Martina said. She knew Grace had never been comfortable around kids.

Her solution to the awkward atmosphere was to pour four stiff gin and tonics.

"Wow, that hit the spot" said Ben, not abstaining as usual.

"Good shot, Martina" said Grace.

"Splendid gin and tonic, Martina" said Hiroshi.

The glasses clinked. Carlo said

"Want a poo, daddy."

Ben smiled indulgently.

"He's started calling me that, recently" he said, leading the boy off to the toilet.

Catherine arrived, wearing a low-cut dress that gave ample exposure to her large, anti-gravity breasts. Catherine had always believed in the motto, which she often quoted, 'if you've got it, flaunt it' and her tits had been exciting boys and girls alike since her mid-teens. There was no sign of sagging in her mid-forties. She was as proud of them as she was of her tenured fellowship at an Oxford college. She was a professor in linguistics and Slavonic languages, a member of Hebdomadal Council, and self-important with it. She didn't like Grace. The feeling was mutual.

Martina managed to deflect Catherine into the kitchen, where she poured sloe gins. By the time Tony arrived, half an hour late, there were five quite pissed people to greet him.

"Tony" shouted Grace.

Hiroshi frowned, and said something to Ben. His intuition had always been to mistrust that man.

"Ah, Hiroshi, delighted to meet you again" said Tony.

"It's a pleasure" said Hiroshi.

Martina tried to push a gin and tonic Tony's way, but he insisted on a beer instead, and had a small bottle of Stella.

"Shall we take our seats for dinner" said Martina, proudly. She was a very fine chef, and she knew it. They sat in a classical pattern, women alternating with men, with Grace between Tony and Ben.

"How are things at the vicarage, Martina?" Hiroshi asked.

"How are things in college?" Grace asked Catherine.

Martina had cracked a bottle of champagne and poured out six flute glasses. She raised her considerable voice.

"Ladies and gentlemen" she said, "I think some congratulations are in order. To Grace, on getting a permanent lectureship!"

Grace blushed.

"Well, it's got a three-year probationary period" she said.

"No problem" said Martina.

"Minor detail" said Catherine.

They clinked their glasses. Grace downed her champagne in one. She was well lit up.

"I hear that congratulations are in order for another achievement, Grace" Tony said.

"Eh" said Grace, with a bleary smile.

"The story's going round Oxford that you've had some very important theory paper published... Some kind of field theory..."

Hiroshi gave Grace a sharp look. He said

"That was submitted a long time ago. Grace has practically forgotten about that work, haven't you, Grace?"

"Well..." said Grace, blearily.

"Anyway" said Hiroshi, "what have you been doing with yourself these past few months, Tony?"

"O, this and that" said Tony. "I'm in the National Audit Office these days."

"But still in Whitehall" said Grace.

"Still in Whitehall" Tony echoed.

"Do you believe in monogamy?" Catherine asked Hiroshi.

"No" Hiroshi replied.

"These sardines are delicious, Martina" Grace said, taking an enormous swig of white wine. "The interview at QEC was a real blast. Five professors seated round a table, including Walter and Cuthbertson. Walter's moved from Cambridge to QEC to set up a new condensed matter physics group. He'll be my official boss, would you believe. Cuthbertson is the head of department at QEC, a real astringent arsehole..."

"Grace!" said Hiroshi.

"You do seem to have problems with authority figures" Catherine said.

"Bollocks" Grace replied. "It's authority figures who have problems with me. They get so used to being surrounded with yes-men that they don't know to deal with a no-woman. Cuthbertson's a bit better than Milton, but still a prick."

"Sounds like you're going to have a great time in London" said Tony with a laugh, egging her on.

"Yeah, Cuthbertson is one of those computer bores who believes you can do science by doing bigger and bigger statistical mechanical computations on faster and faster computers."

"And you can't?" said Tony.

"No" Grace replied. She poured herself another large glass of white wine.

"The most amazing thing" Grace continued, "is that I once wrote to Walter telling him that I thought his void lattice calculations were nonsense..."

"Could you pass the wine, Grace" Hiroshi said.

"So why are you heading into the lion's den?" Catherine asked.

"Oh, Cuthbertson's just an administrator and Walter is just a figurehead for the new condensed matter group. There's some interesting people there... my old mate Len Hopper's moving there, there's a brilliant young theoretician called Thomas More... won the Maxwell prize last year..."

O'Malley hesitated.

"...and it's in London."

"What's so good about London?" Catherine asked.

"Well, the students are great for a start. I'm really looking forward to the lecturing... it's like lecturing the United Nations at QEC... people from all over the planet... and they've encouraged women...

they've got about thirty percent on the physics course… best in the UK…"

O'Malley glugged her wine again.

Catherine seemed needled.

"But what about the standard of scholarship?" she said.

"Well" said Grace, "the way funding has gone over the past decade and the way it will go over the next five years, there's just the two Oxbridge universities and the two big London universities that are feasible bases for doing physics…"

"That's terribly elitist" said Ben. "I have a friend who's doing some excellent work at Bangor University."

Grace looked at Ben with surprise.

"I'm sorry, Ben. I didn't mean to run down people at other universities. It's just the way it's funded by the bureaucrats that have got us by the short and curlies… the big four are way ahead in funding… QEC is second actually, ahead of Oxford…"

"How disappointing, Grace" Catherine said. "I would have expected more altruistic reasons from you."

"Shall I clear the plates?" said Martina.

There were murmurs of assent, and Martina cleared up. She then produced a set of six amazing Siamese Wedgewood plates and carried in a leg of lamb with about forty to fifty cloves of garlic pushed into various cuts in the meat. Martina then fished out a couple of bottles of Gevrey Chambertin. She was really pushing the boat out.

"What did you make of Kinnock's speech attacking Militant?" Martina asked Grace.

"Typical" Grace replied.

"I don't trust Neil Kinnock" Tony said.

"Do you know something we don't know?" Catherine asked.

Tony's face clouded over. He'd seen plenty of files on Neil Kinnock. He wasn't as interesting as Grace, and he wasn't as honest, either.

"No, not at all" he said.

"…but he looks dishonest" he added weakly.

Martina filled the glasses and served the meat. The scramble for vegetables on the over-filled table covered up the embarrassing political conversation. Grace took a big swig of the red wine, and said

"That's great booze, Martina, thanks…"

"Anyway" she continued, "there I was with these five professors, and Avery says to me… Avery's a good guy, by the way… Avery says…"

Here O'Malley put on a ridiculously posh voice.

"Dr O'Malley, you left Oxford in an unseemly rush… what guarantees can you give us that you will not do the same to QEC?"

O'Malley chortled and took another big swig.

"Professor Avery, I replied, how can anyone give guarantees about how her life will develop…"

"You didn't?" said Martina.

"I did" said Grace.

"And they offered you the job?" said Catherine.

"They did indeed" said Grace.

"We're going to America soon" said Hiroshi.

"Oh, where?" said Ben.

"To the mid-west, to Kansas City, Missouri" Hiroshi replied.

"The most boring part" Catherine said.

"Why there?" Ben asked.

"We're visiting a friend of Grace's, called Ron Green. I met him once in Kyoto, last year…"

Hiroshi glazed over for a moment.

"We're going to New York first" he said with a smile "and up to Cornell University. Grace is giving lectures there and in Kansas."

"Are these your new field theory calculations, Grace?" Tony asked. "I've been getting into twister theory myself recently…"

Grace scarcely blinked.

"The new stuff's straight classical calculations, Tony… could have been done by Maxwell and Boltzmann over a century ago… there's no twisters in the polymer work."

"Have you ever calculated with twisters?" Tony asked.

Grace was interrupted as she was about to reply.

"Tony, could you pass me the potatoes?" Hiroshi said. "O, thanks… So, do you have any travel plans this year, Tony?"

"O, this and that" said Tony, vaguely. "I may be off to the Maldives in the autumn…"

"Ben and I are off to St Petersburg… and to Achill Island" said Catherine.

She had had a rich husband who had owned a house in London and a cottage in Ireland. She had got a good divorce settlement.

"You mean Leningrad" said Grace.

"No, St Petersburg" said Catherine. "I prefer to give it its proper name, as no doubt it will be re-named in the future."

"No chance" said Grace.

"The tide of the times" said Tony, pompously, "does seem to be heading in that direction…"

"Bullshit" Grace interrupted, "the old Stalinist regimes in Eastern Europe may be awful, but capitalism still has the usual on offer… war, poverty, hunger…"

"Your nice job in London" said Catherine, "my nice job in Oxford, Martina's research fellowship here… gosh, what a terrible system,

Grace… I know academics in Russia who haven't been paid for months…"

"O, don't let's talk politics" said Hiroshi. "It's so fractious. That was a lovely dinner, Martina."

"There's more to come" said Martina. "Chestnut mousse with Sauternes."

"You're kidding" said Grace.

"I kid you not" said Martina, downing the last of the Gevrey.

During the pudding, Hiroshi, Catherine and Tony got into a conversation about linguistics and Chomsky *et al.* bombed around one side of the table. On the other, Grace, Martina and Ben were reminiscing about a walk in the Cotswolds many moons ago. Tony said

"So, Grace, what have you been doing with yourself all these months since you got back from Japan?"

"O, this and that" said Grace, vaguely.

"A bit of science… a bit of teaching… and I've had time to finish off my book on the Japanese characters…"

"Oh" said Tony, tilting towards Grace.

"Yeah" said Grace. "It's a method I've developed for learning the kanji, the Japanese characters… it's not original… developed from an idea by a bloke called Heisig… it's nice relaxation from physics…"

"Did you know that about seventy percent of the Japanese characters have the same meaning in Chinese?" Tony said.

"Something like that" said Grace. "At the moment, the method is only about meanings, so it would apply to Chinese, too."

"That would be interesting" said Tony. "I learned the Chinese characters by brute force. I'd like to see a different approach."

"It's dead simple" said Grace. "You use basically the radical system of classifying Chinese characters, calling them primitive elements.

You combine these primitive elements into a tale to make more complex characters. It's good fun when you get into it… I've got some tales with me…"

"Do tell me about St Petersburg, Catherine" said Hiroshi. "Why are you going there?"

"For a conference" said Catherine, confidently. "I'm giving a paper on the poetry of Tsvetaeva…"

"Who's he?" Hiroshi asked.

"She" said Catherine impatiently, "was one of the greatest Russian poets of the twentieth century…"

"May I see some of your kanji tales?" Tony asked.

"Sure" said Grace, "but I've only got one copy with me, and I'm taking it to Oxford University Press tomorrow."

"Have they already agreed to publish?" Catherine asked.

"No" Grace replied.

"Shall we go outside for coffee?" said Martina.

It was near the solstice and a lovely, warm evening with beautiful light. The low hills thirty miles away across the flatlands of Oxfordshire stood out sharply.

"I've got to be going" said Catherine.

"So soon?" said Martina.

"So soon?" echoed Tony.

"Yes, I'm giving a seminar tomorrow morning" Catherine said, in a determined way. "I've already ordered a taxi for ten."

"What a pity. The sunset is so beautiful" said Hiroshi.

"I'll see it from the taxi" said Catherine.

She and Ben made their farewells, and headed off with the children.

"Are you staying over, Grace?" Tony asked.

"Yeah" said Grace, "we're both too pissed to drive…"

"I'm afraid I'm somewhat over the limit, too" Tony said. "Martina…"

"Of course you can, Tony" said Martina, "I've no less than three spare bedrooms in the vicarage. I think we can manage…"

Tony was an expert spy. Later that night he sneaked back into the living room and took the kanji tales out of O'Malley's briefcase. It was just a sample, the last two hundred tales from 1840 to 2042. They were handwritten, about three to a page. He photographed the sixty to seventy pages quickly and returned the tales to O'Malley's briefcase.

Back in Pimlico, Tony became aware that the printer was still churning out stuff, reams of it. He got up and pressed the 'Cancel' button on the print monitor. The tray was full of O'Malley's kanji tales. He lit another cigarette. One of the many keyword analyses he had requested was for the tales containing the samurai swords. The first kanji tales he read were

1553. proportion

Harm… sabre

Concrete image of the samurai *swords* we brought back from Japan. No matter how much professors and administrators may *harm* you, you have to keep a sense of *proportion* (science is good, but not that good) to keep yourself from *harming* them with one of these ferocious *sabres*.

1650. publish

Clothesline… sabre

Concrete image of a desperate Grace unable to get the exact mean-field theory solution to the polymer problem *published*. Will she hang herself from the *clothesline* or disembowel herself with the samurai sword that is shaped like the Western *sabre*?

1671. sabre

Awl... sabre

As usual, my concrete image of the *sabre* is of the disembowelling sword used by the samurai. They might have used it as an *awl* for boring holes into their own guts, but I've visualized using this *sabre* for boring holes into other people.

Tony had seen the real thing in O'Malley's eye when he'd burgled the Bibbleton cottage back in '84. Agent Reginald had been happy for him to do the job behind M's back, because of his personal interest in the case. Tony could see them now himself, the short disembowelling sword and the big sword for decapitation, in their beautiful, curved black sheaths.

It was still stiflingly hot in the autumn of '85 when Kamakura read Grace's kanji tales. Many of them seemed to express frustration and resentment at a lack of recognition of her abilities, and there were dark, violent stories involving samurai swords in addition to gloomy political tales. Grace clearly believed she had some kind of mission against the Americans, some kind of messianic belief in her ability to free the world from the oppression of American imperialism.

Kamakura was leaving for Tokyo. As usual the Shinkansen slid into Osaka Station at precisely the appointed time, and he took his comfortable seat in one of the green cars. He hailed a trolley dolly and bought two beakers of whiskey on ice, one for immediate consumption, and one to savour as the bullet train slid out of the metropolis. After the blue roofs of the suburbs had flashed past, Kamakura ordered a third whiskey and opened his briefcase. The first six months of the magnetic multilayers project had been analyzed in meticulous detail, and the final report had been signed, countersigned and countersigned again, and finally delivered to the prime minister's office. He was now going to discuss it with the prime minister. It was the first-generation epsilon twistor project, the most

138

secret and dangerous project in the world, but Kamakura placed the document confidently on the table in front of him. He knew there wasn't anything compromising in its subtly coded format, and no fool had been allowed to stamp 'top secret' on it, marking it out as a document worth stealing. He decided to re-read the attached letter from the prime minister.

6th October 1985

Dear Professor Kamakura,

Thank you for your frank evaluation of the magnetic multilayers project. It seems clear that although O'Malley's idea is being pursued with great determination, there still remains much progress to be made. There are also safety implications to be considered, and we wish to discuss the leadership of this project with you at your earliest possible convenience.

The massive hanko designating the prime minister's personal seal terminated the short letter. Kamakura had been thinking over the candidates. His problem was that he couldn't avoid mentally comparing them with O'Malley, and they fell woefully short. But the key was secrecy, and they couldn't risk Grace coming to Japan and attracting attention. He didn't regret that decision, and the best had to be made of it.

The train was gliding through the Tokyo suburbs. It was time to concentrate on the matter in hand, and convey his decision that they appoint Professor McCall, currently of the Massachusetts Institute of Technology. He knew the prime minister wasn't going to take the idea of a foreigner leading the project at all well, least of all an American. But they had to get the best man available and, after all, wasn't O'Malley a foreigner in the first place? The train was pulling into Tokyo station. Kamakura downed the last of his whiskey, and braced himself for the meeting.

Chapter 7

The Samurai Swords

The Renaissance Fest in Kansas City had been one of the grossest things Hiroshi had ever seen. Huge people wandering about guzzling turkey legs, men with arms thicker than his thighs, mind-numbing 'entertainment' in Ye Olde English style. When it came to the mid-West, Hiroshi was a cultural snob. Cornell had been scary, a bit like being trapped in Stepford, with the ideal wives doing ideal little part time jobs at the university. He thought they'd made an emergency landing in a field when they flew into Ithaca. The Buttermilk Falls were pretty, but not as grand as the Japanese Alps, Hiroshi thought, and camping shops and rich kid students weren't really his scene. He had enjoyed New York the most, taking a childish glee in catching a yellow cab to "Forty-second and Broadway"… images of the Brazilian restaurant, the Guggenheim Museum and the Gotham City style hotel on 65th and Lexington were bobbing meme-ishly around him.

"You're quiet tonight, Grace" he said.

"Yeah, I was thinking about Ron Green…"

"Me, too" said Hiroshi, "well, about America, anyway."

"I really like Ron" said Grace.

"Me, too" said Hiroshi. "He was ever so kind to us in Kansas…"

"Kansas City…" Grace said.

They laughed. It was an in-joke about the way Ron always corrected them.

"…Kansas City, Misooorah…" Hiroshi said, in a ridiculous American accent.

"I loved that Diastole place" he continued, in a normal voice. "It was ever so kind of Ron to put us up there…"

"It was indeed" said Grace.

"I was grossed out by the town, though" Hiroshi said. "You know the way that brochure started defensively 'Kansas City is not just a flat cow town'… well… that's the way it was, I'm afraid… the food was terrible… so much meat…"

Hiroshi and Grace had had a vegetarian spell since grossing out in the States. The massive energy consumption, the out-of-town Walmarts, obese people in huge cars, blocks upon blocks of Black only citizens, followed by blocks of whites only. The overblown air-conditioning, long car drives to out-of-town restaurants where huge slabs of meat served as meals…

Hiroshi gave a shudder.

"But we couldn't wipe them out, could we?" he said.

"No, we couldn't" said Grace. She had a vivid flash of the photograph of the old Einstein in the Eisenstadt book.

Grace was always worried that the house might be bugged, and she put on a record of some old Bowie music, quite loud. Ziggy Stardust and the Spiders from Mars blasted out, and Grace said quietly

"The twistor will be just a deterrent, Hiroshi. To keep American aggression and imperialism from spiralling out of control…"

"But when they've built it" Hiroshi said, "what will they do?"

He put a strong emphasis on the word 'they'.

"Do we have any control over that?"

"No" Grace said.

"And what if they killed Ron Green and three hundred million other Americans?"

"The deterrent works both ways, Hiroshi. The Americans will still have nuclear submarines all around the world. They're immune from attack, too. The new situation will just even things up between East and West… lethal force is lethal force…"

"And how did we get involved in this?" Hiroshi asked.

"Through my pride" Grace replied.

Grace turned the music off. That seventies stuff just annoyed her now. She fished her correspondence with Ron Green out of her briefcase. There was a folder full of it, bursting with drafts of Ron's latest manuscripts, both papers and chapters for his book on 'Polymers in Solution'. Since Grace's visit in August, Ron had been completely wired up on the science. He was pouring it out in a way that hadn't been seen from him since the early seventies. Grace re-read the most recent letter, and let out a deep sigh. Ron was hassling her to proofread his Chapter 4 on Theories of Interaction in Solutions of Semi-Rigid Polymers. Since Ron was discussing her recent Atomic Physics paper with Yamato and Shinoda as well as a couple of her individual theory papers in Physical Review from the seventies, she could hardly refuse. Ron was also hassling her to host a return visit to London. He wanted to come over in the autumn with his girlfriend Lucy. Ron was fifty-odd and Lucy forty-odd. Lucy had never been out of the States. Grace let out a groan. After the hospitality she'd received, she could hardly say no, but the house was going to be very crowded… visions of acting as a tour guide in corny parts of London… visions of shopping with Lucy…

America has a 'star' system in science that Japanese people cannot really understand, Kamakura thought. He looked at the front pages of the five CVs in front of him, spread out on a large desk at the Ministry of Science in Tokyo. They had already agreed to offer the job to McCall, but they had to go through the official motions; advertise the post, draw up a short list of candidates and hold interviews. The other four candidates were two Japanese professors, another Japanese, who headed the research division of Nippon Oil, and a French professor whom Kamakura disliked intensely. He felt vindictive towards a man who had obstinately blocked his new polymer theory for the past decade. The man wouldn't recognize a polymer solution if he took a bath in ketchup, Kamakura thought, bitterly. He was in an irritable mood, because there was no alcohol available in the bare ministry room, and the deadline for completing the paperwork was in twenty minutes' time, when he was to hand it personally to the prime minister upstairs. Yes, the Emmanuel-Canson model of polymers was nonsense, Kamakura thought, unable to let the rancour go. He was grimly pleased with his choice of shortlisting Canson. Picking another foreigner in the short list was good cover for the eventual choice of McCall, and Kamakura would have the pleasure of telling Canson that he had not been offered the post. Maybe it also disguises the paucity of our talent here, Kamakura thought, as he collected up the materials on the four dummies.

The only cv that really interested him was that of McCall, the rising star at MIT. McCall's publicity proudly proclaimed the size of his research group, the value of his state-of-the-art equipment, and the size of his rapidly expanding list of research publications and books, including a best-selling popular science book on gooey, blobby materials. At forty years of age, he was at his peak, with plenty of experience, but still with a burning ambition, the desire for a Nobel Prize. None of this would have interested Kamakura... after all, there were plenty of mediocre wannabes with similar looking American university CVs... but for the unusual features of McCall's theoretical work and political outlook.

Until recently, McCall had seemed a talented, maybe even brilliant, experimentalist, but although he had speculated about causes for the effects he had observed in his careful optical tweezer experiments, he had never written a pure theory paper until a few months ago. Kamakura had the preprint in front of him. It had been accepted by PRL, the leading American physics journal, and was already being hailed on the grapevine as a breakthrough in understanding critical phenomena in magnets. Kamakura couldn't understand the maths, but he understood the conclusion very well. When the Yamato-O'Malley method was applied in this apparently unrelated area of physics, it unified and explained many phenomena, and predicted others. Kamakura had especially liked the way McCall had followed the calculations to their logical conclusion, and had made bold predictions, risking being shot down in flames. He had put his reputation on the line. Yes, the man was a real scientist; he wasn't just going through the motions.

The politics were an unexpected bonus... Kamakura's thoughts got sidetracked again... O'Malley's voice saying that to be at that level as a scientist you would have to be a socialist or an anarchist... an example of her mad arrogance... Kamakura glanced at the clock. The lack of alcohol, and the big meeting coming up, were causing him to sweat. He tried to re-focus. McCall was a friend of Chomsky's at MIT, and had a record as an outspoken opponent of the Reagan regime. He had also engaged in debates with creationism supporters, and fought vigorously for the right of schools to teach Darwin's Theory of Evolution. He seemed to be realistic about his politics, supporting the mainstream Democratic Party, and upheld broadly enlightenment values in his popular science articles. He had a wide correspondence, and wasn't careful about the security of his emails. American intelligence probably intercepted these, given McCall's left-wing politics, and the Japanese Secret Service had been doing this for several months. They painted broadly the same picture. No chink in the armour, Kamakura thought, positively, but then a doubt occurred. Too good to be true, perhaps?

"The question is" said the prime minister "do we tell him about the twistor project at the outset, or do we invite him over for the cover project only?"

"I think we have to tell him at the outset" Kamakura said.

"I disagree" said Maki, the head of the security services.

There were just the three of them in the room, and there were a few moments silence after Maki's blunt statement.

"Present your case first, Kamakura" the prime minister said.

"McCall has made a breakthrough following up O'Malley's field theory work. We must remember that this is the physics behind the epsilon twistor. Now that it has spread from polymers to magnetism, many scientists, good ones, will be looking for other applications. The risk of an independent discovery of the epsilon twistor has become significant. We need to press on rapidly, and get McCall on board at the outset. This capitalizes on his fresh zeal for the O'Malley theory, and will cement a bond of trust between us, if he accepts. If we invite him over on false pretences, then tell him about the twistor project, we will be unable to establish this necessary trust. He will always think we are holding something back from him, and we need his one hundred percent commitment."

He turned from the prime minister towards Maki before continuing

"I don't think we need to worry about being open with McCall. I have checked the details of his personal and political life, and feel confident he will be sympathetic to what we are doing. He has voiced strong criticism of American imperialism. He is a very ambitious man, and I believe he will accept our proposal. If not, it's unlikely he can do much harm with the type of knowledge we will reveal to him. A much greater risk in this respect is if O'Malley's role is discovered in Britain. I digress. I look forward respectfully to your counter-arguments, Maki-san."

Maki coughed.

"Please accept my apologies for my blunt interruption earlier, Kamakura-sensei" he said. "Of course, I must feel strongly about the issue. First, let us assume, as Kamakura-sensei does, that Professor McCall is bona fide. What harm can be done by offering him an ERATO project on his new pet subject, on magnetism? This is already quite an incentive, even for an ambitious man, and is likely to tempt him to accept. Let us also assume that McCall is as rational as Kamakura suggests. If he settles in here for a few months, perhaps a year, on a genuine project on magnets, he'll get to know the ropes without being pressured, and then we tell him about the twistor project. As a reasonable man, he will understand perfectly well why we have been cautious in admitting him to our big secret. If he then decides to leave, we will be no worse off than in the scenario suggested by Kamakura-sensei, and he may be more likely to stay in the circumstances I suggest. For these reasons, I think it is better to leave McCall in the dark about the twistor project, even if he is as he seems. However, my main reason for not telling him now is that he may not be as he seems. He is, after all, a citizen of our major enemy power, of our occupiers. Let me put myself in the place of the head of the CIA. They probably know something about the twistor project and that if we were up to anything secretive here, it would involve Kamakura-sensei. In his shoes, if I wanted to dig deeper, I would prime a scientist with a breakthrough in Kamakura's field, and see if we take the bait. I'm suspicious, because McCall seems too good to be true."

Kamakura gave a start, as this phrase recalled his earlier thought.

"I see" said the prime minister. "I thank both you gentleman for expressing your ideas so clearly. I will consider the matter carefully. When are the interviews, Kamakura?"

"Next week" Kamakura replied. "Professor McCall is arriving on Sunday."

Grace was showing off her samurai swords to Ron and Lucy. Lucy gave them a scared look as they waved the swords around, chuckling.

"Would you like another beer?" said Hiroshi. "Lucy, another Coke?"

"It was great trip, wasn't it?" said Grace.

"I enjoyed Avebury the most" said Lucy.

"Would you like to go to Oxford?" Hiroshi asked.

Lucy looked unsure.

"I think Ron was planning to do things in London" she said.

"Sure am" said Ron. "Did you manage to book the Shakespeare tickets, Grace?"

"Sure did" said Grace. "We've got four tickets for *Troilus and Cressida* on Friday night."

"I'm really looking forward to it" said Hiroshi.

"Me, too" said Lucy, doubtfully. "What's it about?"

"Greeks and Trojans" said Grace.

"Love, war and death" said Hiroshi.

"The usual stuff, then" said Ron, with a laugh.

"Have you seen Kamakura recently?" Grace asked Ron.

"Not since the Gordon Conference" Ron replied.

Grace, Hiroshi and Ron had all been at the Gordon Conference on Polymers and Macromolecular Solutions in Santa Barbara. Grace had promised Hiroshi Californian winter sunshine. They'd got El Nino. Hiroshi could remember the sandbags in front of the hotel door.

"The ocean was beautiful in its rage, wasn't it" Hiroshi said.

"A bit like Grace in her professor's office" Ron said, with a laugh.

Grace had also been showing off her kanji tales to Ron and Lucy, including one in which she had described slapping Professor Milton.

"I can hardly believe you did that, Grace" Lucy said. "You seem such a gentle person."

Visions of a cream tea somewhere between Stonehenge and Avebury floated through her mind, accompanied by Grace's gentle, patient, encouraging face.

"Grace is a gentle person" Hiroshi said.

He shifted uncomfortably in his chair.

"…most of the time."

"We all have our moments" Grace said, with a forced laugh. "Anyway, Ron, what's on the agenda for tomorrow?"

Ron had bought a copy of Time Out and had placed pieces of paper to mark pages of interest. He thumbed through.

"I'd been thinking of taking in a movie. How about *Shakespeare in Love* on the Tottenham Court Road?"

"We'll be getting a bit Shakespeared out" said Grace with a laugh.

"It'll be good for you, Grace" Ron said. "Take your mind of that inaugural lecture of yours... I'm real sorry Lucy and I can't stick around till next week for that."

"It doesn't matter, Ron" Grace said. "It's better that way anyway. I'd feel too nervous if you were in the audience, able to pick up on all my mistakes..."

Ron guffawed, and said "You'll sock it to them, Grace."

Ewan McCall's acquaintance with the epsilon twistor had already put him in great danger, he knew that. Like O'Malley before him, McCall already knew too much, and was now the victim of events. The dean's secretary informed him that the dean was ready to see him. With a physicist's sense of timing, he had arrived at exactly the appointed hour. He had been kept waiting twenty minutes. This was standard procedure for the dean before negotiations with young professors, to establish who was boss.

"Come in, Ewan, come in" the dean said. "Take a seat."

"Thanks, Elliott" McCall said.

He sat down opposite the dean, facing him across a vast expanse of leather that surfaced an antique desk. The dean had a penchant for things European, especially expensive ones, and this was a Chippendale.

"I'll come straight to the point, Elliott" McCall said. "I've received an offer to lead an ERATO project in Japan, and I've decided to accept it. I've come in to tender my resignation."

"Cut the bullshit, Ewan" the dean said. "What is it you really want? Are you unhappy about the progress of the new nanotechnology centre? I thought things were going well."

The dean had plenty of sweeteners up his sleeve, not least the inside track to a cool twenty million NATO grant on the magnetic multilayers that McCall seemed to be getting into. McCall reached into his briefcase and pulled out a short letter.

"Yes, I'll cut the bullshit, Elliott" he said. "I don't care what MIT has on offer, I need a new challenge. I'm leaving."

He placed the letter on the desk, stood up and walked out.

A minute or two later, after gathering his wits, the dean was on the phone to the Defense Department. He had been primed to report on McCall's behaviour, and was put straight through to the secretary of state.

"Ronald, it's Elliott here. I'm afraid I've got some bad news. McCall has just tendered his resignation. He's off to Japan. He made no bones about it."

"I see" the defense secretary said. "How long can you keep him under contract at MIT?"

"He has to give six months' notice" the dean replied. "We can force him to stay until then."

"Make sure you make explicitly clear to him that you intend to hold him to his contract" the defense secretary said. "We'll deal with the rest."

The defense secretary hung up, and immediately dialled the head of the CIA.

"Albert, I want you to organize a burglary of McCall's place, the works, including the safe. I want it done as soon as possible."

"No problem, Ronald" the head of the CIA said. "I'll see to it, now. We're already monitoring his email and phone calls. Anything else?"

"No, that's all" the defense secretary said.

He hung up again, and opened his file on the twistor project, codenamed Operation Snowstorm. They had a new computer wizard nicknamed the Mule, who had cracked Japanese Secret Service codes, and they knew something strange was going on in Hiroshima. The science department had been briefed to check the

Science Citation Index for all papers referring to the Yamato and O'Malley theories. Several American professors had been identified, and illegal wire taps had been placed on them. Now one of these professors was heading off to Japan on a big project, even though he had a top job at home. This was obviously suspicious.

It was the morning of Grace's inaugural lecture, and Hiroshi and Grace were looking after Catherine's children while Catherine and Ben were away in Leningrad.

"It's a pity Ben can't make it to the lecture" Grace said.

Hiroshi made a kind of humph noise.

"Well, I think it's very selfish of him to park Catherine's children on us at a time when you've got such an important event" Hiroshi said.

"Oh, I don't mind" Grace said. "I'm enjoying having them here. It takes my mind off things."

Carlo came in from the kitchen, shouting

"Aunty, Uncle, huge spider!"

"That's nice, Carlo" said Hiroshi. "I'll come and have a look. You'd better get going, Grace. You know what the trains are like."

Six months is a long time to spend commuting into Central London. O'Malley had got used to cycling and walking everywhere in Oxford, and she was already fed up with the train journey. She was waiting on the platform at Kenton for the 12.34 train into town. It was late.

The train finally pulled in, and she was on her way into town, peering at the towers of Wembley Stadium before settling down to the all too familiar trip through Wembley and Queen's Park into the smoke. It had been cleverly done, O'Malley mused, the gradual whittling down of autonomy in the academic world. In a money mad world, being a lecturer in your early thirties isn't high pay, high-status work. What makes a university worth working for is freedom of thought and the leisure time to work on your own ideas. When you're pushed into solving practical industrial problems that better paid industrialists should be doing themselves, and your holidays are cut down to the levels in industry, why continue? She knew her case was different. She had to go on.

The train finally trundled into Euston, and Grace stood indecisively on the concourse. She looked up at the departures board, and the direct service to Holyhead via Crewe and Bangor caught her eye. It was a beautiful autumn day, and she decided to walk to college to clear her head. She found herself in Seven Dials and headed off down St. Martin's Lane. She stopped outside the Slug and Lettuce. It was one-thirty. Grace went in and bought a small bottle of Asahi "Dry" from the bar and twenty Marlboro Lights from the cigarette machine... a Japanese and American world in London... she took a deep drag. The wonderful, multi-cultural, multi-lingual, multi-ethnic society pulsed all around her, and O'Malley had to suppress her emotions in order to concentrate on her lecture, which she had slowly and reluctantly fished out of her briefcase. The words made no sense... nothing made sense.

She entered college by the back entrance, down by the loading bays for the science departments. The security man gave her a cheerful greeting, and commented on the beautiful weather. O'Malley agreed in a desultory way, and headed in the direction of the Ejiri lounge. The irony of the lecture being held in a building bequeathed by a Japanese benefactor, who had been at QEC in the sixties and built up a vast microelectronics empire, was not lost on Grace. She took a deep breath and entered the room. The faculty committee were already in place at a long table at the head of the room. The public gallery... it was only nominally an open meeting, after all... was surprisingly full. Grace had taken her seat, and the dean had already started proceedings, when Grace noticed Tony slip in at the back of the public gallery. Grace lost the plot of the dean's rambling opening address, and tried to search her disoriented mind for the last time she'd seen Tony... yes, of course, the dinner party at Cuddleton... but that was the only time in months. A wan smile passed across Grace's face, then quickly faded… what the hell was Tony doing there?

The proceedings began.

Hiroshi had been expecting Grace to return from her inaugural lecture in the late afternoon. He gave an anxious look at the clock. It was six o'clock already, and still no sign of her. The phone rang. It was Kamakura. Hiroshi switched to the scrambled line.

"Hiroshi?"

"Extremum thermodynamics project" Hiroshi replied.

"There has been a breach in security in the project" Kamakura said. "Please leave London immediately."

"Yes" Hiroshi replied.

He hung up instantly and ran into the back garden, where Roberta and Carlo were playing.

"We have to leave, kids" he said.

"But…"

"No buts. You have to get in the car, now."

Hiroshi had never been rough with the children, but he bundled them unceremoniously into the back of the car, without doing their seatbelts.

"Uncle" Roberta cried, and burst into tears.

A big Telecom van was turning slowly into the street.

"Shut up" Hiroshi snapped, turning the Alfa ignition and pulling off with a jerk. He hadn't even looked up. He saw the van in his mirror.

"Shit" he said, screeching off.

"Uncle" screamed Carlo as he lurched forward and hit his face on the back of Hiroshi's seat.

Hiroshi pulled out dangerously in front of a white van, and headed off down towards Target roundabout.

They'd taken a couple of turns. The Telecom van hadn't followed them.

Hiroshi's palms were sweating… yes, he must stick to the plan… once he'd dropped the car off in Gerrard's Cross, they'd be relatively safe. The Japanese Secret Service would meet them with the limo at Graysheen's Garage on the A40… they just had to get there, first…

Hiroshi turned and blew the sobbing children big kisses and started to play a game of 'I, Spy'. He got round Target at last, and pulled out on to the A40. He switched on his mobile phone, and pressed a single button. It was answered immediately.

"Hiroshi-san?" a Japanese voice said.

"Extreme situation, Graysheen's twenty minutes" Hiroshi said.

"Yes" the voice replied. "Understood."

He hung up. He was keeping to fifty by the roadworks and a lot of big cars and vans were overtaking. Hiroshi had horrible visions of an *Easy Rider* like scene with windows being rolled down and shots fired.

"Are we nearly there yet?" Roberta asked.

'I'll have to take the children with me' he thought.

"No, darling, there's a long drive ahead of us today" said Hiroshi.

The plan was to get to North Wales, then, for him, out by boat from Aberdaron.

"We'll be getting in a nice, big, new car soon, though. That'll be a nice treat, won't it?"

A white minibus had been alongside them for a good half minute. Hiroshi looked across in fear and a young man made an obscene gesture at him. The minibus sped off.

"What a horrid man" said Roberta.

"There are lots of horrid men in the world, Roberta" Hiroshi said, wearily.

He was just getting through Denham, and beginning to relax. He stuck to the speed limit and picked up a tailback of angry BMWs and Mercedes.

The flashing taillights and oncoming headlights were still flashing on Hiroshi's retina, though he'd tried to close his eyes and go to sleep an hour before. He could hear the sea lapping away at the wall below. He was in a hotel in Aberdaron, on the tip of the Lleyn Peninsula in Wales. Amazingly, the escape plan had worked. The Jaguar had sped from Gerrard's Cross to the Ty Newydd in just five hours. He'd even managed to lull the children off on the back seat, with the help of his bodyguards. Hiroshi got up and poured himself a beer. It was an Asahi "Dry". He smiled at this bizarre touch. If the magnetic multilayers project cover had been blown, the safety of Japan would be a long, long way away. He poured the beer into a pint glass and lit a Camel. He went out on to the balcony and saw the boat arrive in the harbour. Hiroshi took a big swig of the beer, then a smoke. He looked out at the moonlight on the open sea, a fugitive, on the run…

Grace had switched her mobile phone off for the proceedings, and had forgotten to switch it back on when she had been persuaded to join a few colleagues for a celebration in the Bricklayers Arms afterwards. It was after seven when she bid her farewells, staggered out on to the Tottenham Court Road, and hailed a taxi. The driver was the chatty type.

"Excuse me" said Grace. "I've got a couple of calls to make."

She fished her mobile phone out of her briefcase, switched it on, and dialled home. There was no reply. She let it ring thirty times… still no reply… the automatic ansaphone switched on.

"Hullo, I'm afraid no one is here to take your call at the moment…"

Grace hung up. She was about to try Hiroshi's mobile number, when her own phone rang.

"Grace-san… extreme situation" the driver of Hiroshi's limo said.

"Is Hiroshi there?"

"Yes."

"Plan B?"

"Plan B."

Grace hung up.

"That sounded like something out of a spy novel" the driver said.

"Mind your own business" Grace snapped.

The taxi was arriving at Euston.

Tony had also switched his mobile off for the hearing, and he hadn't switched it back on till after seven in the evening, either. Back at his flat in Pimlico, he listened to his ansaphone messages. The first one said

"Emergency code X. O'Malley implicated in treason. Apprehend client. Any force justified."

The brief message was followed by the metallic announcement

"The time is 19:05."

Tony cursed. He'd had the bitch within shooting distance earlier. Still, it wouldn't be long. Tony killed the ansaphone, and switched to his secret line. The terribly brief conversation confirmed that four SAS men had already been dispatched to O'Malley's home in Kenton. She should be arriving there any minute.

O'Malley looked up at the departures board at Euston. The next Holyhead train was at 19:55. Just ten minutes to wait. She bought a ticket, picked up a burger and fries on the concourse, and wandered down to the platform. The train was already in. She entered the carriage, sat down, and opened up her Burger King special. The woman opposite gave her a disapproving stare, and moved off to another seat. For the first time in a while, she caught a train that was on time. As the train pulled out, she let out a sigh of relief. The SAS men who arrived a few minutes later at her home in Kenton had to report no sign of their client. The birds had flown, again.

By nine o'clock, it was clear to the security forces that O'Malley and Fujimoto must have received warning of their predicament, and fled. This time, thought Tony, I really am going to trap them. He had now been given full powers in the case, and the airports and channel ports were closed tight.

Tony calculated quickly. Grace and Hiroshi were still in Britain. They probably wouldn't attempt to escape tonight, but would hole up in some safe place with Japanese security people. They might lie low for weeks, and sneak out by some unconventional route, maybe a fishing boat out of Scotland, Wales, Cornwall, something like that. In this case, the security forces would probably need public support in finding them. The old idea of pinning a murder rap on Grace had been one of the plans he'd floated to M. Now was the time to put it into action. A spectacular gruesome murder would be carried out tonight, prime material for the news and Crimewatch UK. O'Malley had referred to attacking Professor Milton with the samurai swords in her kanji tales.

Tony called the unit in Kenton. Two of his top women agents were already inside the house. Breaking in had been trivial. They could have opened the back door with a penknife.

"Smith, Woodbridge here."

"Yes, sir."

"I want you to find a pair of samurai swords."

"I've already seen them, sir."

"Good. Be very careful to handle the swords with gloves. I want you and Jones to go to…"

Tony gave the address of Professor Milton in Boars Hill, and gave them their briefing.

"Smith, it's very important that just one of you do the business. How tall are you?"

"Five-eight, sir."

"And Jones?"

"About six foot, sir."

"Is she slim?"

"Fairly, sir."

"Good, it will have to be Jones then. Put her on."

"Yes, sir."

"Jones?"

"Yes, sir."

"I have a very special killing operation for you."

"Yes, sir."

"Smith has the name and address of the client. He's an old professor. No resistance is anticipated."

"Yes, sir."

"I want you to ring the front doorbell, burst in, and hack the man to pieces with the swords from O'Malley's house."

"Yes, sir."

"Then run off. Smith is not to go within half a mile of the house. She'll act as driver only."

"Yes, sir."

"Use a balaclava, and don't say anything. Phone me back when the client has been disposed of. Remember, Jones, the bloodier, the better."

"Yes, sir... Sir, will there be anyone else at the client's home?"

"Yes" said Tony, "his wife."

"Instructions, sir?"

"Don't touch. We need a witness."

"Yes, sir."

For a woman with her number of kills in Northern Ireland, it sounded like a straightforward job. She'd framed IRA men on several bombings and shootings. She was looking forward to using the swords.

Grace was in the toilet on the train. She phoned Kamakura.

"Hi, Toshiro… have you heard from Hiroshi?"

"Yes, Grace, he is safe. He made a Plan A escape. We are moving him out on a boat tonight. Where are you?"

"On a train out of London. Can you get your agents to meet me at Bangor Station?"

"Yes, Grace. They'll take you to the safe house for tonight."

The train was approaching Milton Keynes. Grace slumped back in her seat, and opened the trashy spy novel she'd bought at Euston. Early on, a suspect was being tortured with electrodes on his genitals, to give information about a ridiculous plot to kill the president of the USA. Grace put the book down, and fell into a fitful, nightmarish doze.

Shortly before ten, the phone rang again in Tony's flat. The slaughter of Milton had gone according to plan. With Grace's attitude about Milton well known… and her murderous kanji tales… and her fingerprints on the swords… and her sudden disappearance that night… there was more than enough evidence to pass the matter on to the police and start a nationwide manhunt.

At six am, Grace awoke from another sweaty nightmare. It was her childhood nightmare. She was falling from the walls of a high castle. She always woke just before the sickening thud into the ground. Grace got up and parted the curtains slightly. The view out over the Menai Straits across to Anglesey was fantastic in the brooding, thundery air. She was in the village of Pen-y-Bont, clinging to the side of a mountain from which slate had been hacked for over a century. It was a poor village, and a harsh landscape.

Grace wandered downstairs and the guard followed her out of the door and up the side of the mountain, to the local peak. The view from there was even more spectacular. A line of seven mountains stretched inland and away in the west, she could see right across Anglesey to the Irish Sea, whose grey colour matched the gashes of the quarries. A sudden storm overtook her, and she slipped as she hurried back down, slashing her hand on a viciously sharp slate. She had a vision of Tony's slate go board. Very likely it had come from here, she mused. Kamakura had warned her to be wary of Tony. Perhaps she hadn't been careful enough.

When she got back to the house, she switched on the breakfast news bulletin on TV. Grace was wanted for the brutal murder of a professor in Oxford. Her photograph appeared on the screen, accompanied by a histrionic appeal for information leading to her arrest.

"Well, fame at last" said Grace.

"Grace-san, don't joke about it" said her guard, Terada-san.

"How is Hiroshi?" asked Grace.

"I do not know" said Terada-san.

"What are we going to do?"

"Just wait, and hope."

Around noon, Kamakura phoned Grace. The news was shattering. Hiroshi's bodyguards had been killed and he had been taken prisoner in Aberdaron during the night.

"Grace, I'm very sorry. We had to try to move Hiroshi last night. They were boarding a boat to Ireland. Our security has been breached at this end too. Even Professor Yamato and I are under protective custody here. We can't move you at the moment…"

"I agree" Grace replied, wearily.

"Grace, all hell has broken loose. The president of the USA has phoned our prime minister, accusing Japan of breaking the Self

Defence Treaty. They seem to know a lot about the epsilon twistor. Our diplomats are denying everything, of course…"

"What about Hiroshi?"

"There are some trumped-up charges against Hiroshi-san of being an accomplice to the murder they charge you with. We will do everything we can for him" Kamakura said.

There was a short silence.

"Grace, are you still there?"

"Yes" Grace replied, wearily.

"Grace, with your permission, we may have to keep you in Britain for weeks…"

"I agree" Grace said.

There was nothing else to say. She hung up.

Grace's spirits sank. She felt utterly alone.

As soon as he left the dean's office, Ewan McCall realized that he was a marked man. He walked briskly out on to the main road across the campus and hailed a taxi. He was back at his flat within minutes, and bolted the doors behind him. He went straight to the safe and took the calculations out. They were the only thing that connected him to the epsilon twistor, and he had to destroy them. First he shredded them, then piled them into a bin bag. I mustn't look guilty, Ewan thought, I must stride confidently across the courtyard to the incinerator. Halfway across, he was intercepted by the janitor.

"Let me take that for you, Professor McCall" the janitor said.

"No, thanks, John" Ewan said, "I need some fresh air."

The janitor seemed to be pursuing him for no apparent reason.

"I'm heading over to the incinerator myself, sir" the janitor said.

"Haven't you got anything better to do with your time?" McCall snapped.

"There's no need to be rude, sir" the janitor said, and sloped off dejectedly.

"I'm sorry, John" Ewan said, to the janitor's retreating back.

The janitor didn't turn round.

After burning the shredded documents, Ewan let out a huge sigh of relief and returned to his apartment. There was no point attempting to delete files and emails from the computer. Doubtless both the American and Japanese security services had seen them anyway, so deleting a bunch of stuff now would just look suspicious.

"Ronald, it's Elliott here. I'm afraid I've got some bad news. McCall is off to Japan on Sunday."

"I know, Elliott" the defense secretary said. "In fact, I was just discussing the matter with the head of the CIA. Look, I'm busy, Elliott, OK."

He hung up.

"Who was that?" the head of the CIA asked.

"A self-important little turkey called Elliott White" the defense secretary said. "He's the dean at MIT. Phoned to tell me McCall's plans, as if we didn't know. Anyway, Albert, what did the Brits tell you?"

"Well, we know that this epsilon twistor project in Japan is real" the head of the CIA said.

"Which is where McCall comes in" the defense secretary said.

"Exactly" the head of the CIA said. "He has already signed a contract to lead a so-called magnetic multilayers ERATO project in Hiroshima, starting in March. It's following up O'Malley's civilian work, so that makes it highly suspicious. Think of the site, too. We've got away with bombing a lot of places since '45, but think of the psychological impact of us bombing Hiroshima again. We've already used a WMD on that city, Ronald."

"Wait a minute" the defense secretary said. "You're running ahead, Albert. There's nothing there to bomb, yet. Let's stick to McCall."

"McCall has a record as a pinko liberal... and he may be tempted to be a traitor. He signed a petition against the Patriot Act" the head of the CIA said.

"What's the update on him?"

"The burglary didn't reveal anything we didn't already know, but we do know he burned some shredded documents just after handing in his resignation. He's suspicious, all right."

"Could we recruit him?" the defense secretary asked.

"I think so" the head of the CIA said. "His personality profile is vain and weak, and I think he could be easily pressured. I think we should let him go to Japan on Sunday, and interview him when he returns."

"If he returns" the defense secretary said.

"If he breaks contract, and stays on in Japan, we'll know what's going on" the head of the CIA said.

Chapter 8

Swn y Gwynt

One of the things that had made Kamakura a great politician as well as a great scientist was his ability to spot talent, and promote it. Even before Ewan McCall had boarded his flight to Tokyo, Kamakura had already decided on his second-in-command. Mizuso Tanaka was the outstanding candidate. As usual, Maki had prepared his file meticulously, and Kamakura scanned it with a complacent smile. He skipped the boring details about her childhood and teens, the fulsome recommendations by schoolteachers and professors, the 'Yes, I remember Mizuso, she always was an outstanding student, very hard-working and reliable' and other anodyne stuff like that. She was reported as being both diligent and respectful as well as brilliant and creative in mathematics. She had graduated with first-class honours in mathematics from Tokyo University in her early twenties, and had immediately set up her own computer company. A decade later, Tanaka Electronics was worth millions, and its head was widely recognized, even by many male Japanese businessmen and professors who resented it, to be the leading computer wizard in Japan.

There were rumours that Mizuso Tanaka had stolen ideas from other companies by 'hacking into their computers', as the new phrase went. When Kamakura had challenged Mizuso about this at her interview, she had not only honestly admitted it, but had expressed pride in it. "If I can get inside other people's computers, and they can't get into mine, why shouldn't I take advantage of it?" she had said. Kamakura had liked her reply. She could do the same to the CIA, too.

Although Maki was an old-fashioned spy, brought up in the days of tapped phone wires and video surveillance, he realized that, now that so much information was stored on computers, including 'top secret' files, digital rather than analogue spying was the coming trend. He was very pleased with Kamakura's choice. He knew they had to get on top of the Americans in the encryption game. He ushered Mizuso Tanaka and Nobuko Brown into Kamakura's spacious office.

Kamakura knew much less about Nobuko Brown. She had a strange ancestry. Her mother's parents had both been born in Shangdong, as her mother had been, but her father's parents were an Australian entrepreneur father and a Japanese mathematics teacher mother. Her parents had moved to Kobe before Nobuko was born, and she was brought up speaking Japanese, Mandarin and English, in all of which she was natively fluent. Kamakura had read in her CV that Nobuko was one metre eighty tall, that she was a strong runner and swimmer, and a slender, supple yoga devotee, but he was struck by her height and poise when she entered the room. She towered above the Japanese Mizuso, her boss at Tanaka Electronics, by twenty centimetres. At age twenty-five, already the second-in-command at a major enterprise, she was clearly a force to be reckoned with.

Rumour had it that Mizuso had wanted to bring Nobuko with her on to the project because the two of them were lovers. In the interview, Mizuso had said that this was not the case. She wanted Nobuko because she was the best. She had graduated in psychology and had a natural, intuitive feel for computing that made her ideas indispensable in the computer hacking game. "Her way and the detached, rational way I understand codes complement each other perfectly. I want to continue working with her" Tanaka had said. "I have been speaking English with American business colleagues for years now, and consider myself fluent, but Nobuko is better than me at languages. She can help here, too."

After the introductions had been made, Kamakura dispensed with formalities about the weather. He wanted to test the two women.

"Are you prepared to go on a dangerous mission immediately?" he asked.

"Yes" Mizuso replied immediately.

"Yes" Nobuko said straight afterwards.

"Good" Kamakura said. "It is about Grace O'Malley's situation in Britain."

Grace's hideout, Swn y Gwynt, was a massive, gloomy house, cut into the side of a craggy hill at the base of Elidir Fawr, the ugliest and most awesome of the Glyders. When the Dinorwig slate quarry had been opened up to large scale commercial exploitation in the 1860s, the manager of the quarry, Lord Vaynol's henchman, had evicted the occupants of the only cottage on the dark upper reaches of the slope of Moel-y-Cath. He took possession of about half an acre of land, mostly on a precipitous slope of trees, heather and bilberries. With manpower and Victorian technology at his disposal, Mr Williams had had the drippy slope at the bottom of the plot blasted out, and the stone quarried for building his new home. The upper piece of land abutted the lane from the village of Pen-y-Bont, where the slate workers' cottages were spreading out along the river, to the slate quarry where they worked for a few pence, and died at an average age in the low forties, notwithstanding Lord Vaynol's physician's report that slate dust was good for the men. It was a perfect vantage point to watch the men trudging up the hill in the early morning. The land around the cottage was flattened, and Swn y Gwynt was constructed with thick walls that had withstood the battering of Atlantic gales for over a century with contempt. The gushing waterfall at the top end of the property was directed under the foundations and the lane in a huge conduit and its upper part made an impressive sight at the back of the property when it rained, as it often does in Snowdonia. Although it was a tall two-storey building that Mr Williams constructed, its roof was below most of the 'garden' that was fenced in to keep the sheep and goats from coming in and munching the plants down to grass. It was like a mediaeval island that garden, with dozens of trees and a nest for a pair of buzzards that often hovered over the valley. Set far back from

165

the lane leading to the quarry, and approachable only by a nearly vertical set of stone steps cut into the rock, with a forbidding rusty, pointed iron gate at the top, it was an ideal place to hide.

Walking up and down, up and down in her hideout in the Glyders, O'Malley could bitterly imagine how Hiroshi's trial would go in the hysteria surrounding the Milton murder, with the judge being primed already. The days dragged on. Grace sank into a deep depression. Only the idea of seeing Hiroshi again, and perhaps, the solicitous attention of her guardians, was keeping Grace from suicide. At her darkest moment, on Friday 13th December 1985, Grace began to calculate. She had never been happy with one aspect of her calculation, now seared on her mind. She had to write, and began to scribble new ideas for the natural introduction of the symmetry-breaking component, rather than its arbitrary introduction into the field tensor. Oyster diagrams started to grin at her, bubble diagrams floated up the page, ladders offered stairways to heaven. A sickening thud of realization hit her. The correct way of introducing the component produced a new factor 3 in the energy release of the twistor. She checked and checked again, using different methods, on the verge of a panic attack. No, the new calculation was the right one; release of a twistor on Earth would destabilize the whole planet.

"God, what have I done?" she murmured.

Grace's head jerked back, and the pen fell from her hand. There had been a noise in the living room, a kind of thud. It had definitely come from indoors and, with a sense beyond ordinary perception, she knew she was no longer alone in the house. 'God' she thought, 'has an MI5 agent got in?... the sounds were in the living room, too... No, it's impossible, no one could have got past Terada... I must have imagined it... there couldn't be... it must be the loneliness making me feel paranoid.' Then she heard a kind of strangled cry from the living room, and what sounded like sobbing. Without thinking, her fight or flight instinct cut in, she grabbed a viciously sharp Sabatier knife from the rack, and tiptoed into the hallway. The door to the living room was open, and she leapt in, brandishing the knife.

On the sofa, a woman dressed in otherworldly fluorescent garb was crying convulsively. She looked up at Grace in wide-eyed horror, and Grace immediately dropped the knife.

"Who the fuck are you?" Grace asked.

"O, gods" the woman said, "don't hurt me. I don't know where I am."

"I feel awful" McCall said.

"We need to see how you react under pressure, Ewan."

"God" McCall said, "you're behaving like the commandant in *Merry Christmas, Mister Lawrence,* Toshiro. Is this really you?"

"We all have dozens of aspects to our personality, Ewan. This is one of mine. I have to be a hard taskmaster to you now, if we are going to come to the best decisions, the best decisions for both of us."

"OK, Toshiro, if you want to play hardball, I'm up for it. I feel awful because I've got a bombshell for you. I've just had a new calculation…"

McCall trailed off.

"I'm intrigued, Ewan. I have a bombshell for you, too. You go first."

"I calculated out the epsilon twistor from first principles" McCall said. "I followed O'Malley's calculations on polymer solutions, and applied them to space-time itself. I know exactly the devastation zone of the device. I destroyed the handwritten calculations, but it's all clear in my head. I could write it all down for you now, Toshiro, if you like. I'm sure there's a factor three missing from O'Malley's calculations. The device would destroy the whole planet."

"I see" Kamakura said gravely. "This is news indeed. While I digest, would you be good enough to pour me a glass of saké? As you know, it is rude here to pour for yourself."

McCall poured Kamakura a large beaker of warm saké, and said

"I've had my turn, Toshiro. What's your news?"

"We are planning to bring Grace O'Malley back to Japan next week" Kamakura said.

"Wow" McCall said, "that's great news, Toshiro."

"Great news?" Kamakura echoed.

"Grace O'Malley is the greatest physicist since Einstein, Toshiro. If ever there was a one-to-one I wanted, this is it."

"Well spoken, Ewan" Kamakura said. "Even if Grace succeeds in getting back to Japan, you will lead the first-generation twistor project. Grace is a marked woman, and you are a dark horse. You are very worked up at the moment, and will need to repeat your calculations when you are calmer. Let's hope you will be able to discuss them with Grace."

'God, I'm really losing it' Grace thought.

It had all seemed so real. The terrified woman, Lisa she had called herself, had claimed to be from another planet (Datonga?) from a thousand years in the future. She'd babbled on about someone called Andrew, and seemed to have accidentally fallen into a time machine. She had disappeared as mysteriously as she had appeared, just after mentioning a mission that had something to do with the epsilon twistor.

'It must have been a full-blown hallucination' Grace thought, 'maybe some kind of flashback from the acid trip. Does that mean the new calculation wasn't real, too?'

Grace went into the room she was using as a study. The notes were still there. She fished them out of the cardboard box where she had stashed them and checked the vital pages of the calculation.

'No, the calculation is correct. I must tell Kamakura' she thought.

"I've got some bad news for you, Kamakura-sensei" Maki said, "the worst possible."

"Fire away, Maki-san" said Kamakura.

168

"I think McCall is working for the CIA" Maki said, without a trace of emotion.

"What is the evidence?" Kamakura asked, in a calm voice.

"We found a transmitter at his house in Hiroshima. It operates at radio frequencies. He built it out of cheap electronic goods he bought at downtown stores over the last few weeks. I have copies of the receipts. It looks bad, Kamakura-sensei. He couldn't have any reason for building such a device unless he were trying to communicate with an outside power."

"And you think he's using it to contact the CIA?" Kamakura asked.

"Who else, Kamakura-sensei?" Maki replied. "They had plenty of time to recruit him in the weeks before he came here. That was always a risk."

"Was the device hidden?" Kamakura asked.

"It was on the roof" Maki said, "disguised as a television antenna."

"Did he think we wouldn't notice?" Kamakura said. "Did he really think he could just set up radio equipment and report to the CIA without us knowing?"

"It does seem strange" Maki said, "but O'Malley-san is a strange woman, too, as well as a brilliant one. Such people often have unrealistic ideas."

Professor Kamakura's temper had been darkening throughout the train journey from Osaka to Hiroshima. Maki had informed him that Hiroshima was crawling with CIA agents. Kamakura banged his fourth whiskey glass down angrily as the train slid into the station. He already had a car booked for the new science centre on the edge of town, where he knew McCall was working on the installation of the X-ray diffractometers. This wasn't a job for his minions. Kamakura intended to confront McCall directly, to accuse him of spying for the Americans.

"Hi, Toshiro" Ewan said.

He looked relaxed and happy.

"It's going great. The USAXS is already in place, and we're just setting up the rotating anode for the Kratky camera. The wide-angle instrument..."

"I haven't come here to discuss the X-ray equipment" Kamakura said, interrupting him. "We have something else very important to talk about, Ewan. Would you come with me, please?"

"What do you mean, Toshiro" Ewan said. "I'm right in the middle of things here. These rotating anodes are always a brute to install."

"That can wait" Kamakura said.

Two big security men appeared in the doorway.

"Please come with me immediately. We are going over to some unoccupied offices nearby, where we can have a private conversation."

McCall eyed the two uniformed men with distaste.

"Are you muscling me, Toshiro?" he asked.

"Yes" Kamakura replied.

When the two men were standing alone in a deserted, furniture-less office, Kamakura said

"I'll come straight to the point, Ewan. I want you to tell me about the radio transmitter on the roof of your penthouse."

"Oh, you mean my SETI receiver?" Ewan said.

"Your what?" Kamakura said.

"My SETI receiver. Come on, Toshiro, you know, the search for extra-terrestrial intelligence. Thousands of scientists worldwide are combing the skies for signals, Toshiro. I'm joining them."

"You're using the equipment to contact aliens?" Kamakura said, in an incredulous tone.

"Look, Toshiro, if there's something intelligent out there, it will be in the electromagnetic spectrum we receive. Maybe it's just that we haven't been looking hard enough. Why shouldn't I join the search?"

"You have serious science to do" Kamakura said.

"O, come off it, Toshiro" Ewan said. "Only the other day you were telling me I had to nurture my creativity. You're not going to deny me my hobbies, are you?"

Kamakura looked nonplussed.

"Why is the equipment disguised as a TV aerial?" he asked, suspiciously.

"It's not disguised as a TV aerial, Toshiro" Ewan said, "it basically *is* a TV aerial. I think people have been too obsessed with the ten-megahertz range. I'm interested in information coded in the hundred-megahertz range. I designed and built my own equipment from scratch, Toshiro."

"I know" Kamakura said.

"So you think I've been using my SETI equipment to contact the CIA?" McCall said. "What a laugh, Toshiro. You could easily intercept my signals, and you know I know it."

"We have had a major breach of security in the twistor project" Kamakura said.

"What!" McCall exclaimed.

"I'll be perfectly frank with you, Ewan. Since we discovered the transmitter on your roof, the CIA have been taking an unnaturally close interest in Hiroshima. How could they have found out?"

"Search me, Toshiro" Ewan said. "Somebody else must have known."

"Just me and Maki" Kamakura said, stonily.

"So someone must have intercepted a communication between you" Ewan said.

"Highly unlikely" Kamakura said.

"When you have eliminated the impossible, whatever remains, however improbable, must be the truth" Ewan said.

"You're talking in riddles" Kamakura said.

"Just quoting" Ewan said. "What I mean is, Toshiro, someone is spying on you and Maki-san, and it isn't me. I never told anyone anything about Hiroshima. Look, Toshiro, I've got nothing to hide. You're welcome to see my calculations and sketches for the new SETI instrument. You're welcome to try it, if you like."

"I don't believe in aliens" Kamakura said.

"The truth is out there" Ewan said.

As soon as the day of her planned escape broke, Friday 20th December 1985, Grace headed off through the top garden and began the ascent of Elidir Fach. She was still perturbed by her strange visitor from another world. It had seemed so real. Now the box with the calculations had gone missing. Had she destroyed them, and couldn't remember?

Swn y Gwynt was eight hundred feet above sea level, and the Carneddau were coming into view, as Grace paused halfway up the dark flanks of the Dinorwig quarry. She had been smoking heavily during two months of high tension... and, wheezing unpleasantly, she stopped and coughed up some blackish spit. Her tongue felt furry, but her head was clearing in the sharp morning air. She knew she had roughly the same distance to go to get up to the ridge. The shattered slate debris barred the direct route, and she skirted it on the grassy edge. A dead sheep was stuck in some ancient, rusty barbed wire, and was rotting incongruously, its face still seeming ridiculously alive. For a while, Grace stood transfixed, unable to break eye contact with the dead sheep, then she suddenly felt a magnetic force pushing her upwards, and with another half hour of swift and steady ascent, she was on the ridge.

The view as she strolled the final flattish part to the cairn was astounding. What luck, what joy! It had been dull, sleeting and drizzling most of December. Now, out of nowhere, was a crisp, clear, blue winter morning. The Snowdon chain stretched away splendidly on the other side of the valley and Grace gazed at it in the remarkably calm air. She'd never been up any of the peaks in such still weather, and the view from the top of Elidir Fawr would be incredible. Grace looked at her watch. It was still only nine o'clock. She'd planned to go straight up and down Elidir Fach only, getting back to Swn y Gwynt by half ten, and starting a leisurely drive to London through the mountains, via Pen y Pass. Grace could see the road snaking along the Llanberis path far below her. But, hell, did she really have to be at the rendezvous with Terada by four for any reason? No, this was her last chance of freedom, maybe of life. The ascent was relatively painless, and Grace was alone on top of the world. The Glyders, Carneddau and Snowdon chain in the foreground, and even a view of the distant Wicklow Mountains in Ireland. God, they must be sixty miles away, Grace thought, as she sat in her second cairn of the day. Grace burst into tears, and sobbed on the mountaintop until her well ran dry. She was just composing himself when a hearty young couple clambered into the cairn to join her.

"Beautiful morning, isn't it?" the man said.

"Yes, isn't it" Grace replied.

"We're on the fourteen-peak walk" the woman said.

"We've done it before" the man said.

"This is my favourite peak" the woman said.

"Mine, too" Grace said. "I'm sorry" she continued, "I have to be leaving. I'm due in London this afternoon."

"London?" the woman echoed, in a surprised tone.

"Yes, I'll be back in the Smoke in a few hours' time." Grace surveyed the panorama one last time. "Have a great walking trip" she said.

"We will" the young couple said in unison. They were holding hands and obviously very much in love. As soon as Grace was out of their sight, on the bristly ridge back to the rest of the world, she burst into tears again.

The steep descent from Elidir Fawr to Swn y Gwynt turned Grace's unfit legs to jelly. She wobbled out of the shower and phoned Terada to say that she'd had a change of plan, and was going to arrive after the rush hour. She was absolutely ravenous, and the cheese and pickle sandwich she made seemed like the most delicious food she'd ever had. She swilled it down with her last bottle of Theakston's Old Peculiar, and selected a few tapes for the trip. As she rounded the big left-hand curve out of Llanberis, and faced the full majesty of Elidir Fawr from below, she put on Nigel Kennedy's recording of Elgar's Violin Concerto at full volume. Grace had once seen Kennedy play. It was the most amazing virtuoso playing Grace had heard in her life. He's like me, Grace thought, a bit of a prat, but a genius. Maybe the two go together. The music was perfect for the scenery, as the quarry disappeared into the past and the glacial desolation of the road to Pen y Pass in midwinter opened up.

The last of the daylight was fading, and Grace was on to some Beethoven piano sonatas, when she crossed from England into Wales around Oswestry. She felt as if she should be winding down the window of her inconspicuous black Passat, and showing her passport to someone, if she'd had one. She was hungry again, and stopped off for a burger at a service station on the outskirts of Oswestry. The traffic around Birmingham would be a nightmare, and she decided to cut across to the M6 toll. With the change of pace in the motoring, Grace picked out her favourite, Lee 'Scratch' Perry's Black Ark in Dub. It had been her first present from Ben, and her most treasured. It carried her through the sticky bit, round the M42, and as far as Banbury on the M40. After a calm period internally, when she'd had the red taillights and the somehow edgy, somehow mellow music filling her mind, Grace became conscious of the nature of the task ahead. Some light distraction was needed, and it was T Rex that saw her down to the Ridgeway, and into the Home Counties. By the time she reached the M25, the Woodstock triple album was well under way and she was accompanied along the final stilted section of the M4, driving into the heart of the Smoke, by Country Joe and

The Fish's *One, two, three, what are we fighting for?* What indeed, Grace thought, consulting the A-Z on her dashboard as the M4 turned into the Great West Road. She was tired, and the trickiest part of the journey would be finding the safe house in Chiswick.

"You look tired" Terada said.

"I'm knackered" Grace said. "The drive took me six hours in the end."

"Fancy a glass of saké?" Terada asked.

Grace woke up to a dream of a dinner party in Cuddleton. She was mumbling "*Expectata dies aderat*" as her consciousness surfaced. The long-awaited day had come.

She'd never see her friends in Oxford again. No more Ben, no more Pru, no more Maya, no more Arne, no more Richard, no more Tom, no more Martina. Still half dozing, and unwilling to get out of bed, she recalled her last trip to Bibbleton. Terada knocked on the door.

"It's nine o'clock, Grace, you asked me to get you up."

"Thanks, Jiro" Grace replied indistinctly through the closed door. "I'm getting my act together."

Grace was not getting her act together. As often happened when she thought of Bibbleton, her mind drifted back to the decisive time when she had discovered the twistor. Suddenly she was with Pru in The Fir Tree, at her favourite window table, downing a couple of pints of bitter and smoking fags.

"Grace, it's quarter past."

Terada's voice from the landing interrupted Grace's reverie.

"Thanks, Jiro, I'm just coming" she said.

Even as she said it, she got an image of Arne giving her a massage. God, I haven't unwound for weeks, she thought, no wonder I'm feeling tense... well, that and the idea that I might get killed this afternoon... they're not going to let me walk away, are they?

"Grace?"

"Just coming, Jiro" Grace said.

She emerged from the bathroom at ten o'clock, and briefly went over the plan with Jiro, for what seemed like the hundredth time. Terada exuded confidence, and promised faithfully to meet Grace at the Japanese Embassy at four, before taking his leave. Grace helped herself to coffee in the massive kitchen. The Beat Takeshi film was at two, finishing at 3.30. Perfect timing for a walk down to the Japanese Embassy on Piccadilly at four. No need to second guess what was going to happen. How should she prepare?

Grace put down the coffee, then washed it down the sink. It would make her too nervous on an empty stomach... she couldn't eat, it was unthinkable. She felt on the verge of a panic attack. Terada had given her some fluoxetine pills for emergencies. It was a new drug that was going to be marketed next year, he had told her. It had been tested, was perfectly safe. It should calm her down.

Grace fished out her sponge bag and removed the bottle of pills. She took one, and immediately felt a bit uneasy. A few minutes later, she felt sick and weird. She staggered to the bathroom and threw up, horrible empty contractions gripping her. Sweating and shaking on the loo fifteen minutes later, she thought, God, I'm not going to have to face the day in this state, am I?

Beat Takeshi removed his heavy revolver from his desk. It was a violent cop film, a throwback to some of his earlier work. The first scene, where he'd poked a petty criminal in the eye with a chopstick, had turned Grace's already sick stomach. She was still sweating and uncomfortable four hours after she had taken the fluoxetine, but beginning to compose herself. Beat Takeshi blew his adversary away in cold blood. 'I can't take this' Grace thought, 'I'm going to be sick again.' She reeled out into the open air, and lurched towards Piccadilly Circus.

"I've spotted O'Malley, sir" an agent said, "she's just left a cinema in Shaftsbury Avenue." He was already looking forward to his reward.

"Have her double-tailed, front and back" Woodbridge said. "Don't hesitate to shoot her if she looks like escaping. I'll be with you shortly."

"Yes, sir."

The agents called in had no difficulty in following Grace, whose slow, unsteady gait wouldn't have thrown off a granny and whose perception was not of this world. Somehow she'd gone down Regent Street instead of Piccadilly, and she instinctively veered off to the right, and emerged on St. James's Square. She knelt down on the grassed area in the middle and was violently sick again. She'd tried some lunch to soak up the poison, and it all came back up in terrible spasms.

"She's being sick, sir" the agent on the corner with Charles II Street said.

"What?" Woodbridge said.

"Sick, sir, it's revolting. She's really ill, believe me."

"Spare me the details" Woodbridge said. "Maintain your positions. I'll be with you in five minutes."

It was a short walk from his office in Whitehall, and when Tony sighted his prey, Grace was still prone on the grass. God, she does look awful, Tony thought, when Grace got up. He tailed her down King Street and St James's Street, back on to Piccadilly. Grace was close to the embassy, could see safety, when her head split with a terrible rending clang. It took her several seconds to realize that the fire alarms were going off in the building, and that people had started streaming out of the door.

God, a diversionary tactic, Woodbridge thought, as Japanese and other people collected uncertainly at the evacuation point. Japs, Woodbridge thought, and immediately unsheathed his heavy army revolver. O'Malley was still standing there uncertainly, and he had plenty of time to take aim. Woodbridge was an excellent shot, and his shot from behind would have passed through O'Malley's back and heart had his prey remained still, but at the very moment when Woodbridge fired, O'Malley lurched sideways to be sick again. The heavy bullet smashed into her shoulder. As Woodbridge re-aimed for the *coup de grace*, Terada fired. At fully twenty yards, with an ordinary handgun, his single shot felled Woodbridge. Grace's prone body was bundled into a waiting limousine.

"She's stopped breathing" the paramedic said.

"It's not just the bullet wound" her colleague said. "Look at the sick around her mouth. She's rigid, too. Looks like some sort of overdose."

The two of them were experts in bullet wounds. That was why they were there. The back of the limousine was kitted out like a mini-ambulance, but O'Malley was dying from the combined effects of the adverse drug reaction, the wound and the shock.

"She's dying" the paramedic said.

"So, the mission was a failure, Kamakura-sensei. *Sumimasen deshita.*"

"You had thought of everything, Maki-san" Kamakura said, "even having the paramedics and the ambulance ready. They could have dealt with the gunshot wound. The one thing you could not have anticipated was that she would have a drug overdose, and would have died if she had not been taken to a hospital. In the end, we had to turn her in. And now she is in the power of the British establishment."

"We must find some way to contact her, Kamakura-sensei. Now that she is officially dead, she has no rights. They may torture her. They must be holding her somewhere in Britain. We must find out where."

"How is the work going on cracking the new MI5 codes?" Kamakura asked.

"Tanaka-san and Brown-san are working on it" Maki replied.

General Mason wasn't admiring the view from his spacious office at MI5 headquarters, overlooking the Thames. The river looked grey and muddy, and Mason was preoccupied with the enormity of his task. Mason's job now was to help prevent humanity from becoming victims of the epsilon twistor.

Not that Mason was a humanitarian. When he had been catapulted to the head of MI5, the O'Malley case had been just another spying job, not a routine one, to be sure, but basically just one of many pressing tasks. Events had unfolded with horrible rapidity last year, and O'Malley's revelation that the epsilon twistor would destabilize the whole planet if realized had been backed up by the communication from his counterpart Maki in Japan about McCall's calculation. It really is true, Mason told himself for the hundredth time, the Japanese really have been working, unwittingly, on a doomsday weapon for more than a year, a top American scientist was leading the project at this very moment, and the British, American, Japanese and Chinese governments were all panicky and confused. He had to stay calm, and do his best. First of all, he had to keep O'Malley alive. Her faked death a few weeks ago had bought them some breathing space, but the danger signs were still on red. The CIA obviously viewed O'Malley as a dangerous communist, and might do something stupid. The night before, he had had a fractious meeting with the head of the armed forces, the Home Secretary, Professor Marmotville for the scientific establishment, and the psychologist assigned to Grace, Peter Johnson. Mason frowned. It was Johnson who had persuaded them to drop the charges against Hiroshi Fujimoto and allow him to see Grace, and so far, they had adopted the softly, softly approach with O'Malley, even allowing her to go out for walks. General Mason's normally confident face showed an unusual trace of doubt. The intuition that made him good at his job told him that this might have been a mistake.

Ewan McCall and Professor Kamakura were in an office, the one off the super-lab in Hiroshima, the nerve centre of the epsilon twistor project.

"I've got some bad news for you, Ewan" Kamakura said.

"Fire away, Toshiro" Ewan said.

"Your second-in-command, Mizuso Tanaka, has disappeared."

"What do you mean?" Ewan asked.

"Exactly what I said" Kamakura said. "She seems to have disappeared off the face of the Earth. We have searched her apartment. Her passport and credit cards are missing, nothing else obvious."

"God" Ewan said, "you don't think she's a double agent, do you?"

"I was hoping you might be able to enlighten me on that, Ewan" Kamakura said, "being as you know her so much better than anyone else."

"What do you mean, Toshiro?" Ewan asked.

"Don't play games with me, Ewan" Kamakura snapped. "Do you think we don't know that the pair of you are lovers?"

"Yes, but..." Ewan trailed away.

"But, what, Ewan?" Kamakura prompted.

"That was just a bit of fun, Toshiro" Ewan said.

"Anyway, Ewan" Kamakura said, "the Americans have lost their superiority in computer spying... their Mule seems to have gone missing, too... and we have intercepted a communication from the head of MI5 to the British Government. Grace O'Malley's death in December was faked. She is being held by MI5 in North Wales. She has also discovered the factor three in the energy release of the device. You are the only man on the planet who could understand her, Ewan. We want you to talk to O'Malley as soon as possible."

"Me?" Ewan said, his jaw dropping.

"Your faked passport and other documents are already prepared. She's surrounded by armed guards, of course, but we'll get you in somehow."

"When?" Ewan asked.

"Tomorrow" Kamakura said. "It's a dangerous mission, Ewan, but we have to know what MI5 are up to, and what O'Malley plans to do. And there may be a bonus for you."

"Bonus?" Ewan echoed.

"I suspect you may also have an opportunity to meet your lover there. I'm sure Mizuso Tanaka is mixed up in this."

As usual, Grace O'Malley was alone at her house in Aberffraw, in the south-west corner of Anglesey. Aberffraw was the main court of the Princes of Gwynedd from the sixth to the thirteenth centuries, and from there they had ruled all of North Wales. In 1986, it was a small village with a Spar shop, a post office and a couple of tiny pubs. O'Malley lived in a nondescript modern housing development on the edge of the village, along the road up the coast. It was a fifteen-year-old bungalow, situated at the end of a T-shaped cul-de-sac of about twenty detached homes, mostly bungalows. Number 18 Swn yr Afon was a typical example, a spacious two hundred square metre house with a beautiful conservatory at the back, affording a splendid view of the near coastline and the rugged mountains of the Lleyn Peninsula across the sea.

Grace was sitting on the sofa, reading *Ends and Means* by Aldous Huxley. She placed the book aside, got up, and walked through to the utility room. Out the back of the house, she thought she caught a glimpse of one of Mason's men in the copse. She fell into a brown study. Images of her friends in Oxford floated into her mind, and she felt a sense of irreparable loss. To them, she was a dead woman. She sat down to scribble at the kitchen table, lit a cigarette and scribbled on and on, now oblivious to her surroundings and the passage of time.

...and the natural introduction of the symmetry-breaking component thus introduces a factor three into the energy release of the epsilon twistor...

Grace walked outdoors, with a sad and serious expression on her face. It was time to face up to her responsibilities, and finish that letter to the heads of the four governments that knew about the twistor. Even without the twistor, there would still be go evenings with Peter. Maybe things would settle down in a year or two. The morning mist had cleared, and it was a glorious, spring day in prospect. Grace went out on to the patio, taking with her a pad of notepaper, a couple of biros, a paperweight, a pair of sunglasses and an old sportsman's floppy hat. A gentle breeze was blowing in off the ocean. Pinning the sheets under a curious green translucent paperweight, she began to scribble.

The folder Grace was using to store the draft of her letter to the Chinese, Japanese, American and British governments was stuffed with scruffy, handwritten notes. The paperweight was pinning down the pad on which she was writing her concluding remarks.

'Thus, in view of the discovery of the factor 3 in the energy release of the device, I urge you most strongly never to proceed with this dangerous project.'

As she stuffed the final sheet into the folder, she heard a voice from the bottom of the garden.

"Grace O'Malley" Ewan said.

Grace looked up, and said "Ewan McCall... how on Earth?"

"Never mind" Ewan said. "Can I join you?"

"Go for it, Ewan" Grace said.

Ewan McCall crossed the lawn, and sat on one of the cheap plastic chairs opposite Grace. Grace put down her cheap plastic biro, and clunked the paperweight down on the cheap plastic folder.

"Still calculating, Grace?" Ewan asked.

"Just writing a letter" Grace said. "Have you got much time?"

182

"A couple of hours" Ewan said, "till they change guards again. We've got that long."

"Good" Grace said. "We've got a lot to talk about."

"We sure have, Grace" Ewan said. "I'll come straight to the point. I discovered the factor 3 in the energy release of the device that's missing from your calculations."

"Brilliant, Ewan" Grace said. "I was just writing to the Chinese, Japanese, American and British governments about it."

"When did you..." Ewan began.

"Friday 13th December, how could I forget?" Grace said, with a wry smile. "And you?"

"Friday 13th December, how could I forget?" Ewan said.

He smiled, too.

"We've got to do everything we can to stop anyone building the thing, Ewan" Grace said.

"I agree" Ewan said. "So does Toshiro."

"Did he send you?" Grace asked.

"Of course" Ewan replied. "As ever, the puppet master, pulling all our strings. But I'm not here just because of him. My second-in-command, Mizuso Tanaka, has disappeared. Do you know where she is?"

"I'm afraid I've no idea, Ewan" Grace replied. "I've never even heard of her, till now."

Ewan looked crestfallen.

"I've had visitors from the future, Ewan" Grace blurted out.

Grace had been meaning to keep it a secret for the rest of her life, just like she had originally intended to always keep the discovery of the epsilon twistor a secret. Like all her secrets, it slipped out all too easily, overcome by her desire to communicate, her deep-seated need to tell the truth, the whole truth.

"You're kidding" Ewan said.

"I kid you not" Grace said. "One came last night. He was a great Chinese mathematician from the thirty-first century, called Hu Song. It's the second time I've had visitors."

Ewan gave Grace a scared look. She was obviously sinking into madness. Suddenly, the early afternoon sun seemed unbearably bright.

"Shall we go inside, Grace?" Ewan suggested.

"Fine" Grace said. "I was going to ask you to do that anyway. It will only take me half an hour to type up the letter. I want you to sign it, too."

"There isn't anything in the letter about the visitors, is there, Grace?" Ewan asked.

"Of course not" Grace said. "I don't want people to think I'm mad."

Ewan gave a nervous laugh, and said

"Let's go in."

Grace got up. When she went back into the living room, she was startled to see two women sitting on the long, grey sofa. One of them was six-foot tall, vaguely Chinese, vaguely Caucasian, the other an ordinary-looking Japanese woman.

"Mizuso" Ewan said, his face lighting up.

"Ewan" Mizuso said, rising to her feet.

Ewan McCall and Mizuso Tanaka embraced in the middle of the room. Ewan suddenly recoiled from Mizuso's prominent bump.

"My God" he said. "You're pregnant."

"Yes" Mizuso said. "It's yours, Ewan."

Ewan was dumbstruck for a moment, and he and Mizuso moved self-consciously apart.

"How on Earth did you get here?" Ewan asked.

184

'They just appeared out of nowhere' Grace thought, 'like Lisa and Hu Song. They must be time travellers.'

"I'll explain things properly later, Ewan" Mizuso said, "but first, may I introduce my companion, Nobuko Brown."

Two hours into a surreal conversation with Grace, Mizuso and Nobuko, which had seriously disturbed his sense of reality, Ewan looked at the clock. The guards had changed. Four SAS men burst into the room. Mizuso screamed.

The four SAS men levelled their guns at Grace, Ewan, Mizuso and Nobuko. After Mizuso's scream, there was an eerie silence and stillness in the room, broken by the arrival of General Mason. The four SAS men, in full combat gear, still had their weapons trained on their targets. They were pathological killers, itching with the desire to kill Earth's two greatest physicists and two harmless women. Mason made a gesture with the palm of his hand, face downwards, his hand descending a few centimetres, and the psychopaths pointed their weapons downwards at the dirty, pink carpet.

"Very interesting conversation, Grace" Mason said. "The last two hours have made fascinating listening for me."

Some of the chronic tension eased out of the atmosphere.

"You promised me the room wasn't bugged" Grace said, shakily.

"I'm a spy" Mason said. "My duty to protect the British public is paramount, and... anyway, Grace, you must introduce me to your guests."

He turned to Ewan, took a pace towards him, and said

"You must be Ewan McCall."

Ewan seemed to be in a trance, and didn't react at first. Then he pulled himself together, and shook Mason's hand briefly, no more than a touching of the two palms.

"Norbert" Grace said, "can you tell your men to leave. They're frightening us."

"Certainly, Grace" Mason said smoothly.

He made a brief motion with his head, flicking it slightly backwards and to one side. The four SAS men withdrew immediately, one to the corridor leading to the kitchen, one to the conservatory, and two to the patio outside.

"They're well trained" Grace said.

"They're well paid" Mason said, "and ready to return, if necessary... anyway, Grace, you must complete the introductions."

He turned to Mizuso, took a pace towards her, extended his hand, and said

"You must be Mizuso Tanaka."

Mizuso looked him straight in the eye, shook him warmly by the hand, and said

"Pleased to meet you, General Mason. I've heard so much about you."

"From your work on the Hiroshima project?" Mason queried.

"Precisely" Mizuso said.

Mason gave out a curious, cackling laugh, turned to Nobuko, and said

"I guess Grace, Ewan, Mizuso and I are all familiar with each other, one way or another, but you have the advantage of me, Miss..."

"Brown" Nobuko said, "Nobuko Brown."

Nobuko stepped confidently across to Mason and shook him firmly by the hand.

"A strange name for a Chinese, if I may make so bold..."

"I'm not Chinese" Nobuko said, "I'm..."

"Ah, yes, Datongan" Mason said, "come back to prevent the end of the universe."

He gave another cackling laugh, and continued with

186

"Shall we go outside? It's rather claustrophobic in here."

"Good idea" Grace said.

Grace led the way outside on to the patio, between the two SAS men, who were standing either side of the French windows. On the way out, Mason whispered to one of his men, and they withdrew discreetly to the two far corners of the garden. The other two SAS men came outside, and guarded the other two corners. The five main players sat around the table in the middle of the patio, and Grace raised the parasol. A fifth guard, Mason's batman, appeared on the patio, bringing Mason a gin and tonic, with ice and a slice.

"I want everyone to be comfortable" Mason said. "What can my man fetch for you ladies?"

"Green tea" Mizuso said.

"Green tea for me, too" Nobuko said.

Grace turned to Mason's batman, who had an oddly vacant expression, like an android, and said

"And could you fetch that bottle of red wine that's on the kitchen table?"

"And another glass for me" Ewan said.

"Good to hear you speak at last, Professor McCall" Mason said. "I understand you must have been alarmed by our dramatic arrival, but we mean you no harm. We don't wish any harm to Maki or his entourage, either. I rather admire the man, and the Japanese Secret Service, generally. Of course Maki and I agreed for you to come here to talk to Grace. You don't think you'd have got in otherwise, do you? Relax. We're all friends here. We need to get to the bottom of things."

Mason's batman deposited a pot of green tea on the table, and filled cups for Mizuso and Nobuko. He also brought the bottle of '76 Gevrey Chambertin, and poured two glasses for Grace and Ewan.

"Cheers" Mason said, lifting his gin and tonic.

The five of them took a sip of their drinks.

"That's great booze, Grace" Ewan said.

"One of the best" Grace said. "It's my last one."

The sunshine in the garden seemed glaring in the following silence. Mason broke it by saying

"What I suggest is that you do type up your letter to the four governments, Grace, and that you do sign it, Ewan. It seems to me that our real problem is that the epsilon twistor is a doomsday weapon, and we must do everything in our power to prevent its development."

"I agree" said Grace. "I can't think of anything else to do."

"Hear, hear" Ewan said. "I'll sign it, too."

Mason's batman brought Grace's PC to the table, and Grace began typing. Mason turned to the others, and said

"Professor McCall, Ewan, would you be prepared to return to the States, to try to persuade the American government to desist with an epsilon twistor project?"

Ewan cast a doubtful glance at Mizuso, and said

"I suppose so."

He knew the Americans might incarcerate him as a traitor, knew he might never see his unborn child, never see Mizuso again. He realized he was chronically in love. Too late?

"I suppose you'll be wanting me to stay here, to try to persuade the British government?" Grace asked.

"Precisely, Grace" Mason said. "And you, Professor Tanaka, Mizuso, would you be prepared to return to Japan, to try to persuade the Japanese government to desist with the epsilon twistor project?"

Mizuso cast a doubtful look at Ewan, and said

"I suppose so."

She could scarcely face seeing Toshiro and Maki again, knew that the Japanese would never trust her after her disappearance, knew that she may be stuck in Japan for the rest of her life, without Ewan. She realized that she might have her baby under house arrest. She realized she was chronically in love. Too late?

"And you, Miss Brown, Nobuko" Mason said. "Would you be prepared to undertake a mission to the Chinese government, to try to persuade them to desist with an epsilon twistor project?"

Nobuko stared gloomily into space. She looked shattered.

"I suppose so" she said wearily.

Mason's batman brought the letter, and Grace and Ewan signed it.

Chapter 9

Thirty-Six Years Later

"Thank God she's signed the letter" Mason said.

"Yes" Peter said. "She seems to be calming down."

"But we need to get her on some tranquillizers and anti-psychotic medication as soon as possible" Mason said, with a trace of contempt.

"You keep treating Grace as if she's mad" Peter said.

"She is mad, Johnson" Mason said. "Mad as a hatter."

"Look" Peter said, "I'm a clinical psychologist, and..."

"...and I'm a spy" Mason said, interrupting him. "And I will now prove to you how mad O'Malley is. We have been bugging her house, and last night she spent the entire time talking to an imaginary friend. Do you want to hear?"

"OK" Peter said, with a doubtful expression.

Mason switched on a tape.

"You must be from Datonga."

Pause.

"Weapon? Oh, sorry, I didn't mean to startle you."

Pause.

"What a coincidence."

Pause.

"I'd offer to make you a cup of tea, but my last visitor disappeared the first time I left her alone."

Pause.

"Never heard of her. Her name was Lisa."

Pause.

"We've got a lot to talk about. I think I will put on a pot of tea."

Pause.

Mason switched the recorder off, and said

"She was alone last night, Johnson, no doubt about it. We've got a noose around the place that's tighter than a gnat's arsehole, and Lisa must be another of her imaginary friends. We bugged her conversation in the garden with McCall, too. Listen to this."

O'MALLEY: I've had visitors from the future, Ewan.

McCALL: You're kidding.

O'MALLEY: I kid you not. One came last night. He was a great Chinese mathematician from the thirty-first century, called Hu Song. It's the second time I've had visitors.

"We need to get her on some medication" Mason said.

"Poor Grace" Peter said.

TRANSCRIPT EXTRACT

Interview date: 9th November 1986

Participants: Dr Peter Johnson and Dr Grace O'Malley

JOHNSON: Are you absolutely sure, Grace?

O'MALLEY: As sure as I've ever been of anything in my life, Peter.

JOHNSON: It will be a massive physical and psychological shock.

O'MALLEY: I know, but I've always felt like I was a man inside and...

JOHNSON: And?

O'MALLEY: And it will make it easier for me to hide.

JOHNSON: O, Grace, you're not getting a sex change with that in mind, are you? It's got to go deeper than that, or it will drive you mad.

O'MALLEY: I'm mad already. You heard Norbert's tape. I've got imaginary friends. I'm schizophrenic. I think I'll be happier as a man. The hiding part is a bonus, not the reason I'm doing it.

JOHNSON: Please think it over, Grace. You're still very disturbed. You've been shot. You are officially dead...

O'MALLEY: ...and I've been visited by time travellers...

JOHNSON: You'll have to let that go, Grace, if you want to establish a new, sane life, either as a man or a woman.

O'MALLEY: I know, but it seemed so real, that night, and Mizuso and Nobuko are real.

JOHNSON: They are. But Mizuso is an ordinary Japanese woman, and Nobuko is the daughter of an ordinary Australian-Japanese man and Chinese woman. Norbert has files on them. They haven't come here from the future, or another planet.

O'MALLEY: Where are they now?

JOHNSON: I'm afraid I can't tell you. Norbert and I have agreed that we need to keep them away from you, at least until you settle down on the new medication. How's that going, Grace?

O'MALLEY: Awful. My muscles ache, I can't calculate, can't even think straight. If I'm going to have these injections every month for the rest of my life, I'd rather have been really shot dead in London.

JOHNSON: I'm sorry, Grace, but we will be able to decrease the dose, when you have recovered from the psychotic episodes...and I don't think this is a good time for you to be deciding on a sex change.

O'MALLEY: I've made my mind up. And the bonus is, it'll be a lot easier to hide as a six-foot tall Black man then as a six-foot tall Black woman. Norbert has even told me that they'll be able to lighten my skin, too, like they've been doing with Michael Jackson...

JOHNSON: You've already discussed it with him?

O'MALLEY: Yes. He's happy with the idea.

JOHNSON: He would be.

O'MALLEY: Of course, establishing a new identity for me as an off-white male will bury Grace O'Malley for ever.

JOHNSON: She'll always be inside you.

O'MALLEY: Will she?

"Something's up, Peter" Mason said.

The last time they had worked together, when Vincent had his sex change and his new identity had been forged, Mason had been the high-flying young head of MI5, in his mid-forties, rippling with energy and self-confidence. Peter had been a top young psychologist, in his late thirties, still a bit hippy round the edges, brilliant at dealing with the difficult Grace, and the even more difficult Vincent, in the mid-eighties. They had been almost enemies then, with Mason contemptuous of Peter's woolly liberalism, and Peter resentful of Mason's harshness. But they had come to realize each other's strengths, and had become friends. They had been in touch on-and-off for decades now, occasionally about Vincent, more often to share their mutual passion for sailing, a passion they indulged more often now that they were retired. They were on the deck of Peter's yacht, moored in Robin Hood's Bay.

"What do you mean, Norbert?" Peter asked.

"That idiot Wilson phoned me yesterday, about Vincent."

Mason's disdain for the new head of MI5 was obvious.

"As if I'm going to interrupt the preparations for my eightieth birthday party to do his job for him. He's good at bullying people, but not much else. Never prepared to take a decision, likes the power but not the responsibility of the job."

Peter waited patiently for the tirade to subside, then asked

"So what was it, about Vincent?"

"Wilson thinks his cover has been blown. No evidence for it, just some vague stuff about him behaving strangely at the university in

York… and a trip to North Wales… apparently he went back to Swn y Gwynt… Anyway, even if it's true, it's his job to deal with it, not mine, at my age."

"So why are you telling me about it?" Peter asked, with a gap-toothed smile.

Over the years, he had taken better care of his patients than his teeth.

"Well" Mason said, "I suppose it could be serious, and Wilson isn't capable of dealing with anything difficult. I have got a nasty feeling that I am going to end up in charge of the case. I was wondering if perhaps you might like to take over as Vincent's psychotherapist again…"

He left the sentence hanging. When Peter didn't respond, he continued with

"You're the only one who could ever get anything out of Vincent, Peter. He trusts you. If something's amiss, well, we both know what's at stake."

Peter looked thoughtful. The awful responsibility of having anything to do with that terrible doomsday project that Vincent had initiated had always worried him. In his seventies, he had fondly believed that he had left all that stuff behind. But then again, Vincent was an interesting man, the strangest of all the strange clients he had dealt with, and…

His train of thought was interrupted when Mason took up the cudgels again.

"It's important, Peter. Maybe you could ask him?"

Peter sighed.

"I suppose so, Norbert."

Peter had been Vincent's best friend for three and a half decades, a beacon of stability in a psychotic world. He genuinely cared for Vincent, and had always tried to keep his medication to a minimum.

The British government, or rather MI5 through Mason, had insisted that Vincent remain on 'calming' and 'anti-psychotic' drugs for the rest of his life. His residence in Britain was a life sentence, too.

By the late 2000s, after twenty years on this regime, during which there was no evidence (and Vincent was under constant surveillance) that he had performed any calculations, or done anything creative at all, Vincent had obviously accepted his fate, and had lost the will to leave Britain, even if he had been provided with the wherewithal. He was deemed safe to take up a minor teaching role at a mediocre university in the north of England, where he was eking out his days. Peter was in his early sixties when Vincent moved to York, and had been offered a lucrative psychology professorship there, with a brief to keep a watchful eye on Vincent. He believed in group therapy, and a book club he had organized had been a successful way of 'normalizing' Vincent.

The most normalizing influence in Vincent's life had been his decade-long relationship with Viola, his Italian partner. Viola was alive and well at sixty, but she had had a difficult life, due to a history of mental health issues in her family. In her late forties, she was in a minor teaching position in London, and on the point of giving up, and returning to Italy after decades in Britain. Then she had met Vincent. They'd had sexual chemistry, intellectual rapport and emotional understanding. Vincent's own problems with mental health had enabled him to establish a relationship with her like no one else Viola had met, and that had clinched the deal when he asked her to come and live with him when he'd got a new job in York. Life hadn't been all hunky dory with him in York, either. She'd found it difficult to find work at first, and Vincent had his own unpredictable moods. Sometimes he muttered incomprehensible science things in his sleep, including something that sounded like an 'epsilon twister'. He always refused to talk about it. She sensed that for all his honesty and loyalty to her, he had some dark secret from his past.

"I've got something to tell you, Viola" Vincent said.

"Go for it, Vincent" Viola said.

"It's about a strange dream I had" Vincent said. "It was so real, a vivid flashback to when I was still a woman, and isolated in the Welsh mountains. They were the most traumatic days of my life, but I also did some amazing calculations then."

"Were they about that 'epsilon twister' that you mutter in your sleep?" Viola asked.

Vincent let out a huge gush of air.

"Yes, it's to do with a thing called the epsilon twistor" he said in a rush. "And in the dream, the name of the awful gloomy place where I did the calculations, Swn y Gwynt, burst into my mind. Then I was Grace again, heading off through the top garden, and beginning my ascent of Elidir Fach. As I woke up, the thought bubble burst through to the present in a sickening, vertiginous moment. The box with the calculations had gone missing."

"What calculations, Vincent?" Viola asked.

"Something to do with the epsilon twistor" Vincent replied, "but I can't remember what. I do remember writing a new inspiration down, and putting the notes in a cardboard box, but they disappeared mysteriously."

He paused, with a puzzled frown, then his face cleared.

"It was so real" Vincent said. "I had realized it at the time. I thought I must have destroyed them. I often burnt calculations in those days, but I somehow know I didn't burn those ones."

He paused again and Viola waited patiently. 'He's in a world of his own' she thought.

"And then I did something stupid" he said. "The idea was driving me crazy. I had to go back to Swn y Gwynt to check, and I did."

"And did you find them, Vincent?" Viola asked.

"No, nothing" Vincent said. "And what's worse, I bet MI5 were tailing me – I'm under strict surveillance. They'll know I went back, and they'll probably keep an even closer eye on me now."

196

'He's just being paranoid' Viola thought. 'Why would MI5 men be watching him?'

"Anyway, the dream was so powerful, I'm sure the calculations were important, and… sorry, I have to come out with it, Viola, this is why I told you about the dream, I want to come off the medication to find out. I can't concentrate… I'm on edge all the time…"

"But won't these MI5 men who you say are watching you notice if you stop taking the lithium and the anti-psychotics?" she asked.

"Not if you help cover for me" Vincent said. "That's why I've told you about the dream, Viola, to ask for your help. If you look out for me, I'll be able to pretend I'm still on the medication."

'For how long?' Viola thought.

"It's important to me" Vincent said.

He looked Viola in the eye, and she returned his gaze steadfastly.

"OK, Vincent, we'll give it a go" she said. "But you will have to stay calm and be mindful not to go off on one down the pub, or at the book club."

Mizuso looked at the old woman in the mirror. Intellectually, she understood what had happened to her. She had been in her early thirties when she had had her baby son. She now looked like women around her in their late sixties. 'I'm in the twilight of my life' she thought. Psychologically, she had found it hard to adapt to the truth that the epsilon twistor had burned away the best part of her life.

Mizuso had been sent to Japan to help wind up the epsilon twistor project in Hiroshima. As she had anticipated, she was treated respectfully by the Japanese prime minister, Maki and Kamakura. She had convinced them that there was no way of controlling the energy release of the device. The fact that both O'Malley and McCall had shown that its uncontrolled release would destroy the planet made it easy for her to convince them not to proceed with any work on its development. Or so she believed. Also as anticipated, she was no longer fully trusted by her Japanese colleagues, and she intuited that she was not privy to important decisions taken by the Japanese government. She had more than intuition on which to base her judgement. She was the greatest computer hacker in the world, and she monitored 'secret' internal communications within the governments of the four nations that knew about the epsilon twistor, as well as 'secret' external communications between them. There was no electronic evidence of covert attempts to develop the doomsday device.

The old woman in the mirror looked back at her with a sad expression, and seemed to suggest 'Perhaps it is the evil you have been witness to, as much as the physical environment, which has aged you.' Being able to crack all the computer codes on Earth had been a double-edged sword. It had helped her keep alive. Indirectly, it had helped keep Nobuko and Vincent alive, too, and Ewan for a while. But knowing the 'secrets' of the imperialist governments about the 9/11 attacks, the invasion of Iraq and, recently, the Ukraine war, had made her sick of the world, had soured her life, had aged her prematurely.

She fell into another reverie about the Fukushima nuclear power plant disaster, and the possible impending one at Zaporizhzhia. 'How can they be so stupid?' she thought. But these strange times had also produced Ewan and Grace (she still thought of Vincent as Grace when she thought about the discovery of the epsilon twistor). This ugly, chaotic world had produced two of the greatest physicists of all time.

Mizuso felt a sharp stab of pain for Grace/Vincent and then a pang of loss for Ewan, who had died of a heart attack in 2004, at the age of sixty. Although she had never met the father of her son since that fateful day in 1986, she had followed his life remotely, mainly though the CIA files. He had been effectively under house arrest for the remaining eighteen years of his life. The records said he had become a cocaine addict, and, who knows, unable to see his son, combined with the frustration of knowing that he would never get the credit he deserved for his great work, he had sought solace in drugs. Maybe not. There were many lies in the CIA documents, and the Americans hated him for having once conspired with the Japanese. There were also suggestions in the MI5 files that Vincent had become a drug addict, and was eking out the rest of his life at a mediocre university. The latter was true, the former probably not. More likely he was still on some awful medication for his 'schizophrenia', diagnosed after he had told people he had had visitors from another world.

Her mind went back to that fateful day in March 1986 again. As soon as she had discovered about the factor three in the energy release of the device from Ewan, she had decided to act independently. She now regretted the impetuous streak of her younger self. She felt it was her duty to save the world from the twistor, irrespective of what Kamakura wanted. She had told Nobuko that she was going to find Grace O'Malley in Britain, to tell Grace that she must help in preventing the development of the epsilon twistor. If only she'd known that Kamakura was of the same opinion, and sent Ewan for the very same reason, it might have led to a better outcome, with less loss of trust.

Mizuso sighed at her greatest loss in her life. Nobuko. Nobuko had always displayed honesty, loyalty and courage. As soon as her sensei had decided on her rash course of action, she had decided to go with her. She wouldn't let Mizuso face danger alone. So, Nobuko had lost Kamakura's trust, too. The two of them had been separated for thirty-six years now, apart from their communications in the cold, electronic world. Nobuko had been twenty-five then. She was sixty-one now, after spending most of her life in China. She, at least, had been allowed to travel, had seen some of the beauties of the Earth. 'A lot of her life had been burned up, too, but she has been better treated than me,' Mizuso thought. There was no hint of envy in this. She loved Nobuko and was proud of her protégé. Perhaps it was only the idea of seeing her again that was keeping Mizuso going. Now, finally, the Japanese government had agreed for Nobuko to come over on a Chinese diplomatic visa, to pay a supervised visit to her in Hiroshima.

Mizuso dragged herself away from the mirror, made a green tea, and sat down reluctantly at her computer. After all these years, there had been a burst of computer noise about Vincent, and she opened her folder on him.

Nobuko had had no trouble in cracking all the computer codes, either. She had also been able to monitor Mizuso's and McCall's progress, and the satisfactory developments, or rather lack of them, in Japan, the USA and the UK. She had been faced with the harder task of convincing the Chinese government of the deadly peril posed by the epsilon twistor. The communist government there believed that the twistor was being developed by their enemies in the capitalist world, and that the story about it destroying the whole Earth had been made up by the imperialist powers to hold China back, while they developed this wonderful new power source themselves. This distrust, and fear, ran very deep.

Nobuko's exceptional skills had impressed her Chinese hosts, especially her fluent use of their language. They wanted to believe her, but the timing of events had conspired to sow the seed of their mistrust. They had found out about the twistor from their top agent, Aiping Li, when O'Malley's raw calculations had suggested its destruction zone was about three thousand miles across – an ultimate deterrent weapon. Then Aiping Li, and her Chinese-American source, had both disappeared. They had only got the story about O'Malley's and McCall's subsequent calculations, the ones that showed it would destroy the whole planet, from the UK, USA and Japanese governments, not their own sources.

Nobuko had made herself indispensable, especially as a computer expert, and had risen to the top of their external advisers. As a foreigner, with Japanese and Australian passports from her father's side, but no Chinese passport from her mother's side, and a six-foot tall, outlandish-looking woman, she had, until now, had no opportunity to gain access to the top levels of Chinese government, an all-national, all-male preserve. Then, out of the blue, had come the message that she was 'invited' (it was an order, in effect) to an audience with Xi Jinping. The timing seemed significant. Mizuso had informed her via their quadruple-encrypted channel that Vincent was back on MI5's radar.

Vincent had only been into town once since coming off the medication, to get a birthday present for Viola. Trendy aromatherapy shops were not his favourite, and he pushed the door open tentatively. He was the only customer in the shop. He was faced by a hippy-looking woman about his own age.

"Can I help you?" the woman said.

The woman had long, grey, straggly hair, but quite a young face and noticeable, almond-shaped eyes.

'My God, it's Pru' Vincent thought. 'This must be the unluckiest coincidence ever.'

Memories of the drinks they'd had together at the window table in The Fir Tree bubbled up, and Grace re-surfaced again. Pru started to say something anodyne about the latest line in scented candles, when she stopped and gave Vincent a curious look.

"Don't we know each other?" Pru asked.

Vincent's deep-seated need to tell the truth had not changed over the years. He found it very hard to lie, even when the circumstances demanded it.

"I'm sorry…" he procrastinated.

"No" Pru said, "I definitely recognize you. My God, Grace, is that really you?"

In the presence of his/her oldest friend from the Oxford days, Vincent was unable to dissemble. He took a couple of quick steps across to her and, tears starting to run down his face, hugged her.

"Yes, it's me" he said, separating himself from Pru, and looking her full in the face.

"God, Grace, it's so wonderful to see you after all these years" Pru said. "We all thought you were dead."

The last time Pru had seen Vincent was at Grace's thirtieth birthday party, nearly four decades earlier, in the mists of time.

"I'll close the shop for a few minutes, Grace. Let's pop round to the pub next door."

The two of them sat at the window table.

"I don't know where to begin, Grace" she said. "Can I get you a drink?"

"Sorry, Pru" Vincent said, "but please could you stop calling me Grace? It's freaking me out. I had a sex change and became Vincent in the eighties."

"O, sorry, Vincent, I didn't mean any harm. It's just that I think of you as…"

"I understand, Pru" Vincent said. "And, yes, I'd love a drink. How about a pot of tea?"

"Wow, you've changed in more ways than one, Vincent. They've got some great beer, even some Welsh whiskey."

"No, thanks" Vincent said. "I'd prefer tea."

Vincent still thought of Pru as the idealistic hippy twenty-something woman he had known in Oxford. Although she still looked like a hippy in York, she had undergone profound change, and not for the better. She had set up an acupuncture clinic in Leamington, and that had failed. Then a reiki centre in Winchester, and that had failed, too. In her late forties, she had been too proud, and untrained and unsuitable, to get one of the wage slave jobs she so detested. Her relationships had failed, too, first with Siobhan, her partner in Leamington, and then with Colin, her partner in Winchester. The fates seemed to have conspired against her. Her moans about the first two decades after their separation went on and on. Then things had turned for the better when she met her current partner. Seb was great in bed, and a nice little earner with his private teaching and freelance translation work.

The two decades Pru and Seb had been together in North Yorkshire had seen a big improvement in her life compared with the previous twenty years, but Pru had become materialistic, and wanted more. She and Seb chugged around in a twenty-year-old car that ran on polluting, expensive petrol. She wanted a new electric car. The house was heated by an ancient, oil-fired Aga. She wanted solar panels on the roof, a windmill in the garden, and a hydroelectric generator running off the torrent behind the house. Her desires for an eco-friendly house could hardly be described as undesirable, but she was now tempted to obtain the money in an evil way. Thirty-six years ago, a man called Tony Woodbridge, a man she had met only once, at Grace's thirtieth birthday party, had phoned her with a bizarre offer. He would give her a lot of money, tens of thousands of pounds, if she could tell him Grace's whereabouts. He had stressed that the offer stood whenever she gave him the information. Pru didn't know that Tony was a trained killer, or that he had shot and nearly killed Grace in 1985, or that he himself had been shot and nearly killed by Grace's bodyguard, or that he had lost his coveted career over the O'Malley fiasco in London and was full of bitterness and hatred about it. But Pru knew deep down that there was something odd, deeply unsavoury, about the offer. It's not an offer you make to keep in touch with an old friend, is it? And then Grace had completely disappeared from her life, and she had forgotten all about it, until now.

Now Grace/Vincent had turned up on her doorstep. She had hardly recognized this new man as her old friend Grace. Could she sell him for thirty pieces of silver, or perhaps as much as a hundred thousand pounds? And perhaps this Tony didn't mean any harm to Vincent, was maybe desperate to contact him for another reason, perhaps a scientific one? Yes, that's probably it, Pru thought, those industrial breakthroughs are worth billions, it must have been something to do with Grace's scientific work. Pru got out her old address book and thumbed it up. 'He's probably moved by now anyway. It's just an old landline number' she thought. She dialled it.

The phone rang in Tony's gloomy, cavernous, basement flat in Pimlico. He was sitting in a battered armchair, smoking a Dunhill and drinking a whiskey, playing through the moves of one of the go games between the AI machine AlphaGo and the world champion Lee Sedol, on his massive, slate go board. He was studying the machine's astonishing 37th move of the second game. He would let the phone ring. Then his ears picked up when he heard a hesitant, unfamiliar voice on the ansaphone.

"Hello, if this is still the phone of Tony Woodbridge, please call me back. My name is Pru, and we discussed some business a long time ago…"

Tony leapt across the room, and picked up.

"Hello, Pru" he said. "Yes, this is Tony Woodbridge."

An hour later, he was on the phone again.

"I've got a job for you, Hugh" he said.

The first Friday of the month saw Peter hosting the book club. Vincent was the first to arrive. 'This is going to be a trial' Vincent thought. He had stopped taking the medication for three weeks now, unbeknown to his minders, and fragments of his old life had been visiting him in chaotic dreams, in which he saw a hundred images of himself, like looking into a shattered mirror. Then, a few nights ago, he had started calculating again, had started to remember his epsilon twistor calculations, and had been scribbling and secreting dozens of pages of notes. He was hyped up, and he knew he had to appear dull and normal as usual, suppressed by the anti-psychotic drugs and the lithium. The pretence was going to be a terrible strain, and he would have to be on his guard.

"Do you fancy a beer?" Peter asked.

Vincent had brought a four pack of Boddingtons.

"I'll have one of these" he said.

"I'm sorry you missed the last meeting, Vincent. I'd have liked to know what you made of *Woman on the Edge of Time*."

"I thought it was brilliant" Vincent said. "I'm glad we decided to take on a female author at last."

"Me, too" Peter said. "The Graves and Primo Levi were great books, but following the First World War with Auschwitz was a bit relentless. I felt battered at the end of *If This Is A Man*."

"Me, too" Vincent said. "Mind you, there's a war going on in the Marge Piercy book, too, isn't there?"

"Do you mean the war in the future, between Luciente's people and the remnants of the capitalist empire?"

"Well, there's that" Vincent said, "but I was thinking of the war between Connie and the staff at the mental hospital."

The doorbell rang. As if on cue, Sean, a clinical psychologist who worked in a secure unit in a mental hospital in North Yorkshire, arrived. He was a former research student of Peter, and gave him a bear hug in the doorway. After Sean had grabbed a beer, Peter said

"We were talking about the Marge Piercy book, Sean. Vincent thought it was brilliant."

"I was shocked at the treatment of the mental patients in Connie's hospital" Sean said, "but I must admit I've seen things like that."

"Oh, come off it Sean" Peter said. "Those scenes were unrealistic."

Peter and Sean, who were sitting on the sofa opposite Vincent, started to speak simultaneously. Peter's seniority prevailed, and he said

"Anyway, things are better now, but I've also seen some terrible things at the Henblest unit where Sean works. It's an awful thing, being sectioned."

Vincent was looking down, but he felt that Peter was looking meaningfully at him when he made his final remark. 'God, I've got two psychology people opposite me' he thought. The silly meme 'They're coming to take me away, ha, ha' floated through his mind. He was relieved when they were interrupted by a knock at the door. Olga and Heinrich had arrived together. They also got drawn into the conversation about last month's book.

"Do you think the scenes in the future were meant to be real?" Heinrich said. "Or just the delusions of a paranoid schizophrenic?"

"Just delusions" Peter said.

Sean made an assenting noise.

"I'm not so sure" said Olga.

Olga had a beautiful, sharp face, and loved science fiction. She had enjoyed discussing the utopian aspects of Connie's future world last time.

"In a way, it would fit in scientifically with that Gödel-Einstein book we read in the autumn. Didn't Gödel prove that there are solutions to Einstein's field equations that allow for time travel? I think these parts of the novel are just as real as the ones in the 1970s."

The doorbell rang again. This time it was Viola. The discussion rumbled on.

"Whichever way" Vincent said, "I thought it was an excellent idea to make the stark contrast between the harsh realities of the modern world, especially with regard to the treatment of poor, non-white people, with the possibilities inherent in the human situation. I really liked the future world she portrays, and whether or not it's 'real' or Connie's delusions doesn't matter."

"I thought her future world was boring" Sean said.

"Me, too" said Peter. "What has happened to masculinity?"

"Withered away" said Viola.

"It just won't happen" said Peter. "Men are naturally aggressive and competitive..."

"When you say naturally, Peter" Viola interrupted, "you have to be very careful what you mean by 'natural'. Do you really mean what's normal in our current patriarchal, capitalist world?"

"No" said Peter. "It has always been that way and always will. There's nothing wrong with being assertive."

"That's different from being aggressive, though, Peter" Viola said. "You can stand up for your rights without being violent or repressive."

"Hear, hear" said Vincent.

While they were speaking, Vincent was thinking how ridiculous it was that the 'other' four members of the group were all high-powered academics – Sean a psychologist, Heinrich a scientist, Olga a mathematician and Viola a linguist. God, was it possible that the whole group was a set up, including even Viola? He already had firm suspicions about Peter and Sean, now the whole group looked like an interrogation committee, probing him about field equations and paranoid schizophrenia. What was 'real' in the book? It was all a story, even if the modern New York parts had been based on interviews with psychiatric patients. God, maybe he was like Connie and his 'epsilon twistor' world and the magic project in Japan was a schizophrenic delusion. The group were all bona fide ordinary people, and his paranoia was the only thing turning them into inquisitors. He could end up getting sectioned, getting the real-world fate of Connie. His reverie was interrupted by another ring at the doorbell. The book club had a new American member, introduced by Peter as Hugh Whitehead.

"Pleased to meet you, Hugh" Vincent said.

"You too, Vincent" Whitehead said, shaking him firmly by the hand.

Heinrich, Olga and Viola were already seated on the huge, multicoloured sofa opposite the anthracite burner, and they greeted Hugh in turn.

"We're all here now" Peter said, "shall we get on to our new book? Maybe you'd like to kick off, Heinrich, as *The Koran* was your idea."

Heinrich put down a bowl of vegetable chips, took a sip of his Hobgoblin Ale, and cleared his throat.

"Well" Heinrich said, "I read *The God Delusion* by Dawkins in the summer, and thought he was basically right about religion. Reading *The Koran* has confirmed my opinion."

"That's a strong opening statement" Olga said.

"I can't stand Dawkins" Vincent said.

Viola laughed, and said

"Talking of strong statements, I think Vincent has gone into the lead there. Any advance in controversial openers?"

"We're not usually like this, Hugh" Peter said to the American, who was sitting in a low chair next to the burner. "We're usually a mellow crowd."

"I don't mind straight talking" Hugh said. "I only heard about the club last week, so I only got the chance to read the first third or so, but I've got my opinions, too."

"What do you make of the story so far, Hugh?" Sean asked.

"I think it is great" Hugh said.

"That's good to hear from an American" Olga said.

"What did you think was great about it?" Peter asked. He sounded surprised.

"People need rules" Hugh said. "Personally I'm a God-fearing Christian, but it's clear from the early stuff... do you mind if I quote you a bit..."

"Go ahead" Olga and Vincent said in unison.

"It's real early on" Hugh said, thumbing up a page. "Ah, here it is...

Believers, those who follow the Jewish Faith, Christians, and Sabaeans – whoever believes in God and the Last Day and does what is right – shall be rewarded by their Lord; they have nothing to fear or to regret.

...It's pretty clear that the Koran backs up the Bible, and whatever differences there are between Christians and Muslims, we're closer together than we think, and against the godless commies..."

"I'm a godless commie" Vincent said.

"*The Bible* and *The Koran*, and other holy books like *The Torah* are all deluded" Peter said. "That's what *The God Delusion* is all about."

"Maybe we should save *The God Delusion* for another book club meeting next year" Vincent said. "So long as I can borrow a copy. I wouldn't want to contribute any royalties to Dawkins."

"What have you got against Dawkins?" Heinrich asked.

"I think *The Selfish Gene* is the worst kind of social Darwinism" Vincent said. "It's the philosophy behind Thatcherism, basically."

"Darwin was a great scientist" Heinrich said.

"And Dawkins is a brilliant exponent of his work" Peter said.

"I read *The Origin of Species* recently" Vincent said, "and I think Dawkins completely misrepresents Darwin's work. I met Dawkins at a college dinner in Oxford and it was all 'me, me, me' all evening. *The Selfish Geneticist* would be a better title for his book."

"Ah, now we're getting down to the real reason you don't like Dawkins, Vincent" Heinrich said. "Did he pass the port the wrong way?"

Vincent laughed.

"Nice one, Heinrich" he said, "but I disagree with your description of Darwin as a great scientist."

"What!" Heinrich and Peter exclaimed in unison.

"Don't get me wrong, Heinrich" Vincent said. "I think *The Origin of Species* is a great book, but I think it's closer to religion than science."

"Nonsense" Peter said.

Vincent got up and dramatically pulled a copy of *The Scientific Letters and Papers of James Clerk Maxwell* from his briefcase.

"This is science" he said, "revealing the mathematical equations underlying phenomena. Maxwell proposed his field equations in 1861, and after 160 years of extensive enquiries and tests, by many fine experimental scientists, no one has ever found an exception."

"I don't think anyone is saying that Maxwell's work isn't science, Vincent" Viola said soothingly, "but surely Darwin's work is great science, too?"

"Is it?" Vincent said. "This comes back to the Gödel book we discussed. Didn't Einstein and Gödel prove that the only universe compatible with the Maxwell equations is a world without time?"

"I'm beginning to see your point" Olga said.

"I'm not" Peter said, grumpily.

"Look, Peter" Vincent said, "our subjective experience of time passing is just our culture. There's nothing corresponding to it in the fundamental laws of the universe. The idea of evolution comes from our prejudice of looking for progress. The causal processes in Darwin's work simply don't exist."

"I once read" Sean said, "by a great occultist, a contemporary of Crowley, that everything runs on magic, and science is the subset of reality that appears to obey causality."

"I don't agree with the occultists" Vincent said, "but I still maintain that Darwin is closer to theology then science."

"So you wouldn't side with the evolutionists against those of us who support creationism?" Hugh said, "because neither of them agree with the work of this guy..."

"Maxwell" Olga said, filling him in. "I agree with Vincent that he was the greatest mathematical physicist of all time, surpassing even Newton and Einstein."

"Was he the guy who had a screw rule?" Hugh asked.

"It's *The Bible* and *The Koran* that have rules about screwing" Vincent said.

There was general laughter, and the tension broke. The seven of them were still discussing life, the universe and everything hours later, when Viola said

"It's been a wonderful evening everyone, but I'm afraid I'm rather tired. I'll have to head off soon. Has anyone got any ideas for next time?"

"I'll pass" Heinrich said, "as *The Koran* was my choice."

"And I chose *Eyes of The Overworld* for October" Sean said, "so I'll pass, too."

"I think *Narziss and Goldmund* was the one before that" Olga said.

"And the Gurdjieff book was in August" Peter said.

"That seems to leave it up to you and Hugh, Vincent" Peter continued, "the returned prodigal and the newcomer."

"You first, Hugh" Vincent said.

"Are you sure?" Hugh said. "I don't like to barge in on you guys."

"Go ahead, Hugh" Peter said.

"Well, I really liked *Blood Meridian* by Cormac McCarthy that I read recently. It's about scalp hunters in the Wild West days. White men hunting Indian scalps."

"Sounds grizzly" Viola said.

"It is" Hugh said, "but it's brilliant."

"How about you, Vincent?" Peter asked.

"Well, I've always liked Aldous Huxley" Vincent said. "Anything by him would be great. How about *Eyeless in Gaza*? I read that in student days. I can't remember much about it, but I think it would be a cracker."

On his way home, Vincent meandered aimlessly around in the backstreets off the Selby Road. Something didn't feel right. He didn't like the new bloke who had turned up at the book club... Hugh Whitehead was it?... He had an unhealthy, dangerous vibe.

Mizuso was well treated materialistically, as befitted a senior scientific adviser to the Japanese government. The meeting with Nobuko had been arranged at the most beautiful, sought-after *onsen* in the Hiroshima region, one where the emperor himself had stayed. Her main room was a hundred square metres of tatami matting, with just a small tokonoma, a withered branch in a vase, for decoration. It was the height of luxury, with an anteroom leading to the indoor baths, and sliding panels giving directly on to the hot pools in the garden. 'I must be careful' she told herself for the ten thousandth time. 'Every word we speak will be recorded and analyzed by both our security services.'

There was a crunch of wheels on the gravel drive, as a huge black limousine with Chinese diplomatic plates pulled up at the front gates of the *onsen*. Nobuko, wearing a smart masculine suit and dark shades, stepped out into the glaring sunshine. Mizuso, dressed in a traditional kimono, felt a wave of excitement when she saw her, but walked calmly up to her and greeted her with a traditional deep bow. 'We mustn't appear too friendly' she thought, while longing to take Nobuko in her arms, and give her a big hug. Nobuko reciprocated the bow, and said

"I have been looking forward to meeting you, Tanaka-san."

'Thank the gods I've practised so many times' she thought. 'Even then, it nearly came out as Tanaka-sensei.'

"And I you, Brown-san" Mizuso replied.

Mizuso and Nobuko had always been interested in languages; computer languages, spoken languages, written languages, sign languages. Aware of the growing surveillance surrounding them at Tanaka Electronics, they had developed their own subtle sign language. They were already beginning to deploy it, imperceptible to both their minders and the video surveillance cameras. Nobuko was longing to give Mizuso a big hug, too.

212

The two of them went through to the vast acreage of tatami, and knelt opposite each other, a few feet apart. One of the minders poured them green tea, then they were left alone, in the relative peace of purely electronic surveillance.

"To what do I owe the honour of this visit from an ambassador of the Chinese government?" Mizuso asked.

"To request a pooling of information about an important matter that affects both our countries" Nobuko replied. "My visit has been personally approved by our great leader, Xi Jinping."

"I am intrigued" Mizuso said. "Please enlighten me. What is the matter at hand?"

All the while, their subtle signals were racing ahead of the stilted conversation, and floating above it, with the joy and wonder of seeing each other again after so many years.

"It concerns the project you worked on here in the 1980s" Nobuko said, "on the ideas of the British scientist, Grace O'Malley."

'And those of the American scientist, Ewan McCall' Mizuso thought.

"How interesting" Mizuso said. "That project was discontinued long ago. How can I help?"

"We have new information" Nobuko said, "and we want to know of any new information you may have."

"On behalf of the Japanese government, I promise to be forthright in my response, if you share your information" Mizuso said.

Nobuko took a deep breath, as if preparing to tell someone something that might shock them, though she knew very well from their private, quadruple-encrypted, untraceable computer communications that the Japanese Secret Service was also privy to the 'news' she was about to announce.

"Very well" she said, and exhaled a full lungful of air. "Grace O'Malley is alive."

Mizuso did not feign surprise.

"We know" she said.

"He is now a man, called Vincent Clerk, working at the University of York, in the north of England" Nobuko said.

"We know" Mizuso said.

"How much more do you know?" Nobuko asked.

"Not much" Mizuso replied. "He seems to be inactive scientifically, and there is no evidence he is doing anything with regard to the 1980s project."

"Is the Japanese government content with this situation?" Nobuko asked.

"Yes" Mizuso replied. "Our proverb for this situation is 'Let sleeping dogs lie'."

"Are you sure this great scientist is sleeping?" Nobuko asked.

"We can never be sure what is going on inside a person's mind, but there is no evidence to the contrary."

After their stilted conversation, carried out for the benefit of the surveillance devices, Mizuso communicated to Nobuko via their quadruple-encrypted channel that she was planning to escape from Japan and go to Britain. She felt intuitively that Vincent was in danger, and that it was her duty to help him. There was nothing more she could achieve in Japan. She had reprogrammed international face recognition software and had a new passport, a new identity with the right to abode in the UK. She was leaving at the next opportunity.

Nobuko was perturbed by Mizuso's plan. She knew her sensei, for all her apparent self-control, had a rash streak, and knew Mizuso wouldn't change her mind. 'Perhaps now is the best time for me, too' she thought. 'What more could I achieve in China?' I will escape from China and join you in Britain, she replied. For both of them, the prospect of meeting in unfettered circumstances outweighed any danger, and Nobuko shared Mizuso's concern for Vincent.

Chapter 10

Grace and Vincent

When she arrived in Britain, the only person Mizuso could one hundred percent trust was Olaf Pedersen. Olaf was the only man she had let in on the secret of the epsilon twistor. He was a morally pure man, and as determined as Mizuso to save the Earth from a catastrophic release of the device. Born in a fishing village in Denmark, his life had taken a strange turn when a businessman friend of his father's, just back from a trip to Tokyo, had left a Japanese newspaper in their home. The young Olaf was fascinated, and became determined to learn this strange and beautiful way of writing. The next twist of fate that befell Olaf was a tragic one. He lost an arm in an accident on his father's boat. Although Olaf's prosthetic arm became so powerful and useful that he could have become a fisherman, his father vowed that his son would not follow him into his dangerous trade. So, it was Olaf's intellectual power that came to the fore, when he studied Japanese at Aarhus University. His college girlfriend was studying computer sciences, and Olaf's fascination turned to computer translation. He was ahead of his time in appreciating how large language models could work, and a reluctant pioneer in the development of artificial intelligence. He understood how much he owed to the pioneering work of Mizuso Tanaka in the mid-eighties, around the time of his birth, and had contacted her as a 'white hat' hacker. The very fact that he had managed to locate her computer had told Mizuso how advanced he was in computing, and they had become internet friends. And Mizuso had shared her burden with him. Olaf knew all about Grace and Vincent, and had been keeping an eye out for Vincent since starting a post-doc in the Mathematics Department at York.

Although Mizuso knew that Olaf was one metre ninety tall and weighed ninety kilograms, she was taken aback by his size when she met him. Although bulky, he moved gracefully, and smiled a lot. 'He seems as calm as an android' she thought.

"I haven't attempted to make contact with him yet" Olaf said.

"That's great, Olaf" Mizuso said, "but I think you'll need to stay closer to him now, try to make friends with him."

"Do you have new information?" Olaf asked.

"Nothing definite" Mizuso replied, "but I picked up that MI5 have put him under increased surveillance, and Peter Johnson has taken over as his psychotherapist. He had Vincent round for a book club meeting recently. Maybe you could check out the other members?"

"Of course" Olaf said, "and I'll get closer to Vincent. I'll do my best to protect him."

"Maybe you could arrange to meet him 'accidentally'" Mizuso said. "He seems to have a fairly fixed schedule at the university, and always takes the same route home."

She paused.

"We mustn't alarm him unduly, but you will have to let him know at the outset that you know he was Grace. Otherwise, he'll never trust you."

Vincent Clerk wheezed as he cycled up to the footbridge on his way back from the university. The Board of Studies meeting had been a disaster. He, along with Olga and Heinrich, had put up fierce arguments against the further dumbing down of the natural sciences course, but to no avail. He reached the top of the elegantly curved bridge out of breath, got off his bike, sat on the wooden bench that ran alongside the arch, fiddled in his rucksack for his cigarettes and lit one, a strange, thin delicious smoke given to him by a grateful Chinese student. 'Thank God this is my last year' he thought. 'I should have retired a couple of years ago, when covid started.'

It was a crisp, clear, winter day and the splendid view down the river lifted his spirits. "I don't think this proposal goes far enough" he had said. "What we should do is introduce a two-year BSc course in CV writing, other professional skills and basket weaving, with a little bit of science." The angry face of the teaching robot, as Heinrich had nicknamed the head of teaching, floated into view, and Vincent burst out laughing, startling away a couple of tourists who had been seated nearby.

He was just about to get up, when a big Scandinavian-looking bloke came up to him, and said "It's Grace O'Malley, isn't it?"

Vincent's heart missed a beat. After thirty-six years, someone had finally blown his cover. He was in a vulnerable spot, could easily be pushed into the river. The man looked strong. But, somehow, he didn't look dangerous. On the contrary, he had a friendly vibe. But that didn't mean anything.

"I'm afraid you're mistaken" Vincent said.

"I understand your reluctance, Grace" the man said. "Please allow me to introduce myself. My name is Olaf."

Vincent had been off the anti-psychotic medicine for weeks, and he could feel an episode coming on. His stomach was churning.

"You're not real" Vincent said. "Please leave me in peace."

Olaf looked around. They were alone on the bridge. Vincent was obviously distressed. Olaf was normally surefooted, but when he moved away from Vincent to give him some space, he slipped and overbalanced. He struck his prosthetic arm on one of the railings, and its surface came away, revealing its metallic interior. Vincent fainted, and Olaf caught him gracefully. When Vincent came to, Olaf was smiling sympathetically at him.

"I'm so sorry I startled you, Vincent, but I needed to convince you that I knew about your past as Grace. I've been sent to meet you by Mizuso, whom you met thirty-six years ago when you signed your letter to the governments. Are you all right, Vincent? Would you like some smelling salts to recover?"

"No, thanks" Vincent said. "Don't tell me, let me guess. You're from Datonga, right?"

Olaf blinked in disbelief. Mizuso had told him about Grace's psychotic episodes, and now he was in one of Vincent's.

"No, Vincent" Olaf said. "I am from Denmark."

"You're an android aren't you, Olaf? I saw your arm."

"I'm sorry I exposed my prosthetic arm to you, Vincent" Olaf said. "I lost an arm as a boy. It's been a huge shock, Vincent. Let's walk back to your home. I'll push the bike."

"I'm still not convinced you're real" Vincent said. "That trick with the arm, that was part of the hallucination, too."

"Allow me to greet your neighbour" Olaf said.

They had walked down the nondescript main road, with its garage, one small café and post office, and turned to cross the railway bridge towards Acomb, where the Terry's chocolate factory workers had lived, in the days when York had manufactured railway carriages and confectionary. Its major industries were now tourism, insurance, and the university.

"What's her name?" Olaf asked.

"Mavis."

Mavis was out dead-heading her hydrangeas.

"Good afternoon, Mavis" Olaf said. "I'm a colleague of Vincent from the university. Pleased to meet you."

After exchanging a few further pleasantries, Vincent and Olaf went in, and sat on the two sofas in the small living room of Vincent's 1930s two-bedroom semi-detached house.

"You see" Olaf said. "Your neighbour perceives me as real, and..."

"OK, OK" Vincent interrupted. "I get the picture. I don't usually indulge these days, but I'm going to have a whiskey and a smoke."

Vincent disappeared into the kitchen, a cheapo 1970s flat roof extension at the back of the house, and stared out of the window, completely disoriented. It didn't look like the same garden at all. It was more vivid, more colourful, more alive, scarier. A couple of small birds were tucking into the pyracantha berries.

As soon as Vincent left the room, Olaf phoned Mizuso on his encrypted mobile.

"I'm at Vincent's home" he said. "He is having a full-blown psychotic episode, thinks I'm an android from another planet. What should I do?"

"Play along with him" Mizuso said. "I've heard MI5 tapes of Grace talking about visitors from the future during her great calculations in the eighties. Perhaps these episodes are inseparably connected to the calculations. Perhaps Vincent has started calculating again?"

"That would explain MI5's renewed interest in him" Olaf said. "By the way, don't worry about time. He's out the back of the house in a world of his own."

"We may be able to turn this weird situation to our advantage" Mizuso said. "If Vincent thinks you're an android from the future, maybe he will be more likely to open up to you. It's worth trying."

"I'll give it a go" Olaf said. "He's coming back."

He hung up.

Vincent sat back down with his whiskey and lit a Camel. He stared moodily down at the dirty, beige carpet.

"Are you calculating, Vincent?" Olaf asked gently.

"No" Vincent said irritably. "I want to be and I'm trying, but I've only just come off some horrible drugs. I'm depressed. It's the years, decades, I've wasted on the medication. I've wasted my life."

"Not at all" Olaf said soothingly. "Mizuso told me that you are one of the greatest mathematical physicists of all time, surpassing even Einstein."

"Nobody else believes that" Vincent said. "Anyway, if it's true, it's for stuff I did back in the eighties. I've done nothing since."

"I've wasted my life" he repeated. "Those fucking anti-psychotic drugs have turned my brain to raisins."

Vincent stared down again, then downed his whiskey in one. There were tears in his eyes.

"Don't talk about it if it's too painful for you, Vincent" Olaf said.

"No, it's good to talk" Vincent said. "It helps me remember, make sense of it all."

He laughed. "Somehow, it's easier to do it with an android. I know you're not going to be judgmental. But you'll remember every single word I say, won't you, Olaf?"

"Yes, Vincent" he said soothingly.

"And you want the story of my life, for your records in the thirty-first century?"

'I must play along with him' Olaf thought. 'He's completely off on one.'

"Only if you are willing, Vincent. All we know about you is up to your disappearance as Grace O'Malley in 1986, and that you are a lecturer in York in 2022. If you want to fill in any of that gap…"

Vincent suddenly blurted out "They put me on some heavy medication in eighty-six, thanks to my 'hallucinations' and I lost the ability to calculate. After a few months, I lost the will to calculate, too…"

He trailed off.

"I'm going to grab a glass of wine" he said.

"Do you mind if I join you?" Olaf asked.

"Of course, Olaf" Vincent said. "I didn't mean to be rude. I must remember to treat you like a person."

"O, please don't treat me that badly!" Olaf said.

Laughing, Vincent came back with a bottle of cheap white Rioja, undid the screw top, and poured a couple of glasses.

"I got a sex change and skin bleaching in eighty-seven. It was pretty traumatic, but I haven't regretted it. I'd always felt like a man inside, anyway."

"How interesting, Vincent. So, Grace O'Malley disappeared from the historical record…"

"…and Vincent Clerk appeared" Vincent said, finishing Olaf's sentence for him.

"I'd promised Mason… the head of MI5, the guy who faked my death… not to do anything scientific. I guess my choice of Clerk as a surname, in honour of James Clerk Maxwell, was my little rebellion. It went unnoticed, and Vincent Clerk I became."

Vincent took a big glug of the wine and lit a cigarette.

"I re-surfaced in Bristol and went into school teaching for a bit."

"As a science teacher?" Olaf asked.

"No, even that was deemed too close to my past for the powers-that-be. I taught languages."

"Did you enjoy it?"

"It was a disaster" Vincent said. "The medication made me slow, and I couldn't cope with all the emotional demands of the children. I became the NUT rep…"

"NUT?"

"Sorry, Olaf, it's an acronym for the National Union of Teachers… anyway, I clashed with the management. It was the start of what we've got now… early Thatcherism… management in schools then was as bad as management in universities is now… sorry, I'm wittering."

"Take your time, Vincent" Olaf said. "This wine is delicious, by the way."

Olaf was being polite. He could perceive that the wine was of poor quality.

"I only stuck it out for a couple of years. I quit my job, and moved down to the end of the Gower peninsula, in South Wales, where I ran my own translation business, through the nineties up to 2006..."

Vincent's face clouded over.

"Then something happened?" Olaf prompted.

"My ex-partner Hiroshi died. I hadn't seen him for years, but something broke inside me... I'd rather not talk about it..."

Vincent stared at the floor, and there was silence for several seconds.

"I was in a bit of a mess for a couple of years, but then I decided to apply for teaching jobs in science at obscure universities. Grace O'Malley had disappeared a quarter of a century ago, and no one would know me in a place like York, where I ended up. I've been here over a decade now. I met my partner Viola quite early on through the UCU branch meetings..."

"UCU?"

"Sorry, Olaf, another acronym, 'the University and College Union', the one I'm in now. Anyway, Viola and I have been partners for years, living happily ever after. I've never told her too much about my past life. She knows I had a sex change in my thirties. I told her I did a PhD and a couple of scientific post-docs in my twenties before giving up research, but nothing about Grace O'Malley..."

Vincent trailed off.

"I think I've lost trust in everyone except Viola" Vincent said, looking down sadly.

He suddenly looked up again, and exclaimed "God, what am I going to tell Viola?"

"About me?" Olaf queried.

"Indeed" Vincent replied.

"If I tell her about the epsilon twistor project, and that you're an alien android, she'll just think I am becoming psychotic after stopping taking the medication. She and her family are prone to mental instability. It's one of the reasons I could relate to her. Her relatives know about schizophrenia, and I get on well with them. Sorry, I'm rambling again. It must be the booze."

"*In vino veritas*" Olaf said.

"I'll think about it. She won't be back from the university till later anyway."

"Certainly, Vincent, but with what you tell me about the mental health issues, it might be worth considering not telling her at all."

"I suppose so" Vincent said. "I'm happy you've come, Olaf, but I must be careful. I tend to blurt the truth out. If I tell anyone that you're an alien android, they'll just think I'm mad. You're a colleague at the university, Olaf."

'I am' Olaf thought.

"Please keep an eye on me if we go down the pub."

"I understand" Olaf said.

One of the things that had kept Vincent relatively stable for the decade since his move to York had been evenings in the pub with his university friends. When Vincent next went down the pub, two of his best friends, Olga and Heinrich, were already seated next to the fire in the back bar at The Silver Globe, their favourite community-run pub just inside the city walls.

"How are your new calculations going, Olga?" Vincent asked.

"I've lost my way" Olga said despondently. "It was going so well over the summer when I was back in Rumania. Now I can't seem to concentrate. I'm so angry about everything at the moment."

"Are you still upset about the Board of Studies meeting?" Heinrich asked.

Without waiting for a reply, he continued with "Don't worry about it. The Board of Studies doesn't have any power anymore, anyway. It's just a rubber stamp for the management. They were going to force this crazy new programme through anyway, whatever happened at the meeting."

Olga had been waiting patiently for him. Heinrich was a good friend, one of her few colleagues she respected as a scientist, and she agreed with a lot of his politics, but he did tend to bang on about their departmental management in particular, and the university management in general, and then the government. 'He'll get on to how it's a microcosm of what's happened in the country in the decade he's been here, the erosion of democracy at every level in society…'

"It's not so much that" Olga said, "as the UCU meeting. It was so pathetic. If we don't go on all-out strike now, after what they've done to the pensions, we never will. That fart from social sciences who banged on about how he couldn't afford to go on an all-out strike, he's got no idea of what poverty is. He should have been born in Ceausescu's Rumania."

"Or Honecker's DDR" Heinrich said. "O, look, there's Viola."

Viola stood uncertainly in the doorway for a moment, then caught sight of her friends. Olga got up and hugged her, then nipped to the bar and bought a round of pale ales. Viola sat down, and raised her glass.

"Cheers" the four of them chorused.

"Olga and I were born into two of the worst Stalinist regimes" Heinrich said, plunging straight into the politics. "I never imagined I'd end up in the same sort of shit in Britain."

"Come off it, Heinrich" Viola said. "I visited the DDR in the early eighties, and it was way more scary and repressive than what we've got here now. Mind you, I am getting very worried about the bullying in the university. There's a nasty case involving that Dr Woolford in your department."

"Yes" Heinrich said, "the Robot has been bullying Alonso for months. He's getting really depressed."

Viola was the UCU rep in the Languages Department, one of the more active groups socially and politically in the university. Natural Sciences was renowned for its apathy, had not even had a departmental rep in the twenty-first century, until Vincent took it on reluctantly in the mid-2010s. Alonso had indeed had some poor student scores for his lecture courses, but instead of helping him, the management had hounded him, and his referral to Human Resources for poor performance had unnerved him. He was on sick leave, ostensibly for long covid. He hadn't come to the pub for weeks.

"I know" Viola said, "but I think UCU is doing a good job in the way they're handling the case."

"I agree" Vincent said.

He spotted Olaf in the doorway and waved him over to their table. Olaf arrived and Vincent made the introductions.

"Olaf is going to be spending the whole term here" he said. "He's on a visiting fellowship from Aarhus."

"Welcome to The Silver Globe team" Heinrich said, "composed of the only sane members of our benighted departments."

"God, Heinrich, don't put Olaf off in his first week here" Olga said. "It's a good place, Olaf. You'll enjoy it."

"Thanks" said Olaf. "I'm looking forward to it. Cheers!"

The glasses were clinked, and the first swigs of pale ales and stouts were downed. The conversation started off bland, but soon took an awkward turn when Heinrich re-started on the politics.

"I've been invited to give a paper at a conference in Beijing" he said, "but I'm not going because of their appalling human rights record."

"Then you shouldn't go anywhere in the world, Heinrich" Vincent said. "I think the Chinese government has got the best human rights record of any country."

"What!" Heinrich and Olga exclaimed in unison.

"Do you know what average life expectancy was in China when the communist party took power in 1949?" Vincent asked.

"You're obviously going to tell us" Olga said.

"Thirty-six" Vincent said, "and now it is in the high seventies, higher than in the USA. The right to live a long life is a fundamental one, I reckon. As is the freedom from living in poverty. In modern terms, average income in China was about a thousand euros in 1949 and now it's ten thousand euros. Raising hundreds of millions of people out of poverty to a good standard of living is a great human rights achievement."

"But what about freedom of the press, Vincent? What about the suppression of freedom in Hong Kong? What about the oppression of the Uyghurs?" Heinrich asked.

"I'll start with the most difficult one first" Vincent said, "what is happening in Xinjiang. We need to put it in a historical context."

"You're not going to stand up for what the Chinese are doing to the Uyghurs, are you, Vincent?" Olga asked.

"I'm against all forms of oppression" Vincent said. "I'm only trying to understand what is happening."

"There's no justification for what's happening there, whatever the context" Heinrich said. "It's a disgrace."

"Is it worse than what's happening in Afghanistan?" Vincent asked. "The Uyghurs live in Xinjiang, the westernmost province of China. It borders Afghanistan. Are women better off there?"

"I don't need a geography lesson, Vincent" Heinrich said. "Where is all this leading?"

"To the problem China believed it faced with Islamic extremism in Xinjiang" Vincent replied. "The Mujahideen probably had visions of marching into Urumqi like they did into Kabul. There was a terrorist attack in Urumqi in 2014 that killed dozens of people and the Chinese government cracked down. They weren't going to let what happened to Afghanistan happen to Xinjiang…"

"And this justifies rape camps?" Olga interrupted.

"Olga, you've known me for ages" Vincent said. "You know I abhor rape as much as you do."

"I know, Vincent, sorry" Olga said. "Go on."

"You're a strong feminist, Olga" Vincent continued. "I think the only real steps forward in women's rights in Afghanistan were under the communists in the 1980s. The Americans undermined them by arming the most reactionary opposition groups, including ones in the mountains bordering on Xinjiang. The point is that I think the people of Xinjiang are much better off under Chinese communist rule than their neighbours in Afghanistan under sharia law. Urumqi has got a good university, higher ranked than our beloved York in maths and sciences. They have women lecturers and students. Comparing that with Kabul, after twenty years of American occupation, women especially are much better off there. The Chinese have over-reacted horribly, and I know the Uyghur people have been treated badly…"

"So you're saying that what's happening in Xinjiang is OK if it's better than Afghanistan, Vincent?" Heinrich asked.

"Look, can we please chill out?" Viola said.

"Yes" Olaf said. "You are all good friends, and it seems strange to me that you should concentrate on the few political issues where you disagree."

"It's the beer talking, Olaf" Viola said.

Olaf laughed. "Do you mind if I classify you as I see your viewpoints?" he asked, with a winning smile.

Heinrich and Olga had been thinking of Olaf as a typical visitor to the mathematics department, a bit introverted, shy and not noticeably socially adequate. They laughed in surprise.

"Go ahead" Heinrich said.

"Yes, go for it, Olaf" Olga said.

Vincent knew more about Olaf, but he was surprised, too. He also laughed, and encouraged Olaf to go on.

"I'll begin with Vincent, because I know him best" Olaf said. "He's also the easiest. A communist. You all hate capitalism, but he's the only one who sees a communist revolution and dictatorship of the proletariat as the way of getting rid of it."

"Spot on, Olaf" Vincent said.

"Viola, I would classify you as a social democrat, within the same spectrum of socialism as Vincent, but not approving of violent revolution, seeking to achieve your aims by gradual social progress."

"I wouldn't argue with that" Viola said.

"Olga, I would classify you as one of the rarest political species on Earth."

"I'm honoured" Olga said, with a beautiful, flashing smile.

"You are an anarchist, a true free spirit, opposed not only to capitalism, but to all forms of oppressive rule."

"I'm good with that" Olga said. "I'd die on the barricades for freedom."

"And you, Heinrich, I would classify as an ecologist. You are deep into science, and realize the damage capitalism is causing the planet. Your response has traces of communist, social democrat and anarchist."

"That's fair enough, too" Heinrich said. "I guess love of nature is deep in the German spirit."

"So, we're a red-black-green alliance then, Olaf?" Vincent said.

"Well" Olaf said, "you've got a lot more in common with each other than with the fascists, conservatives and liberals, haven't you?"

"We sure do" Olga said.

"I'll drink to that" Vincent said.

They all clinked their glasses together, and the third pint went down more harmoniously.

'Happiness is something you have to work at every day' Olaf thought, recalling one of his Aristotle quotes.

"This local pale ale is excellent" he said.

Olaf was pleased the evening was turning out pleasantly, but a part of him was preoccupied with the consequences of a phone call he had tapped. He had tapped the phones of all Vincent's book club members, so easy to do in the world of phones running via the internet, and knew that the new book club member, Hugh Whitehead, was in league with a man called Tony Woodbridge in a plot against Vincent. Mizuso had rescanned her files on Woodbridge. He was obviously a major threat to Vincent, a loose cannon they had not anticipated. Was Olaf disgusted by the reports of the murders perpetrated by Woodbridge? It doesn't matter. He knew his job was to protect Vincent. His mind ran on smoothly, weighing up the possibilities of various course of action.

"You look thoughtful, Olaf" Olga said.

She was lighting up on the effects of the third pint, and was in dazzling form, piling into witty anecdotes about the quantum field theory conference she had just attended in Italy.

"Just enjoying the beer" Olaf said, with a beatific smile.

"Not as good as German beer, of course" Heinrich said, "but not bad at all, I must admit."

"It's great beer" Vincent said. "Anyway, I'm popping out for a fag."

"I'll join you" Olaf said, standing up.

"I didn't know you smoked, Olaf" Viola said.

"Just the occasional puff" Olaf said. "I fancy one now."

Vincent and Olaf went out into the yard, and Olaf said

"There's something I've got to tell you, Vincent…" He paused.

"The thing is, Vincent" Olaf said, "is that you have been betrayed."

"What do you mean?" Vincent asked sharply, a deep, angry frown corrugating his brows.

"A man called Tony Woodbridge has located you. I have his phone tapped."

Olaf could sense that Vincent was very upset.

"I had to tell you, Vincent, for your safety" he continued.

"Do you know this man, Tony Woodbridge?" Olaf asked.

"Only too well" Vincent said. "He's the man who shot me. I thought Terada had killed him."

"Terada?" Olaf prompted.

"My bodyguard" Vincent replied, "many moons ago."

"That's my job now" Olaf said. "You may be in great danger. Perhaps you should go home now?"

"No" Vincent said. "Let's go back in."

The conversation soon became heated again.

"Putin as is as bad as Hitler" Heinrich said. "Germany should send more arms to Ukraine."

"Here, here" Olga said. "All my family are terrified of the Russians."

"I disagree" Viola said. "I think the expansion of NATO is partly to blame for the war."

Viola's father had been a journalist in Sarajevo when it had been bombed with depleted uranium. He had died shortly afterwards. Viola's mother was convinced that it had been from radiation poisoning. Vincent picked up the theme.

"NATO is just a front organization for American imperialism" he said. "I don't condone the invasion, but I can understand why the Russians didn't want Ukraine to join NATO. All Zelensky had to do to prevent the war was to say that Ukraine would remain neutral. Surely not too much to ask."

230

"But the Ukrainians have every right to join NATO. That's what national sovereignty means" Olga said.

"I'm against national sovereignty" Vincent said, "particularly when it's in the hands of people like Putin and Zelensky."

Heinrich snorted.

"You're not comparing Zelensky with Putin, are you?" he asked.

"In the sense that neither of them is fit to lead a state, yes" Vincent replied.

"That's outrageous" Olga said. "Vladimir Putin is a mass murderer and Volodymyr Zelensky is a hero."

The voices of the protagonists had become louder, and sharper. Olaf noticed that their table had attracted the attention of three tough-looking men at a nearby table. His knowledge of languages told him it was an Eastern European language, and he knew that there were many Ukrainian refugees in York, driven out of their country by the Russian invasion. Olaf had an acute sense of danger, and he felt hostile vibes from the men. Understandably, they might not take kindly to what Vincent was saying. 'There's going to be trouble' he thought.

"Well" Vincent said, "he's good at playing the role of heroic leader. He's an actor, after all. I bet he's enjoying every minute of being the most famous actor in the world. He's too fond of the sound of his own voice, that man."

Olga stood up.

"So are you, Vincent. I've had enough of this bullshit. I'm leaving."

"Me, too" Heinrich said. "Sometimes, Vincent, you really go too far."

They stomped off, leaving their friends open-mouthed at the table.

"I'm sorry" Vincent said to Viola and Olaf. "I've spoiled the evening. I don't know what got into me."

'I do' Viola thought. 'It's because you're off the medication.'

"It's OK" Viola said. "Olga and Heinrich are scarred by their experiences under Soviet Russian control. But we've all got our crosses to bear, and if they can't take us having a different opinion to theirs, that's their problem. I think we should leave, too, Vincent, I'm not in the mood for drinking now. Alcohol always does this."

She turned to Olaf, and said

"I'm sorry you've seen us on such bad form, Olaf. We're not usually like this. And I'm sorry we're going so early. Would you like to come back to our place for dinner?"

"I'd be delighted" Olaf said. "Thank you very much, Viola."

The three of them got up, and headed out into the street. The three Ukrainian men got up, and followed them out.

When Vincent and Viola were fiddling with their bike locks, the three men approached them.

"We want a word with you, mate" one of them said.

The atmosphere presaged violence. Olaf stepped between Vincent and the man and, in a calm, pleasant voice, said

"We don't want any trouble."

"Then your friends should keep their big mouths shut" the man said. "Get out of my way."

The man stepped forward, bristling with aggression. There was a blur of motion, and the man was sitting on the pavement, stunned. In the same, calm, pleasant voice, Olaf said to the other two men

"Your friend will need to rest for a while. Please look after him while we leave."

One of the two men rushed at Olaf. There was another blur of motion, following which Olaf had stunned him, too.

"Your friends will both need to rest for a bit" he said to the remaining man. "We really are leaving now."

The third man was obviously in shock, and muttered something, which sounded like a curse. Olaf propped the two prone men up against the pub wall, and said "Let's go" to Vincent and Viola. They got on their bikes, and headed off towards Micklegate. It was obvious to Olaf that Viola was also in shock. 'I must keep an eye on her on the cycle home' he thought.

When they got back, Viola collapsed on the sofa, and said

"I need a tea and a cigarette."

Vincent obliged, and sat next to her on the sofa. Olaf sat on the other sofa.

"I don't feel well" Viola said. "That was a horrible evening, and…"

She turned towards Olaf.

"…although I'm grateful to you, Olaf, I don't understand what you did… it was too weird… what did you do to those men, Olaf?"

"I tasered them" Olaf said.

"I tasered them" Olaf said, finishing his report on the incident to Mizuso. "And it seems as if it has convinced Vincent more than ever that I am some kind of alien android, who can put men to sleep in mid-stride. I can't convince him otherwise, Mizuso. I'm worried he's going to tell Viola, maybe others."

"It's a risk we are going to have to take" Mizuso said. "I think we should engage with his inner world. It's clear that Vincent is frustrated by his inability to calculate. Perhaps you could give him some inspiration by telling him that he is going to discover something incredibly important for the future of humankind. After his years of suppression by the medication, surely he deserves one last chance?"

"It seems unethical" Olaf said, "to use Vincent's fantasies to mislead him in this way."

"But we must consider efficacy first, Olaf" Mizuso said. "If this fantasy gives him the motivation he needs, what can be wrong with it?"

Vincent had not slept well since he started work on the calculations. No matter how hard he tried, his old work had become meaningless hieroglyphics. Gloomily, the realization struck him. Because the anti-psychotics had stopped him calculating, he had assumed that coming off them, he would start calculating again. But it didn't work like that. The calculations had come sporadically, apparently randomly, even when he had been a young woman, and he was an old man now. Then, another cherished hope had gone up in smoke when the trip back to Swn y Gwynt had not provided any inspiration.

"What were you looking for?" Olaf asked.

"Notes of calculations on something to do with the epsilon twistor… notes I made when I was a fugitive in the Welsh mountains. I had a vivid flashback of it in a dream. That was when I decided to come off the medication."

Vincent stared gloomily down at the beige carpet in his nondescript living room. Decades of fog were clearing painfully from his mind.

"I'll never take the anti-psychotics or the lithium again" he said.

"And these notes?" Olaf prompted.

"I went back to where I wrote them, but there was no trace of them, nothing."

"Then you must forget about the notes" Olaf said.

"But what about the calculations?" Vincent responded.

"You will have to start them from scratch."

Vincent looked startled. Somehow, he had taken it for granted that he would just have to edit some old calculations. "I haven't got that kind of energy, anymore" he said. "I haven't done a raw calculation in decades."

"You can try" Olaf said. "If you believe in a good future for humankind, you must."

234

Olaf drew a deep breath. He did not like lying at the best of times, and he had come to like Vincent in the short time he had known him, so he felt uncomfortable when he launched into an improvised version of the script he had agreed with Mizuso.

"My instructions are to tell you as little as possible about the future, but there is something you need to know. The invention you are about to discover will make possible an almost complete clean-up of the Earth's atmosphere in the thirty-first century. Thanks to you, twenty billion people are starting to lead normal lives again, after being trapped under a steel skin. No other human has ever performed such an important calculation. You can do it, Vincent. Take courage."

"Or acid" Vincent said, smiling for the first time during a distressing, fraught morning.

"Acid?" Olaf echoed.

"LSD" Vincent said. "I never told anyone about it, but I made my first discovery of the epsilon twistor on an LSD trip. Maybe it would work again."

Olaf blinked. He had studied a bit of everything at Aarhus, including psychology. He knew there was a connection between LSD and psychosis. Vincent had only just come off anti-psychotic medicine, and might be prone to instability, perhaps even madness, under its effects. A placebo might work wonders, however, or perhaps something milder.

"Or perhaps something milder" Vincent said, taking the thought out of Olaf's mind. "I've taken magic mushrooms, too."

Olaf blinked again, and decided to prevaricate.

"We'll see, Vincent" he said.

"So" Olaf said, making his report on the conversation to Mizuso, "he wants to take hallucinogenic drugs for inspiration."

Mizuso gasped.

"He told me" Olaf continued, "that he discovered the epsilon twistor originally under the effects of LSD, and ended up suggesting psilocybin mushrooms as a milder alternative."

"Gods" Mizuso said, "he's only recently come off anti-psychotic medicine. Anything could happen."

"Perhaps we could get the best of both worlds" Olaf said. "If Vincent were to prove successful, and discover something dangerous, we could bury the calculations but preserve them for posterity, in a quadruple-encrypted file, destroying the originals and the scanned files. In this case, perhaps the mushrooms would be a good idea. Then, we'd know exactly when he is going to be doing the calculation, and could execute our plan. I have checked various files on psilocybin mushrooms, and they are indeed milder than LSD. They grow plentifully at this time of year in woodlands all over Britain, including in the nearby Wheldrake Woods. I could easily get some for him."

"It's a high-risk strategy." Mizuso said. "It might drive him over the edge."

"I'm afraid the alternative is that he goes on staring at the ground, looking depressed" Olaf said.

"Didn't your speech about how his calculations were important for future mankind lift his spirits?" Mizuso asked.

"I'm not sure if it went in at all" Olaf said. "It just set him off talking about the drugs."

"Perhaps you'll have to be more explicit next time. Tell him outright that he's known to have written a great paper in 2022. Surely that will motivate him."

"And the drugs?" Olaf asked.

"It may be a high-risk strategy" Mizuso said, "but it's the only plausible one."

Vincent was feeling depressed again.

"I've wasted my life" he said.

Olaf had heard this before. His reply this time was more imaginative.

"Then everyone in the universe has wasted their lives" Olaf said. "You have done great things, and you have one more great thing still to do. You write a breakthrough paper in 2022, one that will make you revered as one of the greatest mathematical physicists of all time."

Vincent's eyes flashed. To Olaf, it seemed that the back of Vincent's eyes had become reflective for a moment, like a cat's, and a definite gleam had emerged.

"Perhaps I should try the inspiration. Will you get me some magic mushrooms, Olaf?"

"I could get some for you, if you want, Vincent" he said.

"Let's go for it" Vincent said. "I'll start work straightway, see how far I can get when I'm sober, start focusing on the problem."

Olaf's sense perceptions were unusually sharp, and he was aware of the sound of a bicycle turning off the road into the short drive at the front of the house, well before Vincent heard Viola turning the key in the front door lock.

"My last class was cancelled" Viola called out, through the living room door. "I'll see you in a minute" she said, "I'm popping upstairs for a shower."

They heard her footsteps going up the stairs.

"I'm going to tell her everything" Vincent said.

'O, no!' Olaf thought.

Viola had already had some misgivings about Vincent's relationship with Olaf. At first, she had been pleased that Vincent had made a new friend. But then Olaf seemed to be hanging around him all the time, and now Vincent had really gone off on one, telling her that Olaf was an android from the future, and that he had

237

had other visitors from Olaf's world…and that he was planning to take hallucinogenic drugs. In a flash, a decade of her life that had brought relative stability and happiness was falling apart. She told Vincent that he was mad, and went to stay overnight with one of her Buddhist friends in Acomb.

An hour after eating the magic mushrooms, Vincent looked into a rose and had a hallucination, with the flower opening up to football size. He felt in the spiritual harmony with all things... his long slow breaths drew in space, in time, in space, in time, in space… and then he began to calculate.

As if Olaf had ceased to exist, Vincent walked through into the dining room, plonked a wad of paper on the table, picked up a biro, and started to scribble. Following him as far as the doorway, Olaf immediately recognized that Vincent had gone into a different state of consciousness.

When the first wave of calculations hit him, he felt physically sick and was unable to write, but when he'd smoked a cigarette to calm down, the biro grew wings and started to fly across the pages. You can't imagine the four-dimensional integrals he took on, the way the four-dimensional second-rank tensors gave way to higher-order tensors, to completely ripping away the veil that surrounds reality, to seeing it raw, in its pure, pristine mathematical completeness. If you could do that, you'd have climbed K2 and Everest in one night, like he did. Maybe instead imagine being on a Pacific beach and huge rollers crashing in, leaving you gasping for breath, certain that you're going to drown, then suddenly receding and you come up for air, amazed to be alive… and that happening for hours on end.

He handwrote over a hundred pages in one night, always scribbling, scribbling, the arcane symbols piling up on the floor, the calculation following its own logic and his body locked into a simple rhythm – fifty minutes writing, ten minutes cigarette break – hour after hour. Around four o'clock in the morning he realized that there was a way to make the epsilon twistor release its energy like a laser, but so much energy that controlling it was way beyond modern technology. Then, a further leap down the rabbit hole. He recognized with a sickening sense of vertigo that the first discovery led to another, which made it clear *how* to catalyze the release of the epsilon twistor. He had to check. He was driven on and on and didn't really feel he'd resolved the tension racking his body until around six. By then he was sure. He knew how to catalyze the release of the twistor, and destroy the planet.

"God, what have I done?" Vincent said out loud to himself.

The knowledge was perilous, and Vincent was aware he had to hide the calculation, but suddenly, exhaustion set in and he was overwhelmed by the sleep demon. Peter had been right. Grace was still inside him.

Grace was thirty-one. She was walking down a long hall, a hall of mirrors. But the mirrors weren't showing her reflection, or reflections of each other across the corridor, they were peopled by scenes in her life arranged in chronological order.

She stopped, as a scene on her left drew her attention. She had just come home from a hockey match, aged fifteen, and was slightly drunk after drinking a couple of cans of beer with her friends after the game. Her father was in a bad mood, as he often was with his dyspeptic ulcer, and was threatening Grace. As Grace stepped into the frame, with her thirty-one year-old mind, she became conscious of how strong her fifteen year-old body was, how she had just propelled a hockey ball at seventy mph to great effect, how she could also propel her fist at high speed. As Grace stepped towards her father, she stumbled, and was back in the corridor.

This time she was on a travellator, like the kind used at airports. It seemed to be going faster and faster, propelling her into the future, then came to a jarring stop. In the mirror on her right, Grace was twenty-one and in a park with Brendan, her childhood sweetheart, then eighteen and on the way to college himself. Grace had just taken a brilliant first in physics at Oxford, and they were sitting in the Parks on a gorgeous, sunny day, drinking champagne. As the thirty-one-year-old Grace entered the mirror, she wanted to change the course of history by proposing to Brendan. But her twenty-one-year-old lips froze, and suddenly she was back in the corridor, still with the taste of champagne in her mouth. The travellator moved on, then came to a stop. The corridor had reached an end. There was an empty raised dais there; nothing, nobody else.

But Vincent was not alone in his little two-bed semi in York. Two men, Tony Woodbridge and Hugh Whitehead, had broken in downstairs, intent on killing him.

Chapter 11

Imaginary Friends

Tony Woodbridge was still alive at eighty, but not well. Following the fiasco outside the Japanese embassy, Tony's career had already been marked as blocked. When Mason had discovered about Tony's involvement in the murder of Hiroshi Fujimoto, he had hushed it up, of course, but had decided that Woodbridge's psychotic streak was incurable, and a danger to the best interests of MI5. Woodbridge had been dismissed dishonourably from the service, and all establishment career pathways were closed to him. He had a pension, and found lucrative contract work, but no more. He was an angry old man and still longed to get his revenge on Grace. His thinking was all in the past, and he scarcely considered that Grace had morphed into Vincent.

He had known, deep down in his guts, all through those years since he had been nearly fatally wounded in London, that the bitch was still alive. When he received the providential phone call from that hippy woman Pru, now paid her thirty pieces of silver, after hanging up he lit a Dunhill, and poured himself a Chivas Regal. He might have failed in London, he thought, but he'd finish the job in York. It was a job he couldn't contract out. He had a burning desire to kill his adversary personally, to see the expression on their face when he finished them off. But he knew Grace had been a violent, dangerous woman, and Vincent would probably still be formidable, even approaching seventy. Too formidable for an eighty-year-old man with a gammy leg. He would need help. Who could he trust? Living in a degraded world of dishonesty, disloyalty and violence, everyone was suspect, may report him to MI5. MI5 would doubtless be protecting Grace, and would have trained killers as good as Tony had been in his prime. They would have him killed for sure, if he chose the wrong man. It took Tony just a couple of cigarettes and a slug of whiskey to decide on Hugh Whitehead. They had worked together, assassinating communists, in the days when Hugh had been a CIA agent. Although he wouldn't have put it to himself this way, Tony intuited that Hugh's career had been blocked for the same reason as his, the psychotic violence and love of personal vendettas compromising their judgment. They had worked together as freelance operators over the years. In their own strange way they liked each other, admired each other.

Hugh had accepted the offer readily. The size of the reward Tony offered him had surprised him. He would have done it for less. Tony's intense personal interest in the case piqued him. Finding the target had been trivially easy. Once you knew what you are looking for, locating a seventy-year-old half-caste, probably connected to the university, was not a difficult task. Whitehead could have staked out Vincent Clerk's house, and arranged the kill, without meeting Vincent. But, like Tony, he loved to see the expression on the face of the people he killed when they were dying, and that meant so much more when you had met them alive, and knew what you were cutting off. He had infiltrated Peter's book club, and was looking forward to killing this big-headed godless commie. Of course, part of the deal was that Tony would deliver the *coup de grace*.

Vincent woke up groggily, the dream still echoing in his mind. 'God, what time is it' he thought. 'I need a coffee.' He went downstairs and opened the door of the living room. Something didn't feel right. He had an uncanny feeling that he was not alone in the house. He walked tentatively through into the dining room, where two men were pointing guns at him.

One of the things that had kept Viola going through hard times had been her Buddhist practice, and the relationships she had forged with the local Buddhist group in York. It was to the best of these friends, Amanda, that she had gone that fateful night, and opened her heart out about Vincent's psychotic revelations.

"We need to chant for him" Amanda said.

"Let's do gongyo" Viola said. "Could you lead?"

The two of them sat down before Amanda's gohonzon, and started to chant, pledging themselves to the teachings of the Lotus Sutra.

"Nam myou hou renge kyoo."
"Nam myou hou renge kyoo."
"Nam myou hou renge kyoo."

The monotonous chanting calmed Viola down, as it often did, and turned her mind to more positive thoughts.

"It's probably just a temporary blip" Amanda said. "Why don't you go back home and see how he is?"

"I'm a bit frightened about how I might find him" Viola replied.

"All the more reason to go" Amanda said. "I'll chant for the success of your meeting."

Thus fortified, Viola set out for Tradescant Road in the middle of the afternoon.

Mizuso and Nobuko met at York railway station. They had intended to go straight to Tradescant Road, but their joy at seeing each other had overwhelmed them. Although genetically unrelated, they had had a loving mother-daughter relationship, and their separation from each other had been the hardest thing for them to bear in their thirty-six years stuck in a violent, cruel, chaotic world they found difficult to comprehend. Had they proceeded directly to Vincent's, they might have been in time to wake him after his trip and calculations.

"Sit down, Vincent" Tony said, gesturing to the empty chair opposite him and Whitehead. "I want to take a good look at you. Still the same old ugly half-caste."

"Tony, how…" Vincent stammered.

"I said sit down, Vincent. Otherwise, I'll shoot you now. They say being shot in the stomach is the most painful way to die."

Vincent sat down, unsteadily, almost knocking the chair over.

"You're shaking, Vincent" Hugh said.

They were three paces away, too far to lunge at them, even if Vincent had had the energy, but he was exhausted by the trip and the calculation.

'God, I'm fucked' Vincent thought. 'This bastard Woodbridge has caught up with me at last. What a way to go.'

"You beat me in the endgame in London, Vincent" Tony said, "but he who laughs last laughs loudest."

He gave out an unpleasant cackle. Vincent stared at them, silently, stonily.

"You had plenty to say for yourself the other night, Vincent" Hugh said. "Cat got your tongue?"

"You're both mad" Vincent said.

He closed his eyes, and decided to lunge. 'Better to get it over with quickly' he thought. He braced himself.

When he re-opened his eyes, coiling his body to leap, his view of Tony and Hugh was blocked by Olaf, standing squarely in front of him. Olaf had appeared out of nowhere.

"What the fuck!" Whitehead exclaimed.

Tony fired. The bullet must have struck Olaf full in the chest, but he didn't fall. There was a kind of blur of motion.

Vincent blinked and shivered. Olaf was standing next to him, an arm around his shoulders. Tony and Hugh were still sitting opposite him, but disarmed, slumped in their chairs.

"This can't be real" Vincent said.

"It's real" Olaf said. "I realize I have a lot of explaining to do. But first, let me render these two men harmless."

244

Olaf bound the two men into their hard-backed chairs, took out a syringe and injected them both in the arm.

"They will be out for several hours" Olaf said. "We can leave them alone in here. Let's go out into the garden. I'll make you a cup of coffee."

Very shakily, Vincent took his cup of coffee out into the garden. When he passed the end of the extension, he was startled to see Mizuso Tanaka and Nobuko Brown sitting on two of the iron chairs on the patio.

'What the fuck is going on?' Vincent thought. 'Did I eat some more mushrooms this morning, and this is just a weird bad trip. But hadn't Mizuso and Nobuko really turned up that time, in eighty-six?'

"Vincent" Mizuso said, "what a pleasure to meet you again."

She gave him a flashing smile.

"Yes, Vincent" Nobuko said, "it's a pleasure and an honour for me, too."

"It's great to see you both" Vincent said. "The last time was a bit fraught."

"I'm afraid this one will be a bit fraught, too…" Mizuso said.

She was interrupted by the arrival of Viola, who had come through the house and was standing white-faced and trembling near the back door. She looked at Vincent with tears in her eyes, and said

"Who are those two men indoors, Vincent? And who are these people?"

She shot a distrustful look at Mizuso and Nobuko.

Vincent groaned.

"I'm terribly, sorry, Viola" he said, "but you must prepare yourself for another shock. Mizuso and Nobuko are from Datonga, like Olaf."

Tears started to stream down Viola's face.

"O, Vincent, why did you stop taking the anti-psychotics?" she gasped out between sobs.

"I'll explain everything" Olaf said. "I'm terribly sorry, Viola, but I encouraged a fantasy of Vincent that I'm an android from the future, to help free his mind for the calculations he has been so desperate to complete…"

"But what about your arm?" Vincent said, interrupting him, "and what you did to those men outside the pub, and how you saved me from those bastards in there?"

Vincent made an angry gesture with his head towards the house.

"Please calm yourself, Vincent" Olaf said. "It's an ordinary prosthetic arm, and I simply tasered those men in the street and the ones indoors. I…"

Vincent interrupted him again.

"But you appeared out of nowhere, and Woodbridge shot you without injuring you."

"I'm a secret service agent, Vincent" Olaf said patiently. "I was out in the garden office scanning your notes when I noticed you come downstairs. I move very fast compared with old men like that, and I'm wearing a bullet-proof vest. That's all there is to it."

Viola sobbed, and groaned.

"A secret service agent?" she echoed. "What are you doing here?"

"It's a long story, Viola" Mizuso said, "connected with some calculations Vincent did a long time ago…"

She trailed off, uncertain how to continue. Nobuko picked up the thread.

"They were some of the greatest calculations in the history of science" she said, "but they had to be buried because of their consequences for the future of humanity, and Vincent became the victim of his creativity. Mizuso and I have been keeping a watchful eye on him from afar for thirty-six years now, and we have reached a turning point with his new calculations, the ones he did last night. That's why we're here."

Viola's face was still registering disbelief, and Vincent was looking gloomily down at the cracked patio tiles. He suddenly looked up with fear in his eyes when he heard a noise from the next-door garden. It was Mavis, hanging out her laundry. Mavis peered myopically over the low fence, and said

"Hello, Vincent. Hi, Viola. I see you've got visitors."

Vincent suppressed what would have been a hysterical laugh, and said

"O, hi, Mavis. Yes, please allow me to introduce my guests, Mizuso and Nobuko, friends from when I worked in Japan."

Mizuso and Nobuko bowed towards Mavis in the traditional Japanese style as their names were mentioned.

"You met Olaf the other day, didn't you?"

Various pleasantries were exchanged, including the weather, and the progress of Mavis's latest illness, her favourite topic of conversation. When she had finished pegging up her laundry on the line, Mavis said

"Well, I'll leave you to it. My daughter is coming round."

When she went back indoors, it was Mizuso who spoke next.

"Viola" Mizuso said soothingly, "we believe that Vincent may have just performed an even greater calculation. Olaf has told me how you stabilized Vincent's life and have made this great thing possible. We have enormous powers and can help you. Please believe in us."

Viola, shaking and white as a sheet, did not look convinced.

"I would love to explain things more fully, Viola" Mizuso said, "but we have urgent matters to attend to. We have to deal with the two men indoors."

Vincent looked nervously in through the window, and Mizuso followed his glance.

"Please don't worry about the physical threat, Vincent" she said. "Woodbridge and Whitehead will not awake from the narcotics Olaf has given them for several hours. You won't get hurt."

"You can trust me, Viola. I will do everything to look after Vincent, and will protect you, too" Olaf said.

"However" Mizuso said, "although Olaf has disarmed these men, and put them to sleep, they may try again, and maybe find Vincent when Olaf is not around."

"Try what again?" Viola asked shakily. "Why do we need protection?"

"It's a long story" Vincent said, with a sigh. "Let's go for a walk in the park. We can leave our visitors to decide what to do with those two men inside."

He led Viola round the side of the house, obviating the need to go past the weird sight of the two ugly men sleeping indoors. They crossed the little back road and headed off for a much-needed breath of fresh air. Viola looked shattered. Before Vincent could even attempt to explain about Woodbridge and Whitehead, she said

"Could you walk me round to Amanda's, Vincent? I need to lie down and rest for a bit."

"Of course, Viola" Vincent said. "Please don't tell her anything about what has happened. Just say I'm OK."

"Are you?" Viola asked.

Vincent looked shattered, too. The trip, the calculation, the dream, the murder attempt and the effect of the new visitors were all taking their effect.

"Sort of" he said, with a wan smile.

They walked across the park in a stunned silence. When they were within eyesight of Amanda's, Vincent said "I'd better go back."

Life had become agony and ecstasy at the same time.

"Love you, Vincent" Viola said.

"I love you, too" Vincent said. "I'll call you later."

When Vincent got back to Tradescant Road, Woodbridge and Whitehead had disappeared, Olaf was in the back garden, and Mizuso and Nobuko were in the living room. Tears were streaming down Nobuko's face.

"What's wrong?" Vincent asked.

"I've just had to give Nobuko some bad news" Mizuso said. "How about you? Is Viola OK?"

"No" Vincent replied. "I've dropped her off at a friend's. She's exhausted."

"This is a difficult moment" Mizuso said. "First, the easy part. Olaf has dealt with the two killers…"

She hesitated. Now did not seem to be the time to tell Vincent that she had used his computer to contact Mason, and that MI5 would exact the ultimate reprisal for their attempt to murder Vincent.

"Where are they now?" Vincent asked.

"Olaf took them back to Whitehead's flat in York" Mizuso replied.

'And Mason's men will already be on their way there' she thought.

"Don't worry, Vincent, Woodbridge and Whitehead will never bother you again."

Mizuso paused and took a deep breath.

"The next step is more difficult, because it depends on what you want to do. Before you decide, I've got to tell you something about us. Nobuko and I were partners in Japan in the early eighties, before we got involved with you and the epsilon twistor. Since 1986, I have been basically a prisoner of the Japanese government, and Nobuko of the Chinese. Now is not the time for false modesty. We are the two top computer hackers in the world and can access any computer on Earth. We have forged new identities for ourselves. I already have a complete history as a Japanese-UK citizen, and passports that no one could connect with Mizuso Tanaka. I have a UK residence permit and have reprogrammed international face recognition software at all passport controls to pose as a UK citizen. We escaped to help you, and I have decided to remain in Britain, initially as a Japanese tourist."

Vincent looked up excitedly, a glimmer of hope in a brighter future already lightening his expression. The prospect of a companion who understood his calculations was uplifting.

"God, Mizuso, I can't believe my luck" he said. "I've got a new sense of purpose in life. A feeling that I can help change things for the better. I feel like a new man."

"You've done such incredible things with your calculations, Vincent" Mizuso said, "I think you deserve some help. The problem is, Nobuko thought we might live together, but she is too striking to hide in plain sight, like me. I have just told her we must part, for our own good."

Mizuso turned towards Nobuko, and said

"Nobuko, I am so sorry to have told you like this, at the last moment, but I couldn't spoil our final time together at the station with too much sweet sorrow."

Nobuko had been gloomily silent till this moment.

"O, Mizuso" she said. "I still can't believe it."

"Of course" Mizuso said, smiling at her closest friend, "our worldlines are joined forever. The parting of the ways is apparent."

"But painful" Nobuko said.

Tears started to run down her face. To be deprived like this, just after they'd met again.

"Excuse us, Vincent" Mizuso said. "We need some time alone."

"Of course" Vincent said.

He slipped out into the garden, where he found Olaf trimming the hedge.

"I thought I'd do something useful, while you dealt with your emotional stuff" Olaf said.

"Mizuso's staying!" burst out of Vincent.

"I know, Vincent" Olaf said. "She told me of her decision earlier. It must be very difficult for her and Nobuko now."

His glance strayed in the direction of the house. Vincent could tell there were tears in his eyes.

"But the moment was structured this way" Olaf said.

"Did she tell you why she's staying?" Vincent asked.

"She's not obliged to explain things to an agent" Olaf said with a laugh, "but she treats me as an equal and she did say that she felt she could do great things with you in Britain. She said that you had inspired her politically, and that she could use her advanced knowledge of computing to help bring capitalism to an end before the middle of the twenty-first century, and prevent the destruction of the planet. She spoke with conviction."

"That's wonderful. What a woman!" Vincent said.

"I will be leaving with Nobuko" Olaf said. "It's better for all of us you don't know where we're going. We have to go soon, too, as MI5 people might arrive when it's realized that Nobuko and Mizuso have gone missing."

Vincent looked down disconsolately. He had become friends with Olaf as a person and, in view of his newfound identity, he would have been the perfect bodyguard. 'He's just saved my life' Vincent thought, 'and now I'm losing him.'

"I'll miss you, Olaf" Vincent said.

"You, too" Vincent. "But I am happy that you will have a great companion in Britain in Mizuso."

Nobuko and Mizuso joined them in the garden. They had both been crying.

"Our time is up" Mizuso said.

"Yes" Olaf said. "MI5 will be arriving soon."

When Mizuso gave Nobuko one last hug, Vincent started crying, too.

"Shall we go?" Olaf asked Nobuko.

"Yes" Nobuko said.

With one last look over her shoulder, she went indoors with Olaf, and they disappeared.

Mizuso was grief stricken, but now exercising iron self-control.

"So" she said, "to business. Now that Olaf has scanned your calculations, we must burn them. He sent them to me in a quadruple-encrypted file that no one else on Earth could read. I will destroy the entire part of your computer that contains the scanned files, irreparably."

"I'll light the chiminea" Vincent said.

Mizuso darted indoors. Vincent followed her, and fumbled around in the kitchen looking for the firelighters, dug them out from under the sink, and dashed back into the garden and down to the shed. Back with the kindling and some logs, he got the fire going.

Mizuso darted back out, with a sheaf of a hundred pages or so of Vincent's raw calculations bundled under one arm.

"Are you sure the file is safe?" Vincent asked uncertainly.

He had never trusted the world of computers.

"Perfectly" Mizuso replied. "Don't worry, Vincent, the file preserves your handwriting for posterity. May I?"

"I'll do it" Vincent said.

He took the notes, and pushed them into the rising flames.

"We have to wait for them to turn to ashes" Vincent said. "While we do, I want you to tell me more about yourself and the world you come from. Who are you? Why have you appeared at the two most important moments of my life?"

"What difficult questions, Vincent! I'll do my best…"

She drew a long breath.

"Who am I? Philosophers have been pondering that one for millennia, and we haven't got much further in the twenty-first century than the first. I'll spare you any boring details of my early life, but I've survived as a computer wizard. The encryption codes used here are a child's puzzle to me. The same is true for Nobuko. We have been helping the Japanese and Chinese governments to avert any catastrophic attempt to develop the epsilon twistor. I have hacked into terrible communications between secret service agents, and have tried my best to keep an eye on you through MI5 files. I'm sorry, Vincent, to bring it up, but I even know about Woodbridge's involvement in the murder of your friend Hiroshi, from tapping MI5's computers."

"I hated him" Vincent said, "but I'm happy I didn't kill him after Olaf had knocked him out. I couldn't have done that, not in cold blood."

"I'm so happy to hear you say that" Mizuso said, "and I can reassure you that you can live safely in Britain now."

"Is that what I have to do? You said the next step depends on what I want to do. Is there an alternative?"

"Yes" Mizuso replied. "You, or you and Viola, could go into hiding. I can enable you to do this because I can access any computer on Earth. I have two properties in central Italy, a remote farmhouse in Umbria, in acres of its own land, and a flat in Firenze. I am never going back to Japan. Mizuso Tanaka has disappeared. I could do the same for you and Viola."

Momentarily, an eager, excited expression crossed Vincent's face. Then his brows clouded over.

"Could we really disappear, though?" he asked. "Won't the security services keep an eye on Viola's family? She'd never agree to an arrangement where she couldn't see them. She's very devoted to them."

"I see your point, Vincent" Mizuso said. "Does she visit her family regularly?"

"Three or four times a year. She couldn't go into hiding."

"I understand, Vincent" Mizuso said. "I will have to leave it up to you and Viola. In any event, I took the liberty of preparing faked passports for both of you. Whatever you decide, you may need them in case of emergencies. You will be able to sail through all the world's passport controls with them, and can join me in a safe bolthole in Italy if need arises. I made both Jamaican and Italian passports for you and UK and Italian passports for Viola. I have established new identities for both of you, and bank accounts with unlimited resources."

She fished in her handbag, and brought out the passports, along with debit and credit cards. Vincent took the documents. A potential new life was opening up, despite the difficulties.

"That's wonderful, Mizuso" Vincent said. "I may need them if they start to bomb me out with the medication again, or try to get me sectioned. I can't thank you enough."

"The thanks are all on my side, Vincent. These are trivia compared with what you have done for the future of humanity."

Hearing a noise from behind the back fence, Mizuso glanced nervously at her watch.

"I have to go now. Although I took precautions, the security services may have become aware of my disappearance, and here is the first place they will look for me. You can contact me via this quadruple-encrypted number. This is another bitter farewell for me, Vincent. Take care!"

She came and kissed Vincent on the cheek. Suddenly, she turned, headed resolutely to the side gate, and left a bemused Vincent on his own.

Vincent fell into a brown study. Had it all been a dream? Another psychotic episode? He watched a family of blue tits gathering on the bird feeder. Gathering himself, he went indoors. The dining room felt eerily silent. The faked passports and bank cards were on the table. They were real, at least. He picked up the phone.

"O, hi, Amanda" he said. "Is Viola there?"

"Hi, Vincent" Amanda replied. "Yes, she's just woken up. Are you OK?"

"Fine, thanks" Vincent said. "Could you put Viola on?"

"Sure, Vincent. Here she is."

"Are you OK, *cara*?"

"Better, Vincent" Viola replied. "Are you alone?"

"Yes" Vincent replied. "All our strange visitors have left. Everything is safe and sound here now."

"Thank God" Viola said. "I'll see you in a bit."

It took Mizuso Tanaka several months to check Vincent Clerk's calculations. The last twenty pages had been particularly difficult. The handwriting was strange, sometimes almost a horizontal cross bar, with indentations and dots, looking as if a spider with inky legs had crawled madly across the page. She had dared not contact Vincent for clarification. He was not sufficiently computer savvy to use the quadruple-encrypted files, and she could not risk ordinary encryption codes. Using AI analysis, she had deciphered the handwriting style herself, and had reached the same conclusion as Vincent. The new calculations showed how to catalyze the release of the epsilon twistor. Like Vincent, she realized that channelling the vast output of energy was beyond modern human technology, and likely to remain so for a long time.

Mizuso and Nobuko had been working hard for decades to prevent anyone from developing a device to release the twistor.

'If only we could control it' she thought. 'Imagine having a device for turning the little knots of space-time that we call particles into pure waves of energy. There are no by-products. The only thing that comes out of the source is pure energy. No more coal, no more oil, no more gas, no more uranium, no more plutonium, no more acid rain, no more radioactive waste... No more need even for solar power, tidal power, wind power, no more booms across estuaries, no more unsightly, noisy turbines... just unlimited, free, clean energy... in an idyllic future, for a peaceful society with an advanced technology. But too much energy for a chaotic capitalist world. It would destabilize the whole planet. I cannot bear the responsibility for this alone. I must contact Nobuko.'

As they had done most of their lives, Mizuso and Nobuko met in cyberspace.

"I have checked Vincent's calculations" Mizuso said, "and am sure they are correct. It's the most important calculation in the history of physics, and it's a terrible moral decision on what we should do next, the horns of a dilemma. On one horn, we work to suppress Vincent's great creative work, which is anathema to me, and maybe suppress the discovery of knowledge which may be incredibly useful in a world that has become a peaceful place. On this negative horn, we at least ensure everyone's safety for now. On the other horn, we publish Vincent's work in some disguised form, for posterity. Perhaps in the future, in a better world, the twistor could be used to power a pollution-free, energy-rich environment. Should we miss out on that possibility? The knowledge may not be rediscovered for centuries, Vincent is such a one-off. I'm worried that this knowledge could disappear if something happens to us."

"But we can't risk letting it into the public domain in any form" Nobuko said.

"I've had an idea" Mizuso said, "that I want to try out on you. I thought I could disguise the calculation in a paper in an obscure branch of science. I was thinking of writing the new theory in the world of marine biology, and arranging for its publication in a minor journal. It will disappear, but remain to be rediscovered by a wiser generation, if we cannot transmit our encoded knowledge."

"It sounds risky to me, sensei" Nobuko said. "I remember how McCall's work on magnetic multilayers got related to the epsilon twistor."

Mizuso winced at the mention of Ewan's name, but said calmly

"That was in a field being actively researched by thousands of people. I mean something much more obscure. I know someone in the School of Ocean Sciences at Bangor University, a reliable old colleague of Olaf's, who could arrange for the publication in the Journal of Estuarine Pollution."

"It sounds like you have got it all worked out, sensei" Nobuko said.

She was a good enough psychologist to realize that Mizuso had already made her mind up, and that a rift on this decision wasn't worth it. In any event, they had to 'back up' Vincent's calculation somehow, and this seemed as good a plan as any.

"And I agree it is a good plan."

"Thank you, Nobuko" Mizuso said. "It was a great weight on me taking responsibility for this."

"I'm sure it's the right decision, sensei" Nobuko said. "Have you thought about the authorship?"

"Yes" Mizuso replied decisively. "It is going to be by G. O'Malley. We can't use Vincent's name, and connect him with the new calculations, and I have established an alias as a Gail O'Malley. The surname is common enough for the initial not be connected with Grace."

"For the time being anyway" Nobuko said doubtfully.

"And I've got some cheerier news for you, from a surprising source. Mason has agreed for us to spend some time together at a safe house in Italy."

After several months back in the cold world of hyperspace, to meet again in the flesh…

"O, Mizuso, that's wonderful!" Nobuko exclaimed. "When?"

257

"As soon as you can make safe transit" Mizuso replied. "It's incredible, Nobuko. Mason has had some kind of epiphany. He's even discussed how to help Vincent with me, and is allowing Vincent and Viola to go to Italy, too."

"That's great news, too" Nobuko said. "I'd love to meet them again. Vincent is a strange man, but I like him."

"Me, too" Mizuso said. "I had the most bizarre conversation of my life with him recently. He told me that when he had finished the calculation, he was visited by a great thirty-first century mathematician called Hu Song. They went out for a walk and drank saké together. He has completely blanked out of his mind the terrible incident with Woodbridge and Whitehead. To him, it never happened. He is living in a parallel universe to us."

"I've got something to tell you, Peter" Mason said. "But first, could you listen to this?"

Mason switched on a tape.

O'MALLEY: You must be from Datonga.

VISITOR: Datonga? [Pause] Ah, Professor O'Malley, may I ask you the favour of putting down your weapon.

O'MALLEY: Weapon? Oh, sorry, I didn't mean to startle you. [Pause] What a coincidence.

VISITOR: Yes, indeed.

O'MALLEY: I'd offer to make you a cup of tea, but my last visitor disappeared the first time I left her alone.

VISITOR: Her? You mean Nobuko Brown?

O'MALLEY: Never heard of her. Her name was Lisa.

VISITOR: Never heard of her.

O'MALLEY: We've got a lot to talk about. I think I will put on a pot of tea.

VISITOR: Don't worry, I've no intention of leaving.

O'MALLEY: Oh, I should warn you not to open any of the curtains or blinds. The house is surrounded by armed guards. Obviously they don't know you're here, or we'd have heard by now. They're trained killers and particularly twitchy at the moment.

Mason switched the recorder off, and said

"There's more, Peter, but you get the gist…"

"My God" Peter exclaimed. "He wasn't an imaginary friend, then. Poor Grace. Poor Vincent."

"I'm sorry now, Peter" Mason said, "but I felt I was doing my duty at the time. And I suppose I was also influenced by the *impossibility* of anyone getting into her house that night. We had the place completely sealed off."

"So you doctored the tape" Peter said, "and fooled me into believing in Grace's schizophrenia."

"Believe me, Peter" Mason said, "I am truly sorry that I deceived you. It's partly that I wanted to deceive myself. Grace's conversation with her visitor got stranger. Listen to this."

Mason switched the tape back on.

O'MALLEY: I made some Lapsang Souchong. It's a China tea.

VISITOR: I know.

O'MALLEY: Take it easy, I was only trying to be friendly. By the way, may I ask your name?

VISITOR: Ho Chi Yin.

O'MALLEY: Wow, named after the great Vietnamese liberator.

VISITOR: What?

O'MALLEY: Sorry, I guess you're not au fait with twentieth-century Earth history. By the way, may I ask when and where you're from?

VISITOR: I'm from your future, and from your past.

O'MALLEY: I thought I recognized you. You came to my inaugural lecture at QEC, didn't you? [Pause] Yes, that's it, Cuthbertson introduced you as a famous Chinese maths professor.

VISITOR: This is ridiculous.

O'MALLEY: No, I remember it clearly now. Cuthbertson introduced you as Hu Song.

Mason stopped the tape.

"It ends there" he said. "I have been having nightmares about it for years."

"God" Peter exclaimed. "It's as if Vincent is living in a parallel universe to us."

"We'll never know what happened that night" Mason said, "but we checked the guest list for her inaugural lecture, and it included a Hu Song. We also have a film of the lecture, and there was certainly a Chinese man in the audience. It's beyond comprehension what happened that night, Peter."

"Vincent is a very strange man, but he has been done a terrible injustice" Peter said.

"I agree" Mason said. "It has been on my conscience all these years. I have had a kind of epiphany, and have felt the need to confess. I can't take back the wrong I did to you and Grace, but I apologize from the bottom of my heart to you and will do my best to help Vincent now."

"How?" Peter queried.

"We know Vincent is off the medication" Mason said, "and we'll let things be. I have been reassured that no one in the history of mankind has ever produced any new science at Vincent's age. I don't think we're in danger of him discovering any dangerous new inventions now. He seems to be OK off the medication. My motto for this situation is 'Let sleeping dogs lie'. I have even decided to allow Vincent and Viola to go to Italy to visit her family."

"Well done, Norbert!" Peter exclaimed. "I think Vincent deserves some help."

He nearly said "in the final years of his difficult life", but desisted.

Martin Smalley is a scientist and novelist, bringing his deep knowledge of physics to the world of fiction. He has authored dozens of scientific research articles and is the author of Clay Swelling and Colloid Stability (CRC Press, 2006), a respected work in its field. As a former physics lecturer at the University of York, Martin captivated students with his engaging teaching style. His lectures on Electromagnetism and Optics have amassed over 100,000 views on YouTube, demonstrating his ability to make complex physics ideas accessible and intriguing. A lifelong lover of spy thrillers, Martin now brings his passion for both scientific exploration and storytelling to his second novel, *The Epsilon Twistor*, which delves into the political consequences of a scientific discovery. His debut novel, *Datonga*, is a gripping sci-fi adventure that merges real physics with thrilling mystery.

@martinsmalleyauthor

Also by Martin Smalley

DATONGA

MARTIN SMALLEY